More praise for *The Great Mi*

'Jonathan Lee's wily, virtuosic, intimate portrait of a public man that also serves as an X-ray of America. *The Great Mistake* is a great novel of New York, in which the shaping of public space becomes inextricable from the loneliness, longing, and ferocious ambition of a single, damaged man' Garth Greenwell, author of *What Belongs to You*

'A wonderful, compelling, finely tuned and deeply loveable novel, with a central character who is all of those things too. Jonathan Lee has taken the bare facts of a nearly-forgotten life and turned them into a rich and unforgettable story, told with a relish for language and voice. Mr Andrew Haswell Green now has permanent lodgings in my brain, and very welcome he is too' Jon McGregor, author of *Reservoir 13* and *Lean Fall Stand*

'It's perhaps fitting that at a time when the Great American Novel is at a low ebb . . . a Brit should write what is likely to be the best American novel of the year. *The Great Mistake* is a book of extraordinary intelligence and style, written in language at once beautiful and playfully aphoristic. It's a novel whose protagonist – decent, dignified, wounded – will live long in the mind of those that read it, a novel that delivers wholeheartedly on Lee's early promise' Alex Preston, *Observer*

'An exceptional work of historical fiction about one of the key figures in the development of 19th-century New York City . . . A highly satisfying mix of mystery and character portrait, revealing the constrained heart beneath the public carapace' *Kirkus* (starred review)

THE
GREAT MISTAKE

JONATHAN LEE

GRANTA

Granta Publications, 12 Addison Avenue, London W11 4QR

First published in Great Britain by Granta Books, 2021
This edition published by Granta Books, 2022
Originally published in the United States in 2021 as a Borzoi Book by
Alfred A. Knopf, a division of Penguin House LLC, New York

A CIP catalogue record for this book is available from the British
Library.

1 3 5 7 9 10 8 6 4 2

ISBN 978 1 78378 625 1
eISBN 978 1 78378 626 8

Typeset by Scribe, Philadelphia, Pennsylvannia
Offset by Avon DataSet Ltd, Alcester, Warwickshire
Printed and bound by CPI Group (UK) Ltd, Croydon, CR0 4YY
www.granta.com

For A & M

Novels arise out of the shortcomings of history.

—Novalis, from Penelope Fitzgerald's *The Blue Flower*

Do not mourn the dead. They know what they are doing.

—Clarice Lispector, *The Hour of the Star*

THE
GREAT MISTAKE

STRANGERS' GATE

The last attempt on the life of Andrew Haswell Green took place on Park Avenue in 1903. News of his murder filled the front page of the *New York Times*—*"Father of Greater New York" Shot in Front of His Home.* The motive was offstage, unaccounted for. Speculation filled the *Herald,* the *Tribune,* the *Sun.* Some writers got excited by the victim's fame or the five shots fired. Others stared straight-faced at the date of his death: Friday, November thirteenth. Citizens prone to long-necked dreams carried pocket pieces on unlucky days like these, rabbit's feet and rusty screws, Pope Pius IX in a paperweight, the pit of a peach named Stump the World, items mute and immune to worry, charms to protect them from bedlam, but at the age of eighty-three Andrew had no time for fetishes. The things he trusted, late in life, were grass and trees and weeds, buildings and bridges made of stone, and after his absurd ending had faded from the news a marble bench was erected in his name in Central Park. This small memorial can still be found overlooking the open greenery of Fort Fish. On Tuesday mornings a person with cleaning supplies arrives to remove last week's bird shit with a brush.

On Andrew's *fateful final morning,* as the *Times* would describe it, he woke early and spent a long time preparing to move. Then he descended sixteen stairs with care and sat down at his table of Massachusetts maple under an electric-only chandelier. Park Avenue was waking beyond the window. Dust rose and fell behind passing carts. Wheels creaked as they carried Friday loads across the cobbles. Coffee made with thirty-six beans was best—this was his conclusion after decades of private research—and he sipped steadily from his favorite cup, painted the yellow of elm leaves in fall, until Mrs. Bray came in with breakfast.

How did you sleep? she asked.

Like the dead, he said.

They shared the smile they always shared, then together lifted knives and forks. His housekeeper was a sprightly seventy-nine-year-old, her once-fiery Irish curls now resembling coiled metal. Jokes about his advancing years were usual between them, and she prided herself on being skilled in the art of foretelling misfortunes—had in fact told him several times in recent years that jealous gods were watching his rise to fame and might soon begin searching for a flaw. But on Friday the thirteenth, a few hours before she was to witness his murder, Mrs. Bray voiced no warnings over their omelets. As she would later explain to Acting Captain Daly of the East Thirty-Fifth Street police station, an officer itching for an advancement to Actual, her parting words to her employer that morning were merely that his full white beard had become unruly of late, that a visit to the barber this week was essential, and that she expected him back at the house today by one thirty at the latest, preferably smelling of witch hazel and hair oil, for the recent trend in this city toward emancipation from lunch would not hold in a man of his age.

Hearing all this, Andrew smiled and nodded, then did the awkward dance of getting his greatcoat onto his aching body. He hated going to the barber. A friend of his had died last year of an exploded heart while listening to the scraping of a neighbor's jowls. Didn't sound like a good way to go.

4

He rinsed his cup out in the sink, then traveled to his office near City Hall, where he remained until one o'clock. Several tasks were accomplished in a neat four hours at his desk: making plans to honor Mary Lindley Murray with a plaque; responding to idiotic correspondence from politicians whose principal wish this week was that the Statue of Liberty, *her complexion seasick,* should be made brown as a penny again; and imagining a route for the new subway cars, large and copper-bottomed, vestibuled, to be carried on floats up the Harlem River, the kind of gleaming image that recedes to leave the rest of your day looking ordinary, ordinary, ordinary.

He walked out into the bustle of Broadway and took a moment to catch his breath. The *Herald* would describe the impending crime as occurring on one of those *well-cut November afternoons when the sun shines bright and the wind blows cold, when it is fall in the light and winter in the shade.* The *Sun* would maintain that the skies were *darkly overcast.* The *Brooklyn Daily Eagle* would stand entirely alone in claiming it was raining.

In this unreliable weather Andrew *rode the Fourth Avenue streetcar uptown,* as would later be recorded in the police report, with a look of amused determination on his face, the sharp features that made his moods look worse than they were, his white beard flickering in the wind as he went. He loved the press of cold air against his face. The way it seemed to tighten the skin. Only the skyline upset him as he moved through the city. The showy mess of buildings of different heights which stood, he felt, in increasingly incoherent argument with one another.

He was on track to meet Mrs. Bray's one thirty lunch curfew as he *alighted at the Thirty-Eighth Street stop* at twenty minutes past the hour. Succeeded in stepping around a stinking puddle formed by the fishmonger's discarded ice.

5

A particular pleasure Fridays brought him was the prospect of freshness—the week ahead did not yet contain any mistakes!—but why did every halibut seller in this city seem to share the impression New Yorkers had no sense of smell? Andrew looked up. Could see Mr. Hepiner now on the steps of his shop. An amphibian figure forever rooted in his little rubber boots, clutching that fishy bucket as if it contained the nation.

Oh, hello! Hepiner said, waving.

But Andrew did not wave back. There are certain grudges that are every bit as irrational as they are uplifting. A person must protect them at all costs, especially in old age.

He was eager now to be at home, in silence. To eat lunch, in silence. To read his new book, *The Literary Guillotine*, a record of the Literary Emergency Court, presided over by Mark Twain, within which execution was duly done upon the most overrated authors of the day, in silence. He saw on the stretch of sidewalk ahead a destroyed newspaper page, accompanied yet again by a constellation of chestnut shells (who exactly was this chestnut tosser?) and he stooped down now—ah—to gather all these items up, then crushed them carefully into his leftmost coat pocket, the one he'd asked his tailor to line with easily cleanable material designed with this particular purpose in mind. Tidying the streets, the ritual of it, gave him comfort. But there was never less trash. Each day brought more.

Those who saw him pausing to pick up those chestnut shells on this final journey would soon be cast as witnesses. They would decide he looked tired, that his back was hurting, that his character of late could be glimpsed in his gait—awkward, listing, the right hand dropping low as the foot beneath it fell, an old man who always appeared to be trying to catch objects falling from his grasp. And he did feel some of their eyes upon him. Felt embarrassed to be recognized

6

like this every day, but also grateful to be seen, for he feared of late that he was fading away, that President Roosevelt was taking longer and longer to reply to his letters. There had been talk last year of renaming a great bridge or building in his honor, but he was concerned he had burned such plans down by being curmudgeonly instead of ingratiating, and making comments to politicians which only he found funny. That unwise remark, for example, about Mayor Low's mustache looking like it had crawled onto his top lip in the search for a warm place to die.

A few minutes before the confrontation that would kill him, he walked north along Park Avenue without the aid of the cane Mrs. Bray always tried to make him take, past the usual butcher selling crimson cuts of beef and the tailor in his window making PANTS TO MEASURE, and past the candy store and the dental practice adjoining and the shady red-and-white awning they shared, and crossed the street in a shadow cast by the Murray Hill Hotel, its Cape Ann granite and Philadelphia pressed brick, its Corinthian columns carved with festoons of foliage, and looked at his home, number 91, and wondered what horrors Mrs. Bray had cooked up. He only hoped it would not be Hepiner's halibut again. She tortured him with this, her insistence on fish. She felt it was good for his knees and his eyes, for the thinning soles of his feet, for the creak in his joints in the morning—but what of a man's morale? At the age of eighty-three he had the self-awareness necessary to be patient with other people, but not always the facility to disguise the effort.

He loved this city. He hated it. It was a cathedral of possibilities, it would never settle down, it might remember him or it might forget him, there was a sense of no control, and for some reason he hesitated now, thinking city thoughts or lunch thoughts or other thoughts entirely, standing with his left hand settled upon the *little iron railing which ran along the front of his home,* and because of this hesitation, and a thousand other factors, a raw sprawl of coincidences and missteps and mistakes, a measure of bad luck and a degree of design, he would soon be lying on the ground with his face to the sky, sprawled and embarrassed, twitching, well on his way to becoming, in the words of one cab driver across the street, *dead as a tent-peg.* Or in the formulation of Mr. Anton the florist, a man who claimed to love nature despite what it had done to his face, *dead as a herring.* As dead as a sightless eye. As dead as a soulless sentence. As dead as a doornail, or a cliché, or a lucky rabbit's foot, or the pit of a peach named Stump the World. As lifeless as all the newspapers that would bear his name in the morning.

2

CHILDREN'S GATE

In their coverage of *the murder of the century*—the century being only three years old—several writers noted that the victim hadn't always seemed destined for fame. Andrew had been born in 1820 into a respected Massachusetts family that then fell, during his youth, into debt. Seventh child of eleven. As invisible then as he is today, in twenty-first-century New York. But there are still details to be found. A childhood never fully dies. Stories of life come up through cracks in the accounts, the spaces between death sentences, the pauses in obituaries, finding light and air to grow.

Weedy, Andrew was. Rawboned. A skinny child, quiet but stubborn, possessed of a shy self-reliance that could look like arrogance. Frown that sometimes made him seem superior. A tendency to impose order on his brothers' mud-caked boots, left there by the door each day in dirty disarray, a mess he hated to look upon, that he felt an urge to solve, lining them up by size and type at night, telling nobody what he had done. He was a boy who appeared at times too old for his years, one uncle said, and who had a gaze too intense for his own good. A tendency to stroke his chin when engaged in thinking or dreaming, as if trying to conjure under his fingertips the first hints of the beard that would grace his face later in life. Child with a quiet wisdom in his voice. In the slowness of his blink. A curl of amusement in those thin lips, at times—as if he thought, little bastard, that he was better than you. He liked to draw things. Note details down. Make up names for imaginary friends and places, towns which even now you will not find on maps: *Fernfoss, Skystead, Dignidale*. His family feared he might one day succumb to the catastrophe of being a poet.

Some thought his strangeness came from having entered the world in a leap year. Did this quirk of the calendar somehow contribute to his character, investing him with an understated self-sufficiency, like a tree that has survived a lightning strike? He was known in his boyhood to never cry when beaten by his brothers, but to always look a little lost, disoriented, a finish of innocence to the eyes, like he'd been born into the wrong century, or family, or body. It took several years for anyone to discover a simpler solution: his eyes were bad, he was farsighted; for immediate, intimate truths, Andrew needed spectacles to see.

He was not allowed to attend the school in Worcester fulltime. His energies were needed on Green Hill, the family farm. He learned how to finish a chicken coop in superior style. He took his turn at the plow, at cutting corn, at mowing and raking hay, at picking and storing fruit, at gunning and fishing and nut gathering, at preparing loads for market. He became strong and fast in the execution of these tasks, but was nonetheless told he performed them with a kind of dreamy distance, an observation which he struggled to reconcile with the facts of his productivity.

Andrew was not unhappy at dawn feeding the pigs their potatoes mixed with meal, corn and cold water, cider apples. But the real joy of each day was being released into individual liberty for two hours in the afternoon. In these hours of recreation Andrew liked to climb trees alone, perch in branches alone, sketching the landscape he saw before him, inventing whatever scenic details were hidden from view, filling out gaps in the facts.

He began to feel irritated, and then somewhat angry, at the way his father had laid out the land. He felt he could see a better way, a plan more beautiful but also more fruitful, so he drew out alternative arrangements in his notebooks, then crossed them through with one clean line and resolved to start again. When finally he showed the best plan to his father, laughter taught him to do better next time, but he did then notice, after a decent interval had passed, that the sheep pen was moved around to the back of the house, just as he had suggested in his sketches, so that the sheep would have greater protection from the wind, and would be able to move more freely between dark and light, a contrast which Andrew had come to realize such animals enjoyed.

After church on Sundays, he liked to escape his siblings by taking long walks in the hills. Sometimes on these walks he ventured all the way to Auburn, Leicester, Paxton, Holden, Rutland, Princeton, Harvard, Boylston, West Boylston, Shrewsbury, and Grafton. The longest of these adventures saw him sleeping in barns or moonlit open fields, riding in carts when distance demanded, that feeling of the friction of travel in his teeth, a whole world waiting to be discovered. When his one true school friend, Samuel Allen, asked if he might join him on the next such adventure—*keep you company, Andrew, take air together!*—he felt his own smile dissolve into the expression of one who felt he had already been robbed. Couldn't help it. Walking, to him, was walking alone. A precious thing you did not want to spoil with talk. He walked until his toes snagged and bled, his soles ached, his legs were bags of sand. He walked until fatigue sent him falling face-first into glorious hay, until the birds sang ugly songs to make him awake, until his mind got carried away—it was always getting carried away—and the church clock struck five and it was time to feed the pigs again. He walked until he stopped wondering why his parents were not concerned with where he was walking. If he was back in the house on Monday morning, preparing breakfast for his younger siblings, his attention somehow sharpened by the sleeplessness, as if being awake to the world was a trait built by habit, like tolerance to certain poisons, or an ability to climb, no one seemed to mind. In the mornings he was always trying to unpack his father's face, find the affection behind the sunburn.

He ascended Mount Wachusett at the age of eleven. Sitting at the summit in a knife of sunlight, he ate an apple carefully. Let voices filter through his thoughts. *Wipe that smile from your face. Set your jaw like a man. An ax is to be gripped like an ax.*

And yet at other times the stern surface of his father's face fell slack, and he held Andrew in his arms and kissed his ear, the usual distance between them destroyed, intimacy arriving without complaint. Those were the best of all moments, when he was drunk but not too drunk.

He looked at his father sometimes, ruddy skin, burned lips, breath sour from the second-worst wine in the cupboard, and thought: I can only hold things the way I hold them. But to say this out loud would be too heavy, so he tried his best to change. His ax work was more effective than that of his brothers, he cut faster and deeper and longer too, but he was beginning to realize that adults were largely blind to results. Everything for them was a question of method. All the world cared about was style—and his was apparently feminine.

In a usual week, his father would hit him only once, an outburst of violence occasioned by the drinking, or released by it. There was often the chance, therefore, to smell the back-of-the-hand blows coming, and sometimes to duck out of their way. If it were not for the ridgy power of that wedding ring, no blood would be drawn at all, but you had to let him achieve contact once in a while, for there is nothing more anger-making than effort which misses its mark. Even then, Andrew sensed this.

Mother died when he was twelve. He did not want sympathy, he only wanted her back. She was feverish one day, and then she wasn't. One of his sisters found her body in the bed. There were arguments in later years over which of them had first realized she was truly gone, each sibling remembering differently, so that the event of her death took on the specter of a tiny myth, a world of perspectives without a stable center.

His first thought, when his turn to enter the bedroom came on that day in his twelfth year, was that the air smelled of turned milk. His second thought was that they, he and his mother, would never be able to speak again.

It was not her cold face that was so shocking. It was the small fact of her silence. The bland reality of it—that all their conversations were now closed—came to him in a sickening rush. Never again in the morning would he be permitted to climb into her bed and huddle close after claiming that he was cold. Never again would the dog, which was named Dog, also jump up onto the bed, and be fed yesterday's bread, and be taught things Andrew had learned at school, his mother smiling while he pretended to be the teacher to the beast. Sometimes the dog barked twice when asked to calculate the sum of one plus one. Other times it made mistakes, which he forgave.

Andrew spoke rather rarely in the months after her death, or so he was later told. Words were still possible for him during the thickest part of his grief, but the audience seemed somehow unworthy. Sadness had made him selfish.

His mind hopped between packed impressions of the past like a child on burning sand. Silence wasn't a decision, not exactly, but he would come to think it had been a choice, an attempt to get closer to her, the state she was in, an absence more vivid than a presence. Briefly he thought of drowning himself in the river, but what if one day she sought to speak to him through the night? There would be better years. It would take a long time to swim toward them. He wasn't sure, at first, that he had the energy. The breakthrough was realizing that there would be days when he did and days when he didn't, days to avoid the water at all costs and days to dive in, bold.

His father soon brought in a replacement. For this he could not be blamed, the house needed to run, but was it necessary, truly, to marry four times in all? Andrew saw, earlier than most, the ways in which a family can drain itself of members, new mothers arriving to replace the old, bringing half siblings, pet rabbits, new cousins, appetites, growing bodies competing to breathe. Most of the women entering his father's life treated Andrew with the same cool reserve which they applied to the sheep and the pigs and the weeds, and this was fine. In his thirteenth year Andrew decided to pretend to everyone, all the time, that he felt fine. Oddly this worked—on them, and on him. He discovered there was a real buoyancy to be drawn from the act of seeming buoyant.

The house he grew up in was a plain wooden dwelling that stood on a little-frequented lane, two-storied but low in the ceilings, of decent length and breadth, and anchored by a chimney of needless proportions which, in certain lights, looked like a set of steps trying to rise into the sky. The effect, if one squinted in strong sunlight, was of a home built upside down. He stared at it on his fourteenth birthday as if he had never seen it before. Blinked. Wondered if there were better places to live, functional but also striking. He thought he might like to become a builder.

What else from his past might a reader of the *New York Times* not have been told? Perhaps that his eldest sister, Lucy, was his favorite sibling on account of three things: she did not beat him like his brothers did when he lined up shoes by the door, she told the truth whenever it mattered, and she had somehow escaped Massachusetts. But one day she wrote a letter home to their father in which she admitted that she feared that her little brother Andrew *might never become an elegant man on account of his distaste for reading.*

Finding this letter on his father's desk, feeling heat rising through his throat, a shame in his stomach that would never fully cool, Andrew resolved to apply himself to books, night and day, so that he might not merit what his sister had said. This despite the trouble with his eyes, the creamy haze which all proximate objects seemed to be bathed in, and the headaches that attention by candlelight caused. He developed a habit of reading five pages from the opening of a book, and then five pages from the end, going back and forth like this for some time until he could picture the raw sprawl of story in the middle.

It was one thing not to be a manly man, to fail to grip the ax a certain way, but if he could not become an elegant man instead, what exactly was left?

Under his bed was a box of leaves, varieties from trees he had met on his travels by foot. English elms. Tulip trees. Linden and sycamore. Oak. He could tell you the position each leaf had occupied on the tree when he'd picked it, but not yet why they had grown in that direction, nor what the use of the midrib and veins might be. He had begun to feel the first stirrings of it, the longing to transform himself into someone new, that special American itch for the future which, even now, so often afflicts the young. But in his bones Andrew also felt something even more alarming: a draw toward present beauty which he knew he should probably conceal or kill, for he imagined his life would give him no way to satisfy it.

3

GATE OF ALL SAINTS

Every murder invites a murderer, just as every egg invites a spoon or knife. The thin white shell would not make any sense unless breakage was part of its plan.

A little before one thirty in the afternoon on Friday, November 13, 1903, Andrew arrived at his home, number 91. He was, by now, much looking forward to lunch. He had his hand on the gate and his mind on boiled eggs when he noticed a stranger pacing back and forth on the corner of Fortieth and Park Avenue. A black bowler hat was perched at an odd angle on this man's head and he was glancing periodically at his pocket watch with the depressed intensity of someone who has been waiting far too long for their moment of action. Then the man looked up from his watch. Seemed to see Andrew. He smiled and waved and then began to jog in Andrew's direction.

The man looked perfectly cool as he approached, neatly dressed in a dark suit. Roughly five feet eight inches in height. Dark skin. A mustache which was turning slightly gray. It became obvious to Andrew, with the fresh perspective proximity sometimes brings, that the bowler hat was at an odd angle because it was too small, and therefore sat too high. As the man came to a stop he adjusted the hat in a somewhat self-conscious manner—or so Andrew, feeling self-conscious, decided.

Andrew thought he could see a hint of affection within the man's expression—a desire to transmit more than this occasion might allow?—so after a short awkward pause had passed he said, Hello, do I know you?

You know me, the man replied.

They stared at each other for longer than was common. Andrew began to wonder what outcome the stranger was envisaging. A certain percentage of the public liked to imagine themselves into Andrew's life. It was probably the same with most public figures in the consolidated city, but there was no way of getting used to the *feeling* of being seen, guessed at, measured and assessed, trespassed upon, invaded and altered by other people's perspectives, however positive or negative those perspectives might be, and however gently applied. Strangers shaped out their own idea of him and called this creation by his name. They made him an outcast of his own universe and a bit player in theirs. They approached him in the street like this and said, *Andrew Green, you have ruined this city!* Or they said, *Mr. Green, you have made us great!* Praise and censure went down exactly the same drain, though he admittedly preferred the friendly trickle of the former. Everybody all the time wanted to tell you about your successes and mistakes, everyone had an opinion to share, it was as though they were afraid that withholding speech could be a kind of death, or a cause of death, that they would expire on the spot if they did not speak speak speak. And now the stranger in the bowler hat stepped closer, and closer still, so close that Andrew could smell his breath—mint scent, lemons, pleasant—as two cab drivers across the street, standing in a strip of cool sunlight, loudly debated whether Jimmy Sheckard's best hours of baseball lay in the past or the future.

Have I really met this man before? Andrew thought now.

Am I mistaken in thinking I have not? I do not forget a face. I do not feel like an old man who has begun to forget faces. And yet . . .

He hated the idea he might slowly be losing his ability to hold other people in his head: neighbors, politicians, players of pointless sports. Was this man in the too-small bowler hat about to rob him of something more or less than memory?

Andrew avoided the intensity of the stranger's gaze by focusing instead on the space above the man's right ear. It was an old trick from childhood. A way to control embarrassment and fear when confronted by his father. And it was in this moment of temporary calm that Andrew decided to say goodbye to the man, to now turn and finally walk through the gate to his own home, but something continued to hold him back, an uncanny sensation. He was not the god of his body, let alone his fate, but what rooted him to the spot was perhaps a combination of two qualities, both sometimes dismissed as slight: nervousness and curiosity. Nervous of what the man might do if he turned his back on him, but also simply nervous of offending someone who was most likely a well-meaning stranger. Curious what the man might say if given further time, but also simply curious how long the present silence might continue. Other factors too, maybe. The culmination of a lifetime of unfulfilled intimacy. The desire, late in life, to see every project through to its conclusion, however doomed that end might be. At a certain age we forget to be afraid of people. We start to dread, instead, their absence.

A shift of cloud threw sunlight on the ground between them. Andrew noticed, in this new light, a spot of dirt on the man's otherwise shiny left shoe. It took all the willpower in the world not to kneel down now and scrub it clean. And what impulse was this within him, he wondered. What did it say about him, this constant desire to remove signs of dirt, in himself and in other people?

Across the street several cabs were standing before the Murray Hill Hotel. Some of the drivers of these cabs were in their seats, perhaps reading the racing news. Others were talking on the sidewalk nearby. Now more and more of them were looking up, taking in this odd partnership between Andrew and the man in the bowler hat. Did these spectators fear for his safety? Did they perhaps know, better than he, that this man was, say, a local thief? Was everyone wondering how much money he was carrying today, and how quickly he might be persuaded to part with it? He was known to be generous in matters of charity, but a famously frugal old bachelor in other respects, and on one occasion on the El train last year—still discussed in this neighborhood—he clobbered an aspiring thief around the head with an umbrella until the young man ran for cover. The headline in the *Sun: Famous "Father" Puts to Rout a Robber: A. H. Green Swings Umbrella with Telling Effect.* (Dollars protected from theft: two.)

The stranger adjusted his bowler hat again. Then he said, low and clear: Tell me where she is, Mr. Green.

And Andrew—an error—suddenly felt rather irritated, hot, bothered, bored, for this whole event was just the kind of minor misunderstanding that could shift in shape and waste half a day away. So he said, Who are you, anyway? And who is *she*? It may be helpful to be specific.

This last sentence did not go down well. The man sighed heavily, as if a decision had now been weighed and made. And Andrew, in his nervousness, realizing his mistake, glanced down at the ground again and said automatically, You have . . .

Yes? the man said.

Dirt. On your shoe.

The stranger in the bowler hat frowned. Observed his own shoes, the spot of dirt. Then he puffed out his chest, as if trying to reinflate his punctured pride, and began reaching into his pocket for something—heavy-looking, a first glint of metal in the sunlight?—until a noise from the street seemed to give him pause.

It was Mrs. Bray.

He was grateful to see her!

And then that gratitude turned to fear for her safety. She was whistling as she walked back from wherever she had been, perhaps a conversation with the what's-the-word *director* of Et Cetera Et Cetera about her daughter's performance tomorrow night. She slowed as she approached, staring at the stranger. Seemed determined to find meaning in the man's face—perhaps she recognized him, or wanted to? The whites of her eyes shone bright as paper, clean little breaks in the text of the day, and from a parcel tucked under her awkward left arm an appalling smell did drift.

Mr. Green? she said. Julia asked me to fetch fish for your—

Go inside, Mrs. Bray.

He watched with rising regret as, for the first time in living memory, Mrs. Bray did as she was told. She was inserting her key, drawing open the door, the warmth of the house rushing out to greet her experienced skin, all the well-lit rooms within which old objects drowsed, the glass figurines and heavy books, the maps and sketches on the walls, framed pages from the Greensward Plan, so many bachelor surfaces to be wiped and swept, and Mrs. Bray, for her part, had a strange feeling of being at the center of things now, an inkling that events were about to turn on her perspective. A moment later she heard five shots fired, and knew beyond doubt that he was dead.

At the bottom of the steps the stranger in the bowler hat

was holding a gun—one of those with a cylinder, Mrs. Bray saw. Mr. Green was lying on the ground with his face to the sky.

Cold Mr. Green . . . Cantankerous . . . A man you surely have not warmed to, Mrs. Bray.

These were things people had said to her about her employer. But now he looked, perversely, warmer and more accessible than ever before. That at least was how she would picture, in hindsight, his final face. He wore the expression of an old man interrupted midtask, or trying to hear a joke that remained out of range. His right hand was trying to shield his eyes, as if it thought it was the sunlight that was killing him. There was blood in his white beard, and on his shirt, but—small mercies—his lovely emerald-green cravat seemed to have been saved. He owned a dozen such neckties, all in different colors, as if this one public concession to brightness, to the idea of putting one's personality on display, might make him feel better about keeping other aspects of his self in shadow.

Mrs. Bray felt ready to faint. To fall down these steps and arrive at the murderer's feet. But she also felt acutely alive to detail. Her employer's killer was staring up at her. He looked confused by what he'd done.

It was then that a street pig came running around the corner, excited perhaps by the smell of blood. And oh, the animal did not care for the question of motive! That, she decided later, was what gave it such power. The real cruelty of dying was not the way your own obscene dreams went gray. It was the fact you lost the chance to tell your story. The animals rushed in, and they never agreed on what they saw, for the past was as much a work of imagination as the future.

The gun, Mrs. Bray heard herself say.

She discovered that her forefinger was pointing to the ground.

The murderer frowned. He aimed his revolver at her head, her chest, and then at her left leg, which was her better. Finally, just as she'd resigned herself to death, he laid the weapon down, with tenderness, in the exact spot that she had gestured toward.

Later Mrs. Bray would vomit into the sink. Later she would weep and write it all down. A letter to the woman she loved, a Mrs. Margaret R. Ellis, the one her husband no longer let her see, telling her everything that had happened, giving events a color and a shape on the page. Funny how, as you write a letter to a person who matters, you start to exist within the architecture of your own account, doctored details becoming true in the telling. In her correspondence with Mrs. Ellis, Mrs. Bray was not trying to solve the crime. She only wanted what every witness in history wants—to ascertain where she stood in relation to fate.

She shivered. Thought she felt the first ghost of Mr. Green already hanging over her head. The art of soothsaying had been passed from the Chaldeans to the Grecians, and from the Grecians to the Tuscans, and from the Tuscans to the Latins and to the Romans, and now it was clear to Mrs. Bray that the curse of foresight resided here, at 91 Park Avenue, on Friday the thirteenth, with her. She saw that flags on public buildings would fly at half-mast on the instructions of Mayor Low. She saw that Mr. Green's body would be dressed in his best suit so that funeral-goers could imagine he had consented to attend. She saw that President Roosevelt would deliver a tribute to the deceased under uninspiring skies, the leavings of a meal in his walrus mustache, patting his vest as if to double-check that the shooting hadn't happened to him.

BOYS' GATE

Shortly before Andrew's fifteenth birthday, two miracles happened: a gift of spectacles transformed his vision and his friend Samuel Allen stole a cartload of wine. The wine was red and tasted red. Sam got it from an uncle of his who ran a business which had an anachronistic name no one except its owner could remember. This man, Andrew understood, was such an enthusiastic consumer of his own product that taking inventory of the bottles had become less a science than an art, a very fluid process over which (to bracket his problems) he had lately given his young nephew some influence.

An August night. The moon was about as full as their heads were with the wine. The buzzing of bugs, the chirping of crickets, the croak of a toad or a midsummer frog, the possibility of a nighthawk in the sky. All this filled the evening air as flowers swayed in the leftover heat—the kinds of details one might remember or imagine later, much later, with the hunger of hindsight or heartache. He and Sam Allen were playing on the grass behind the Allen house, stomping out the last embers of a fire. Then an argument over who had climbed a tree quicker ensued and all of a sudden the two of them were fighting, rolling onto a patch of bare soil where another fire had once been, breathless, laughing, Andrew inhaling the scent of his friend's sun-touched skin, desperate for air and for relief, for a night to match the glorious warm day that had passed, lips burned by July and breath enlivened by the wine, more drink than he had ever in his life drunk before—at least two cups, perhaps even three?—and it had made them stupid, the drink had, and Sam's shirt was unbuttoned now, partway, his chest, that bone, its hard name—clavicle?—and Andrew now felt a strange burst of joy in his heart, a blood rush that had been absent these last few years since his mother went to bones.

Straddling Sam Allen, holding his friend's wrists to the dirt, he looked into those unblinking green eyes in that thick handsome face, and he thought, Disgust or desire? In which proportions was Sam, in this moment, experiencing these adjoining feelings? Andrew couldn't see, he didn't know, because his new spectacles had fallen off his face.

Where were the spectacles? For a moment he did not care. He was full of the excitement that thrives in the seconds before rejection or acceptance are announced.

What magnifies the world will at the same time diminish the person whose vision it benefits. The old family doctor had warned him of this months ago, told him to wear the spectacles only for an hour each day, since the work which spectacles do to correct one's God-given vision, the manner in which they accommodate mistakes of the eye, will over time have an utterly annihilating effect upon a young man's sight. And now perhaps he had worn them too much, because they had fallen off and he could see almost nothing of where they might be. Except, oh, *there* they were, by the embers of the fire in which he and Samuel had burned, only an hour ago, grotesque pictures they had drawn of girls, the Redman girl for instance, her imagined nether parts, frightening openings, suspicious spaces. She showed you if you asked, but they were too afraid to ask. Or perhaps not sufficiently interested.

He realized, to his surprise, when he got up onto his wine-legs to retrieve the spectacles, that Sam had closed his eyes. And so, although it seemed absurd, he came back with clearer sight and lay down next to his friend.

Every breath was a world. He felt his own lips drawn down toward Sam's ear or the space just above it—by force or inclination, he could not quite say.

Then a certainty. A clear, unmistakable feeling, as he nuzzled his nose against Sam's ear, of being watched from afar. And now Sam's eyes were opening, opening wide with fear, and Sam's mouth was opening too—lips stained bloodred—saying, What are you doing? What are you . . .

Doing. Sam pushed him away. Pushed him. And only then did Andrew turn and see her for sure: Sam's mother in the window, holding a candle. A glimpse of her horrified face. Flicker of curtain, then gone.

And he had known, hadn't he? That someone was there, or could be there. For a second, even a minute, during, or before. It was almost like he had wanted to be caught with his lips so close to Sam's skin. As if he had decided to become an adult, had been seeking out an annihilating effect on his own immaturity, his own youth. As if he knew already that life amounts, above all else, to the recruiting of witnesses. But then again, he might just have been drunk.

———

Nothing was said for several weeks. Andrew kept the incident in his stomach, a squirming humiliation he could see no way to exorcise, and when he resolved to stop thinking upon it, he of course only thought upon it more. Then one night, as his father sat nodding in his chair, seemingly drifting into the edges of sleep, words came. It was like seeing a dead man speak, someone who is finally free to say the things he could not while alive, though his father was too stubborn and grizzled to ever die—he'd live forever, Andrew felt.

His father said, eyes still closed, You are not friends with the Allen boy anymore.

The sound of the fire. The crackle, the glow. His father's face, his thick wrinkled skin, looked indestructible in the firelight. The scar on his wrist shone.

Andrew found he could not respond. Could not swallow, think. Then his father spoke again:

The Allen boy, his mother. She remarked upon a fight.

A rush of relief. A fight, a fight! And then his father opened his eyes and stared at him for a long time, long enough to undercut the seeming innocence of the remark that had been uttered, until Andrew saw those blank eyes beginning to close again, just as Sam's eyes had closed that evening in the field. In full sleep, Andrew's father wore the bitter expression that had come upon him so soon after he was widowed, overnight almost, like a disease it seemed, one which made the muscles needed for a smile go slack—that was it, the whole of it; the man no longer smiled, except in anger—and Andrew realized he had been wrong. His father *would* die one day, of course he would, and he'd be afraid of dying alone, as everyone is, so he would try to take others with him. His father would fail in this aim for one reason alone: he had always been bad at parties. Not even the sheep in the field followed him.

———

That summer, aided by his gift of vision, Andrew's grudging commitment to reading began to edge its way into pleasure, and then into obsession, as most hard habits eventually do. But then September darkened the green in the leaves, and his new devotion to literature was cut short over breakfast.

He was informed by his father that he would soon be sent away to New York to make money and be useful.

Andrew blinked. Looked for humor in his father's face. Scanned the pale, frozen expressions of his assembled siblings too. It was a relief—though not a big one—to see they shared his shock.

An apprenticeship at a general store has been arranged, his father said. An establishment by the name of . . . Hinsdale & Atkins, I believe.

As his father kept talking, Andrew watched the lazy effort of his lips, wet with milk from a glass at his side, and knew that the moment with Sam Allen in the field was connected to this banishment. It was as if each word were something heavy rolled out over the valleys of the mouth.

You will send half of your wages home, his father said, and this will be . . .

A chicken had got in. It was pecking at a cupboard door.

His father threw a spoon at it, and missed.

———

Over the weeks that followed, the first stirrings of a kind of hard regard started to form. Over the skin of him. His innocence. Scar tissue over a wound—or, to continue the theme less grandly, wine stain over a lower lip? He was tired of being shamed for his grip on the ax. For the drawings he liked to make of the fields. For the fact he had currently no great interest in girls. For his supposedly feminine handwriting.

All right, he thought. If you want to lose me, your best worker on the farm, so be it. The prospect of his father being eaten by regret began to seem delicious. The blunt fact of his having delivered the apprenticeship news at breakfast time, with the whole family there, stopped aching and began simply to sting.

He would go to the city. He would take the apprentice-ship as if it were his choice. Perhaps there would even be, somewhere in New York, opportunities for walking and climbing. To eventually make some serious money to send home, to be the outcast who becomes the savior! He was not sure. He knew nothing. He cared and did not care. He was afraid. He never remembered crying in his sleep, but he woke up often with his cheeks wet, even in the dead of winter. He was innocent, for the most part, of appetites, and yet he also felt a wild hunger growing in his gut. It might be nice, perhaps even productive, to turn himself into a ghost and start again.

At times what he felt, late at night, during these years, was a kind of helpless nostalgia, an emotion that he knew he had not yet earned. But it wasn't nostalgia for times he had already lived through. It was nostalgia for versions of himself he hadn't yet been. Though he did not want to leave everyone behind and go and work at a store in New York, perhaps it would prove to be—he winced at the phrase as it bloomed in his head—a gateway, to some other kind of existence?

Much later in life, Andrew would decide that his father, a failed lawyer who briefly became a failed essayist before turning his hand to becoming a failure at farming, had never lacked intelligence. No. What he had lacked were the tools of empathy needed to cultivate an understanding of other people. That, and a talent for forgiveness.

His father could never see why Andrew was so upset by what his sister Lucy had written in her letter—her assess-ment that he might *never become an elegant man.* This was a boy, after all, who had never shown much reaction to insult or punishment from him, William Elijah Green, a supposed figure of actual authority. A boy who, indeed, went on to display no hurt in his eyes at all when reminded, shortly before his banishment to New York, that if he had aspirations to become a fancy gentleman in the so-called metropolis, then he ought to forget about them quickly and entirely, for the only category available to him in this bitter world of unequal wealth would be, at best, gentleman of four outs.

Without money, his father said. Without credit. Without wit.

That is three, Andrew said.

Without manners.

And in his father's eyes, as he concluded his assessment, were there not signs of a smile? Love was present, Andrew felt, but its shine was hard to find.

He would go looking for it everywhere in the years to come. Love, love, love. As if it were a coin to be found in a field, or a park. As if it could be obtained without forfeiture.

5

GIRLS' GATE

At the East Thirty-Fifth Street police station, Mrs. Bray was required to repeat, over several hours, for a constantly changing audience of officers with good or moderate or supremely bad breath, the bare facts of what she had witnessed on Friday the thirteenth.

For the last of these interviews she was alone with Inspector McClusky. He had emerged as the apparent leader of proceedings.

McClusky was a manly man. Deep of voice. Confident. And smelled only of coffee. All the other officers had looked, Mrs. Bray thought, like the lightbulbs hanging down in this dreary interview room—bulbous at the hips, narrow at the head, dusty, inadequate, flickering in and out of attention. Whereas Inspector McClusky, when he had first walked into the room, had an utterly different aura. A sparkle to the eyes. A brighter bulb, certainly, and thicker in the chest than the gut, balancing capably on delicate feet. The handkerchief intermittently at his nose was an off-putting presence, but at least it looked clean. When she complained that the drinking water in the chipped cup she'd been given tasted rather disconcertingly of cheese, it was he, Inspector McClusky, who replaced it immediately, relying on a different faucet, and a smile. She thought she heard him mutter something about cabbage, but perhaps it was *savage*.

How did it *truly* happen, Mrs. Bray, so to speak, he said. Your full perspective will be very valuable.

Valuable! He was exactly right, she thought. Valuable was the word. His use of it made her happy, as a term of praise, but more importantly it was a reminder that she had a selection of morsels of information at her disposal that a less public-spirited citizen might only serve up at a picnic for a price. Time to draw it all out a bit, get to know him. Build a bond—of trust. Might the inspector even need a housekeeper?

Have you not already spoken to officers Houghtaling and Kelly? she said, careful to be blunt but not too blunt. Your colleagues were there for much of the drama.

He had, he said. He had. But they were—he smiled again— inevitably confined to their own particular perspectives.

Mrs. Bray liked this. Own particular perspectives.

Do you need a housekeeper? she asked.

He frowned and did not immediately answer. Then he said, Perhaps? One day . . .

Well, here was how it happened.

She had been hurrying along Park Avenue at a time approaching one thirty in the afternoon on Friday, swinging a walking stick she did not really need, one which she had in fact purchased for Mr. Green but which he refused to use, and as she walked she was whistling a tune she could not have described if asked, a mingling of various rhythms she had lived her life by, her feet moving at speeds that younger people seemed to find surprising, most probably because they associated old age with infirmity—whereas Experience, the experience of it, in her experience, in fact made you not an invalid but a warrior.

Yes, she was tired. Tired but determined. And given she had been delayed just now by a conversation in the street about her daughter's musical career, which had to date been full of discord, she also knew that she was late, a minute or two behind schedule with regard to lunch preparations, perhaps even three or four, or seven, or nine, or ten, and that Mr. Green never was tardy, not where Friday lunch was concerned, since she had invested so much time over the last few decades in instructing him, in quite clear terms, not to be. He would be back from the office by now and wondering where his meal was. So she rushed. She daydreamed. She carried under her left arm the stinking fillet of fish Mr. Hepiner, the monger, had offered, wrapped in wax paper, the freshest offering he had for sale in the shallow end of the week. It was fat, this fillet. Would take a full twenty minutes to fry. Regrettable, certainly, regrettable.

Here Mrs. Bray thought to pause in her account. I am a very good cook, Inspector, she said, making sure to smile.

Inspector McClusky nodded. Oh very good, very good. It was clear he was fascinated by her. He was writing *everything* down.

And then she saw him up ahead: her employer—now, today, no longer her employer, as he was dead—Mr. Green. Her first feeling was elation: He was only now arriving home! And then: Who was the man he was talking to?

Mr. Green was standing with his left hand resting on the little iron railing that ran along the front of his home. Something about his posture was peculiar—more upright than he had been in years, looking like a bird trying to scare off a rival, or else one locked in a mating ritual, even as his hand sought out that support. At first she could not see the face of the man he was conversing with, but then she drew closer and she could. Several decades younger than Mr. Green, this stranger, and neatly dressed in a dark suit. Dark skin, she explained to the inspector. I would say a black man . . .

The inspector nodded gravely.

A mustache which held some gray, she added, watching him scribble it down and—delightfully!—drawing a little mustache in his margin. He wore a black bowler. Every few seconds his hand had seemed to succumb to a great urge to touch it.

Mr. Green was out of sorts. This she could plainly tell as she approached. His famous calm had been ruffled by whatever the stranger in the bowler hat—an odd thing to be wearing, but people in the metropolis were, weren't they? Odd—was saying to him now, or perhaps not saying. In the end a silence can be every bit as devastating as a sentence; this lesson she had learned from her own losses. Her employer's arms had extended in a gesture of confusion—she watched his palms opening their faces to the sky—and she heard him say to the man, though she later doubted her own account, Who are you, anyway? And who is Miss Davis?

The rumble of a passing cart. The dust kicked up by constant deliveries to the Murray Hill Hotel! The way clouds of filth drifted across the avenue and clung to the windows of the house she had to somehow keep clean for her obsessive employer, a man who had created so much of this city but still seemed, even now, so concerned with irrelevant detail—the opposite of what a Great Man, whatever that was, should surely be like. Insisted on folding his own clothes, oh so precisely, like he was in the army. And he never had been in the army. Mr. Green had been ready to participate in Mr. Lincoln's war, but his special friend, Mr. Samuel Tilden, had wanted him to stay in New York, keep working on the Central Park, remain safe . . . And it was true, Mrs. Bray supposed, that certain people can contribute more in life than in death?

Inspector McClusky scratched his handsome chin. I've always thought so, he said.

He had family, did Mr. Green. He did not live entirely

alone. This she now emphasized to the inspector. That her employer's loneliness was not entire, that the fish she was due to cook for him for lunch was big enough for others too, the young ones, who would want to eat if they were home. They came in and out of the house unannounced all the time, for he had decided, against her advice, to give them all keys. For some time he had shared number 91 with his nephew, Timothy R. Green, and his three nieces, the misses Lucy M., Julia E., and Mary R. Green. It was something he could offer them in his affluent years, Mrs. Bray supposed: a comfortable base from which to make their own way in New York. But there might also have been a selfish motive, a desire for atonement? An apology, perhaps, for missing so much of their childhoods on account of his work, or for his uneven relationships over the years with their parents, his siblings, his whole family.

Mr. Green only now seemed to see her approaching, so wrapped up was he in whatever conversation with the stranger was taking place. He nodded to her slowly, strangely, and then briefly glanced at the parcel she was carrying, and she thought he looked a little angry at the sight of it.

Then he fixed his gaze upon her with an expression that now played into panic and said, Go inside, Mrs. Bray.

His voice shook a little, and that was shocking. To realize that he was scared. She could not recall another instance in all of eternity. Every politician who had ever visited the house, even President Roosevelt himself, had taken the part of being the terrified one, for it was well known that Mr. Green could be stinging. She would often recall with her friends how Roosevelt, surrounded by his staff, had stood on these very steps, the ones she was climbing now with the fish in its paper pressed to her chest, and when Mr. Green had opened the door to him, the president had said something that was small even for small talk, a remark about a very peculiar chimney on a building next to the Murray Hill Hotel, and how it had attracted his attention just now, as he came past it. Mr. Green had blinked. Said nothing. And so the president, rather keen to fill a silence now, continued: Still, Andrew, I suppose a chimney like that draws well, doesn't it? Whereupon Mr. Green delivered this unblinking retort: Yes, Mr. President, it draws the attention of every damned fool who comes down the avenue. Would you care for coffee?

So yes, he could be funny. If you thought such things were funny. And the coffee had to be made with a specific number of beans. He could taste any errors in arithmetic.

For a moment, she considered defying her employer's instructions and raising her walking stick high, striking the stranger with it. But would that not humiliate the man who paid her wages? Could he not, if he could deal with presidents so well, easily manage a stranger in an unfashionable hat, even one who looked so much younger, and stronger?

So she left Mr. Green to fend for himself in his hour of need, taking her final steps toward the front door, her right hand touching the keys in her coat pocket, the quick comfort of a change in temperature and texture, and despite today's unlucky date she did not, in this moment, feel greatly afraid for him, only somewhat uneasy.

Friday the thirteenth! She had thought the bad luck would take the form of a broken bone, or a lost parakeet, or perhaps an explosion at a house across the street, a rude remark from one of the cab drivers who sat all day long outside the Murray Hill Hotel praying for rain, the kind of profitable weather November promises but does not always deliver. She had foreseen, that morning, over a breakfast omelet which she had shared with Mr. Green—they had reached a stage of her service that was *closer* to friendship—only the general tone of the day, absurdity mixed with tragedy, but not the sly specifics.

Mr. Green had this gift. He was possessed, she knew, of different talents from hers, an eye for the small things, for how to bring them together into a whole. He did not foresee events, he instigated them. A man obsessed with what New York could become. A person who loved a detailed plan. No flowers for my funeral, he had told her with a smile on several occasions this last year, as if seeing his ending approaching. *No living thing to die for my final performance—except, quite naturally, me.*

In the moment before the shots rang out, she turned her attention back toward the open front door of the house, and gazed into the interior, which expanded in her mind.

The brightest wall of the corridor was hung with a framed document that remained untouched by the tragedy that had happened outside. It was a list of the gate names Mr. Green had chosen for his Central Park in the final stages of his work in making the Greensward Plan real. Early jottings on a yellowing piece of paper, words from a time when he had decided he was tired of the city's lack of space and air, the way it had become a tangled belt of shipyards and docks, commerce eating up the coastal spaces, every backyard built over, no place to walk or play or breathe—a metropolis, as he had said, *with no heart and no lungs.*

Boys' Gate
Children's Gate
Girls' Gate
Women's Gate
Engineers' Gate
Farmers' Gate
Gate of All Saints
Hunters' Gate

Mariners' Gate
Miners' Gate
Merchants' Gate
Naturalists' Gate
Woodman's Gate
Pioneers' Gate
Scholars' Gate
Warriors' Gate
Strangers' Gate
Inventors' Gate
Artisans' Gate
Artists' Gate

Each name a gateway onto the city's character, he had felt. And they opened a space, too, onto Mrs. Bray's own past now. She had worked with Mr. Green for half of her life. She remembered now the pressure he had come under to give the gates other names, names belonging to rich and wealthy men, surnames set in stone, a form of family patronage. And he had declined, and perhaps made posterity angry? He had adhered to the idea of ordinary access even at personal cost.

The gunshots marked the start of the circus. A race and a farce, no time to dwell and dream.

The murderer seemed much disturbed by what he had done. He kept saying, He deserved it, he deserved it, he . . .

And everything from that point unfolded in an instant, asking to be reimagined later on.

Officer Kelly and Officer Houghtaling came running around the corner. They flew into the murderer, pinned him to the ground.

Once handcuffs were tightened on the wrists of Cornelius Williams (who had by now announced that this was his name), Mrs. Bray watched with horror as Officer Kelly stood tall, as if satisfied his work was entirely done, and puffed out

his chest, trying to make himself hero-shaped—though in reality (and this she did not tell the inspector) he still looked like a horse scrotum.

Cornelius Williams said again, He made me do it.

Who? replied Officer Kelly, irritation shining from his eyes.

Him, Mr. Green! He was protecting her. He would not give me her address!

And Officer Kelly said, Whose address?

Hers, the murderer replied.

Hers?

Then a voice—perhaps the other policeman?—told Mrs. Bray to run and fetch Dr. Forbes. She did not want to run to fetch Dr. Forbes. Dr. Forbes was the only thing worse than a fool, which is a fool who likes to touch your shoulder while he talks. But in the circumstances . . .

A particular image came to mind as she hurried down the avenue to fetch the doctor, one she would keep private forever. It was a memory of a light gray felt hat often worn by her friend Maggie in the months before they were separated. On afternoons when they were free of their husbands they would sometimes lie in bed together, and she would ask Maggie to describe the clothes she had sewed that morning. The words themselves were colorful. Soft to touch.

When Mrs. Bray reached the stoop to number 96, it transpired that the doctor was already sitting there in the open air, waiting for a call to action.

This stoop-sitting was, Mrs. Bray knew, a very unusual practice indeed for Dr. Forbes, for he was a great believer in the importance of staying adequately hydrated, and also a great despiser of the pigeons that loved to defecate with such success on this section of the city, and these two individual tenets of preference had combined over time to make a single, thick quality supporting his whole character: an extreme reluctance to linger outside his own home, even in the most pleasant of weather, for fear that bird feces might contaminate the glass of water that he felt a man should always have at his side. Their awful feathers. Their beaks. Their feet! She knew the doctor had dreamed about them, for she was able to access some men's dreams.

Mrs. Bray said, Dr. Forbes, you must come. Mr. Green has been shot!

The doctor's face opened up in something like delight, as if an old familiar excitement was stirring within him, a fire he himself had thought was too pissed upon to ever spark again. And he said, I knew I heard something!

He had dealt with so many sore throats since leaving the army, she thought. So very many sore throats! Now a real adventure required his attention. His medical skill, his grandeur, might be allowed to shine! She was unexpectedly happy for him for a heartbeat, then reminded herself it was almost certainly too late.

As Mrs. Bray walked with Dr. Forbes toward Mr. Green's dead body, pigeons were alighting on various roofs. The doctor glanced at them, as if knew what would await him, later, in the glass of water he had abandoned on his stoop.

A crowd by now had gathered. Nine people, ten, perhaps fifteen. Mrs. Bray watched Officer Kelly managing this fact—the fact of bodies. It seemed he had punched the murderer in the face while she had been gone—Cornelius Williams's nose was now bleeding profusely—and he and Officer Houghtaling were currently preparing, it seemed, to deliver a little speech to the neighbors and cab drivers and Murray Hill Hotel guests who had gathered on Park Avenue in shock, or grief, or expectation of further excitement.

Officer Kelly shifted his weight from foot to foot. He cleared his throat. Only when he had the full attention of the crowd did he seem willing to begin. He recalled news that had reached him years ago from Holmes County, Mississippi.

The negroes there, he said, pausing to cough, took the law into their own hands one day and lynched a member of their own race.

As he spoke he pointed to the murderer, who at this time, in addition to still bleeding heavily from his nose, had begun to look nervous, glancing from side to side, as if, Mrs. Bray thought, by witnessing the special type of insanity possessed by public officials, he himself had suddenly become very sober.

The lynched man on that long-gone day, Officer Kelly continued, was named Wolsey or Wesley. He had been suspected of assault on a girl, if I remember . . . He was in the custody of a good constable, who was taking him to jail, when a crowd of other dark people came in sight, overpowered the officer without harm, and hanged the prisoner on a tree right there in the open. Justice to one of their own!

Here Officer Kelly paused for effect. Mrs. Bray watched him carefully. The air all around her suddenly felt tight. Stretched thin with the possibility of further horror. And it seemed everyone had already forgotten about her dead employer, lying just a few paces away with his coat over his face.

The crowd there on that day, Officer Kelly continued, like you all here now, I am sayin', was respectful of the white officer, taking their hats off to him, as should happen, but were very rough in their behavior toward the prisoner. I am thinking of that story now . . .

What was it that he had in mind, Mrs. Bray wondered, as the silence grew more and more uneasy. An assault on the murderer, or an actual killing? An act to save the city the costs of paperwork, prosecution, imprisonment?

Whatever it was, none of the cab drivers came forward to

comply. Pigeons circled overhead. Officer Kelly now looked rather embarrassed. Mrs. Bray felt her blood cooling just a little, and then an interruption arrived.

Everyone had turned, so Mrs. Bray turned too. It was not clear to her what noise or gesture had first caught the crowd's attention, but their gazes had now settled, as hers did, on an unusual old man standing thirty or forty feet away.

He was made up as a professor, this old man. He carried a cane under his arm. He had a white beard. Was smartly dressed. Some of the gathered cab drivers whispered to each other as they stared at him. Was this the ghost of Andrew Green?

And, as they did so, this old man stood there, in view of them all, but pretending they were not there, or mere invisible spirits, and proceeded to read a newspaper! As if that were the most natural thing in the world. Mrs. Bray made a sign of the cross on her chest.

The old man now took a long porcelain pipe from his pocket and went to light it. But in doing so—a great mistake!—he lit his newspaper on fire.

Some in the crowd began to shout. Others rushed forward, then stopped. Put out that fire! Help that old man!

But instead of helping, most only talked about helping, from varying degrees of proximity. The poor old man struck wildly at the flaming newspaper with his pipe and stick. He threw the paper in the air to try and rid himself of it. Soon the pipe and stick were also in the air! And he kept them there, in the air, although the paper was continuously changing weight. He juggled them, apparently in desperation, until it became clear that the whole incident had not come about by any error. He juggled, and he juggled still, with extraordinary skill, until the last atom of flaming newspaper was consumed. Then the irascible old gentleman caught the pipe in his mouth and the cane in his hand, smooth and sure in his every motion, and hobbled off down Park Avenue, smoking and smiling.

Perhaps he had never noticed the dead body on the ground, Mrs. Bray thought. Or perhaps the murder was exactly what had occasioned his performance? The other question on Mrs. Bray's mind was whether the old man would be glimpsed again before the year was out, as the *Tribune* speculated he would, or whether this artist of extraordinary talent was now ready to disappear from the record forever.

Mrs. Bray looked at Inspector McClusky, and he looked back at her.

Shall we go over some of those details again? he said.

MERCHANTS' GATE

G*ood luck.* This is what his father says to him as bags are settled on the ground. They stand on the path beside the carriage, blinking in the sunlight. *Good luck to you, in the mercantile trade.* As if it were all a question of circumstance. Of fortune. No human will involved at all. And then, after a moment of hesitation, comes the embrace—one that seems to lack a center. A feeling of being held only by the very edges of who you are. Of wanting, so intensely, to be brought into the heart. All of Andrew's courage evaporated in an instant. He was ready to fall to his knees and beg. Do not send me away.

Are you cold in that coat? his father says.

No, Andrew tells him. I am not cold.

Good, his father says. The air today . . . that is good.

The day is warm. The comment makes no sense. His father steps back and lifts a hand to his brow, protecting his eyes from the light. His wrist scar draws the sun. It is a long pink mark that arrived shortly after Andrew's mother died, when his father had an accident with a saw. For a while it was bandaged and rebandaged by the doctor, who came every day, whispers through the door.

It's time, the driver says. It is time, it's time.

The stagecoach to Providence, then a steamboat to the city.

He steps aboard. The horses snort. His father soon gets

smaller, his figure receding in the window, shrinking everywhere except in the mind. Andrew takes his spectacles off, then puts them back on, and off, and on. When he settles them on his nose for a final time, blinking, arching his neck to look again, his father has vanished and he feels it is his fault.

Gas in his gut. The roar of it. Stomachache for the whole journey. Strange bread his father's latest heartache likes to bake. She is less pliant than the others were. Andrew feels she will be fine.

Rise and fall. The knead, the punch. Falling asleep and whipping awake, head like heavy, heavy dough. He is wearing the better of the two worst shirts his third-favorite brother let him borrow. Privately, to pass the time and to get it right, he rehearses what he might say to Mr. Hinsdale, his new employer, formulations shifting as the coach jolts and sways.

I would like to succeed at the . . .

I would like to . . .

It is my intention, Mr. Hinsdale, to succeed in mercantile pursuits . . .

To find a situation in which I can . . .

(Thrive? Feel less embarrassed by who I am? Save my bitter father from financial disaster? Swap my thick-soled shoes for a pair less awkward? Correct the youthful errors in my education?)

Sometimes, during this journey, he thinks of his mother. And sometimes he thinks of that saw.

———

Most mornings, during that first summer in the city, he wakes at 5:00 a.m. in the windowless basement room that comprises his lodgings, a cupboard-like space set off from the cellar, barely bigger than a coffin, his mother's coffin, a coffin of Massachusetts maple that allows her soul no room to breathe, with his skin thick with sweat and his head prematurely pounding. Sometimes what wakes him is the sound of a dog whining in the street. Then a gunshot, and the whining stops, or else it increases.

He tries to resist the temptation to scratch the insect bites that have emerged down one side of his body ever since he started sleeping on the soggy mattress he's been assigned by the Hinsdales, its brown spots and red stains, but he gives in to the dirty urge in the end to relieve his itch and the bites are turning to sores that bleed and make more stains. He is thirsty, always so thirsty, and he'll remember that sensation for the rest of his life, but the water here is bad, he is afraid of it. He sleeps on his socks at night to try and dry them, has a cough that keeps him barking in the dark, but he earns a dollar each week plus meals and sleep, and he has not yet been fired, a fate he has learned has been frequent and quick for many of Mr. Hinsdale's previous apprentices. Half of his wages he sends home in letters his father replies to only rarely. But the mere fact of his survival here, overlaid with his first independent income, gives Andrew a thrilling sense of satisfaction that surprises him afresh each day and wraps his loneliness in something smooth.

At 5:15 a.m. it is time to brush his teeth with his finger and climb the stairs, get on his knees, and clean the floor of the store.

Beyond the large display window, the sun is coming up. Heat is always already creeping in under the front door of the store. It takes a conscious effort to breathe as the day begins to burn. Stink summer. Sweat summer. Suffocate-to-death summer. In such conditions it is impossible for him to imagine this city in the winter, the slow silence that the cold back home has always held, but as he cleans, and coughs, and climbs the little creaky ladder to restock the higher shelves each day, something in his chest does seem to loosen, and his arms seem to lengthen, and a pressure lifts from his bones and brain and, as if held by no ties at all, he relaxes into the pleasures of repetition.

Perishables have to be prioritized at this early hour. The drawback is you have dirt under your nails for the rest of the day. He handles the containers of coffee beans and spices, cool and smooth. He restocks the milk and eggs, the honey and molasses. Sweating, he unpacks the crackers, the cheese, the butter. Sweating, he addresses bolts of cloth, pins and needles, threads. The unpacking of great bags of dried beans is next. They become less dry as he leans over them, dripping, and the sight of this, of his own body dirtying the produce that he knows should be enjoyed by other people, deserving people, people whose families are whole, parents who are not ashamed of their sons, upsets him a little, irritates his need for a perfect process, so he begins to tie a towel around his head while doing this particular task, to soak up any moistness, prevent the spillage of sweat, forestall the ruination of these beans, their pleasingly uniform size and shape and texture, thousands of them, huddled like a whole city's population in need of care, and when he catches himself in the mirror, unfurling into adulthood, he laughs, because he is tired, and he always laughs when he is tired.

He finds his favorite thing is window work. Arranging jars of foreign teas in a tower. Imagines he is building a vertical village. He has it all just right.

He notices he is still good at construction, but also suited to erasure. Talented, he might almost say, at spotting what does not belong, at making cluttered spaces clean, at removing mess so a place can gleam in a way Green Hill never gleamed. He likes the way the slightest impressions are magnified at this early hour: the distant crack of a crate-maker's hammer; the flat beauty of a flake of downtrodden tobacco; the vendor pulling a cart out of the shack on the other side of the street, ears all aquiver with the effort. This is an area of hatters and druggists, of print shops and bookstores, of hackney coachmen waiting on corners praying for rain.

There is a taxidermied raccoon on the counter. Its eyes shine with a dull displeasure this morning. He sees on the wall clock that it is already half past six, so he performs the task of laying yesterday's newspapers at its feet. Stories of death and disaster. He thinks of his mother. Why are some victims newsworthy, and others not? That dog outside is howling again.

His morning solitude is broken always in stages. First he hears an upstairs window opening. Then comes the bright sound of liquid hitting the street. Finally there is the stair-case creak. Without deciding to be scared, he is scared.

Mr. Hinsdale emerges in the doorway holding a candle in a little dish. He has not yet changed out of his nightclothes. Prefers to dress after breakfast. He looks at this time of day like nothing so much as a giant, buttoned-up baby. He yawns. The candle flame gutters. He yawns again. The flame recovers. When the mouth is open, revealing those surprisingly neat, sharp teeth, Andrew thinks of an overfed otter. Soft bearing, and even softer whiskers. But vicious, should it feel provoked.

As he stands there with the candlelight coloring his hairy chins, Mr. Hinsdale's attention—which is always quicker than his body—rushes to the counter, to the newspapers Andrew has laid out for his perusal. Mr. Hinsdale makes a habit of reading the latest death notices daily. He establishes addresses, then visits bereaved families to pay his respects. When the mood seems right (and to Mr. Hinsdale, it almost always seems to seem right) he arrives at the doorstep of a mourning wife or child and offers to relieve them of certain salable items belonging to—his favorite phrase—the No Longer Living.

Greatcoats. Medicines. Good quality canes. The objects of dead men surround Andrew now. People possess so many *things*. He wants a few too. Not too many. But some. A little ownership, eventually.

Andy Green, Mr. Hinsdale says in his morning voice, one of basic disapproval with compound interest added. Green as grass! But in time you will learn. Why are you wearing a towel?

Andrew's hand reaches up to his head. Indeed, there it is.

I forgot to remove it, he explains, wondering if it is acceptable to ask not to be called Andy.

But . . . why is it there? Mr. Hinsdale asks. There is nothing he likes less than being in the dark.

Andrew shrugs, thinks of the sweat-free beans, then apologizes for shrugging.

Sometimes Mr. Hinsdale can be almost amiable. There are occasions when he even asks questions about Andrew's past. Today, for instance, he wants to know from which part of England the founder of the Green family first came. He is impressed, clearly, by the idea of having an apprentice whose name bore, once upon a time, a noble history, and Andrew on this subject is pleased to have information he can impart. An ancestor of his, the first Thomas Green, before coming to Worcester and choosing Green Hill as his residence, had been contemporary with very troublesome times in England, whose monarch was by then already framing the timbers for his own scaffold. This English ancestor might have left his English home, Andrew tells Mr. Hinsdale now, partly on account of a desire for a life of exemption from religious constraint, and settled in Massachusetts on that account.

Mr. Hinsdale puts his candle down in order to better blow his nose. Exemption from religious constraint, he repeats. Where did you learn all this, little Green?

From books, Andrew explains.

Mr. Hinsdale pockets his handkerchief. Clutches the crucifix around his neck. He sleeps with that crucifix on, Andrew has ascertained. There is a shallow imprint of self-sacrifice visible on the pink flesh above his collarbone.

Books will not help you, he says.

The pre-American annals of the family have always been important to Andrew's father. This is probably because, Andrew suspects, they made his father think there had been gentlemen among the Greens before, and therefore could be again. Though it is always clear, too, that his father is as conflicted in this as he is in most matters; he is surely not sure he wants his children to rise up above him.

One book Andrew found last year, while searching for evidence to make his father happy, had affirmed that one Thomas Green was a relative of and fellow comedian with William Shakespeare, and that Shakespeare's father may in turn have once possessed an estate which was known as Green Hill. It was also suggested in the pages that Thomas Green may have known John Milton, poet, statesman, scholar. So yes, there are suggestions of a literary lineage to the farm, even if such evidence could not be supported in a court of law. The current reality of Green Hill is very different—a site of drunken disrepair—but Andrew, too, takes comfort in imagining a better past, even if he cannot picture, just yet, a better future.

Night falls. It always does. The shop closes. Mr. Hinsdale retires to bed. Andrew sweeps the floor a final time. He hears the sound of Mr. Hinsdale's daughter screaming upstairs, the one who is an adult with the mind of a child, and his wife softly singing to her, and the awfulness of this, night after night, is punctured by further gunshots outside, cracking through the dark.

7

HUNTERS' GATE

One night, out walking, unable to sleep, and more fatigued than usual by his endlessly unfolding apprenticeship, the eighteen-hour days, the bugs that puncture his skin every night, the lack of money for real milk or for visiting his favorite sister, Andrew saw a man in the street who was raising a gun and pointing it at what?

A young mastiff, thin and weary-looking, staggering for a place to sleep.

It was the summer of shooting dogs. The mayor, deciding there were too many strays on the street, had offered an inducement to exertion of fifty cents per death. This generous sum had encouraged certain enterprising New Yorkers to import dogs into the city in the dark of night from Flushing and Oyster Bay, from Crane Neck and Mount Misery, from Saugatuck and Sachem's Head, all along the shores of Long Island Sound, in order to kill them and drag their bodies to the central payout points.

In a few months, the Great Fire—how keen some men are, he thought, to call destructive things *great*—would sweep through this street and bring it all to ash. But for now, Andrew's eyes adjusted to the dark only enough to see what was directly in front of him.

The dog, too, now saw the gunman. Yet it did not run away, was too tired or dumb. The difference, in the end, between life and death is perhaps nothing more than movement? Life on the farm had taught him this, even if he did not quite know how to express such a truth, and Andrew decided to move on the dog's behalf. He said to the gunman, Wait!

He did not want another harmless dog to die just so the hunter could claim fifty cents from the city. And the man with the gun—this was the strange thing—did exactly as he was told.

Andrew's fingers began fumbling for coins. He seized, among all the gullyfluff that gathers in a good apprentice's pocket, fifty suitable cents. This was money which he was otherwise going to spend on bread to fill his roaring stomach, sink himself into a deeper than usual sleep.

He offered the coins to the man, who laughed, and took the money. What a boy! he said. Then he apologized and shot the dog anyway.

Profit and loss. Andrew went hungry for two days on account of this stupid expenditure. New York lessons are quick-learned. An instinct is a propensity prior to experience. Only the dog in a wild state howls for no reason. He watched it being dragged away.

———

He started to think, after this dog event, that the trick to living here was to find a form of distance from the city itself. To see it only as a place, not a life. An area that could change and be changed in the mind, transformed through private unspoken effort. Pick your way through the alleys like a dog in a dream. Do it as poisonous steam rises into an indifferent sky. Inside his head, his own version of the city began to grow.

The sophisticated citizens his father had told him so much about back home threw their waste out of windows each morning. It splashed and spread into puddles which

bubbled as the sun sought to reach its peak. Heaps of gar-
bage decomposed in doorways. Rats danced in the alleys.
He watched laborers returning home with dinner kettles.
Ragpickers bothering apple ladies. Horses set to collapse
under the products of commerce they had carried back and
forth, back and forth, all day long. New York didn't set out
to charm you. It was like God that way. You had to bring a
lot of the enthusiasm yourself. He liked the idea of that. Of
being somewhere that would not pander to him, but which
would not single him out for any special cruelty either. Any
harm would be randomly applied.

Or at least, randomly applied within a given area of social
standing. The rich could afford to avoid a good deal of cruelty. They could choose where to put their feet, and what to
eat. The constant hunger in Andrew sometimes dwindled to
a manageable pit of pain in his gut as he waited each night
for Mrs. Hinsdale to bring him a small supper—two potatoes and a strip of boiled shad, six days a week. On Sundays,
the potatoes numbered three. And on Sundays, too, the
Hinsdales allowed him some time to walk and worship God.

Andrew believed in walking more firmly than he believed
in a higher being. Was even more hungry for motion here
than he had been at home. So he walked to the Presbyte-
rian churches and the Episcopalian churches, to the Bap-
tist churches and the Methodist churches, to the Wesleyan
and Independent churches, to the Dutch Reformed and the
Roman Catholic churches, to the Universalist and Orthodox
and Quaker churches, to the Hicksite and Congregational-
ist and Unitarian churches, to the Lutheran and Moravian
and Swedenborgian churches, and, on one swiftly regretted
occasion, even the German Reformed. A sermon was much
cheaper than the theater. It was also a lesson in the way city
gentlemen moved. Their phrases, gestures. An opportunity
to watch and imitate, which had to be the first stage of pos-

session? In the rearmost pews his lips moved in mimicry. Performance. And sometimes desire. He loved the energy of the hymns, the sense of belonging they seemed to offer. He memorized words in foreign languages, faithful only to their sounds, and wondered if his own occasional doubts about the existence of God might in some way be mutual. Did anyone in the heavens really believe in him, Andrew Green, this awkward boy below, his spirit, his potential for good? His own question frightened him into muteness, the kind of silence the living rarely know, the moon hanging sullied by smoke in the sky, filthy with the expulsions of men.

Tonight, if his legs had any strength left, he would climb up onto the roof of the store again and watch all the action that Broadway occasioned, the chaos of carts and animals, the hawkers and homeless, the worse off and the better off, the luckier than him and the far less lucky, ladies in their interminable coats braving the dirt simply to be seen. The rich leapt over suspicious puddles in their beautiful clothes. Up and down they strolled, no discernible destination in mind, and that, he decided, must be a thing that money can buy: the freedom from needing direction.

Half-built houses. Whale-oil illumination. An alleyway is a disappointed road, waiting for someone to widen it. He made sketches of the surrounding streets. He was not yet quite sure why.

Even at night there was the sound of breaking stone. It aggravated him, and yet it also stirred an excitement. New buildings gleamed like lines in the Bible, poetic, lovely, as true as fact or fiction. Stony-faced fashionables seeking dinner marched from Union Square to Howard Street and back, their stirring silks, their varnished boots, their Paris bonnets. The rattle of omnibuses, the smell of waste, the constant filth kicked up at crossings, the cigar smoke on the balconies of the cafés overhead, too much detail to

54

see at once, too much to note down, impressions fighting for space in his lists and diaries and letters. He was always writing now. Reading was more problematic. He needed somewhere to obtain actual books. He needed knowledge. He needed, desperately, to escape the smallness of the store.

And standing up high on the roof of Hinsdale & Atkins on those thick summer nights, long before he suspected he might one day become accidentally famous, he looked north across the city as the day declined. Enjoyed a giddy, godly sense of a cooling breeze. The sky up beyond Houston Street became a purer black, a thing one ought to be able to touch or feel, like a piece of coal or a length of slate, a field on Green Hill after burning. It signaled the wilderness this island would still accommodate for a while: the swill-milk, hog-feeding, and bone-boiling establishments; the rocks and swamps and ponds and rills; the dogs and pigs that thrilled their way through the vast northern reaches of New York.

8

PIONEERS' GATE

Many of the tributes Mrs. Bray had imagined did indeed appear. Powerful people described her employer as a pioneer. Each found a different point of entry for their eulogy, separate gateways through which to revisit his achievements—his parks, bridges, museums; his work to create a fairer, more orderly public school system in New York when he was president of the city's Board of Education; his tireless cleaning out of corruption when he served as New York's comptroller; his essential role in founding New York's first great public library after the death of his book-obsessed friend Samuel Tilden in 1886; or his almost single-handed bringing together, late in life, of the existing City of New York with Brooklyn, western Queens County, and Staten Island, to create the consolidated New York we now know, a project his critics described as the Great Mistake of 1898, questioning how such work, the stealing of Brooklyn's independence, could make him deserving of the title of Father of Greater New York when he did not even have children of his own. Personal anecdotes and rumors were shared too when news of his murder came, but on each occasion the thing that had caused those paying tribute to speak was the same: Death. His death, to be precise. His silence. The opportunity it presented. The lively words of condolence mourners performed tended to reveal more about the speakers than their disappearing subject. Some wanted, in death, to put themselves close to him. Others decided there was nothing to lose. If his reputation lasted and grew, they would be golden by association. Whereas if the circumstances of his murder or his sometimes secretive personal life led to the slow obliteration of his mostly good name, the mourners could simply disown him later. The beautiful fact was that he would not answer back.

Mayor Low set the flags on City Hall to half-mast. He reminded Americans that there would be no Central Park without Andrew Haswell Green, who had a greater claim to being the park's chief creator than *any other single man*. Together with his *intimate friend*, Samuel Tilden, Green had also helped to bring the city back from the brink of financial and moral bankruptcy, the mayor said, and played a key role in throwing Boss Tweed in jail. All this before his career had culminated in a vast and extraordinary act: bringing about, in 1898, after several decades of stubborn campaigning, the union between New York and Brooklyn. The consolidated city, the mayor said, in some of its most beautiful and enduring features, should be grateful to Andrew Green, for it was the *monument of his love*. The Father of Greater New York's fanatics and critics could agree on one thing, the mayor felt: the name Andrew Haswell Green would be remembered forever.

When President Henry A. Rogers, of the Board of Education, saw the flags on City Hall flying at half-mast, he cursed himself for his slowness. He sent out a general order that all flags on all public school buildings be similarly set. The gesture was necessary, he announced later to the press, blowing his nose heavily on account of a cold, in respect for Mr. Green's great services to the public school system of this city.

Justice Vernon M. Davis, in the Criminal Branch of the

Supreme Court, heard of the murder while adjudicating the trial of Annie Caruso, who stood accused of stabbing Joseph Polumbo of 128 Hester Street. He had always thought of Andrew Haswell Green as a friend, he said, though it was also true that the word *friend* usually implied a person who responded to invitations to dinner.

I have just received word that a distinguished member of the bar, the hardest-working man I ever knew, has been shot in cold blood, he said. A great philanthropist. One who has done a great deal for the advancement of the material and moral interests of the community. The deceased was a true gentleman, a person of great character and indomitable energy in every relation in life. Andrew H. Green was, among many other things, the chairman of the board of directors of the New York Society for the Prevention of Cruelty to Children, of which I, Vernon M. Davis, was of course also a member. I feel unwell to find out just now that a man such as Andrew Green has been shot dead outside his own home. It is only proper to adjourn the court out of respect to Mr. Green's memory.

Ex-congressman Thomas J. Creamer, who over the last decade had suffered greatly on account of his name—cruel, fashionable jokes about the thick and rich rising to the top, and some other remarks he couldn't even understand—said that he was also much affected by the tragedy. He could, in truth, hardly appreciate that Mr. Green was truly dead—especially at the hands of *a man of the kind* he understood the murderer was. He could not really bring himself to speak of such a tragic event, truly, he said, and then went on to speak of it at length.

Creamer said that Mr. Green was a prominent presence in the lives of all the lawmakers of the period immediately after the close of the Civil War, when he, ex-congressman Creamer—with some success, it should be noted—had represented the Tenth New York District in the Assembly, and the Sixth District in the Senate, between the years 1865 and 1869. Mr. Green was wont to bring bills to the legislature for consideration and passage throughout this time, Creamer said. Then, and ever after, until the day of his death, it was clear that Mr. Green kept a very close eye on legislation by the state lawmakers, exercising the kind of attention to detail he had probably honed as a young man put in charge of bookkeeping for various New York stores, before then transforming himself, somehow, into a sharp and hardworking attorney, and then later a famous advocate for fairer education and greater public space for all. Mr. Green was never a nuisance. No, no, not that. But he was, it might be said, a very particular man, and perhaps there was a strangeness to his character too, or what might even be described as an emptiness—a quality indefinable, and perhaps nonexistent. Green was a lifelong bachelor who had guarded his own private life with care, Creamer said, while bringing great public works into being.

Ex–district attorney W. M. K. Olcott was also among those who called at the Green residence to express deep-felt sorrow. Olcott told Andrew's younger brother, Oliver, who had by then arrived from Chicago by train, that he had come into close relations with Andrew during the Greater New York consolidation times, as a result of taking a role on Mayor Strong's Sinking Fund Commission. He could hardly speak highly enough of Andrew Green, who had always lived up to his ideals. Olcott felt sure that Posterity, *that pitiless bitch*, would in due course be kind to the man *a vicious negro* had murdered on Park Avenue on Friday the thirteenth. He also wondered if by chance there was cake? At which point, Mrs. Bray obliged.

Words and words and words. Prejudice. Public funeral. Column inches. Weeping in the street among people who had known him, and people who had never even heard of him.

There was speculation over whether the murderer was truly insane, as opposed to untruly insane, or not insane at all, and whether Andrew Haswell Green might have known him somehow. Was it a crime of passion, or a political assassination, or some kind of great mistake? Was it true that the truth will out, as white moralists liked to say it would, as if they somehow had an eye on all of society's lies, the disclosed but also the undisclosed, a survey of the whole surely being the only way to make any assessment of absolutes?

There was talk among many politicians of erecting a great memorial to Andrew, just as there had been at the eightieth-birthday party the mayor had thrown for him, the one which Green rudely had neglected to attend, saying he was in the end too busy with work and planned to eat alone with his nephew. But what if new information came to light—a revelation that he really had known his killer, in some insalubrious way, or else knew the woman, Bessie Davis, whom the killer seemed to be raving about, and whom detectives, even the rising star known as Inspector McClusky, had not yet tracked down? It had been said before, and was now said again, that during his life Andrew had perhaps associated with society's underclass too freely, campaigning for improvements to the conditions of colored people even as he failed to prevent so many of them being removed from their land to make way for his Central Park, and people recalled Green on at least one occasion late in life speaking—in a rather pathetic way, some said—of guilt he felt about a year he had spent in Trinidad in his youth, when he had been desperate for money, as a supervisor on a sugar plantation where not all the workers had been treated well. A certain kind of personal atonement, the quest for it, tends to implicate everyone else. In New York his campaigns for equality were, in high society, often as unpopular as salad, and the itch.

And had Andrew, some of the politicians reflected as the days and weeks of scandal and speculation continued, not been a somewhat patronizing individual, after all? Distant? Superior? Aloof?

Did he not, perhaps, from one perspective or another, deserve to die? Or—to glance at the issue from another direction—did he truly deserve to stay alive?

A man dies at twenty and it is a great shame. He dies at thirty or forty and he has been taken from us too soon. But if one reaches the age of eighty-three, all the shock eventually begins to flow the other way, even in a murder case. The chief question becomes: How on earth did he survive so long?

9

ENGINEERS' GATE

The first attempt on the life of Andrew Green had occurred on Thanksgiving Day in 1873, when he was a mere fifty-three years old. He would believe, until the day of his actual death, thirty years later, that the assassination plan had been occasioned by his work with Samuel Tilden to expose the corruption of William Tweed, a member of the New York Senate who had used the full extent of his ingenuity to become the third-largest land-owner in New York.

By this time Andrew had risen to the position of comp-troller for the city. His task was comprehensive, yet simple: to save New York from financial ruin. You have done it with your park, the politicians begrudgingly said, so why not with the city itself? We need you. You are needed.

Need. What a powerful word when it is not framed as a command: I need you to unpack the dried beans, I need you to muck out the pigs, I need you to leave me in peace, I need you to arrange your face and not cry at your mother's funeral.

Today his work in clearing up the catastrophe that was the city's finances would be, regrettably, interrupted by a personal appointment. He had made a commitment to eat too much turkey this afternoon with two of his surviving sis-ters and their children. He cursed himself for this promise, but it was too late to break it, and he arrived at the office at 5:00 a.m. in order to ensure that the wasteful Thanksgiving meal that lay ahead of him might at least feel somewhat earned.

The only other person in the office was, it transpired, a messenger boy. This boy happened to be yet another Samuel.

Did this young Samuel not wish to spend the day with his family? Andrew asked him. Reminded the boy, whose skin was marked by a pink scar across his cheek, that a circular had been sent to all employees relieving them of the need to come in today. Apparently some people did not like to work all day and all night. Had other needs, lives, families they liked. He had been trying to be respectful of that.

The boy Samuel shrugged. He was cradling various packages in his arms. Andrew felt a rush of love, or connection, however mistaken. Another person putting labor before life.

The side table, please, Andrew said.

The boy now placed most of the packages on the side table, but he kept one box in his hands.

I wasn't sure, sir, he said.

Sure of what?

The boy straightened. Swallowed. Mr. Comptroller, he said, his voice breaking a little. I believe that this, this particular package . . . looks suspicious, Comptroller Green?

He looked in the boy's eyes, saw confusion meeting fear.

The box in question was perhaps ten inches long and six inches wide. Two inches thick, or perhaps two and a half. It was wrapped in thick brown paper, prepaid at letter rates, and addressed by means of characters that had clearly been cut from newspaper pages.

Well, the boy was right, Andrew thought. They might as well have written *bomb* on the front.

The boy's expression now clouded with doubt. Sir, what should we do?

Andrew thought for a moment. I will tell you what we must do, he said.

The boy, for a few seconds, looked extremely relieved.

We must, Andrew continued, encourage this package to brave the harsh elements of a storm-tossed sea, relying on our own firm purpose in wetting its deadliness. We must ask Divine Providence for a safe landing place—a rock of defused certainty upon which we might embark.

Sir? the boy said, shifting his weight from foot to foot.

And Andrew heard himself say: Come with me, if you like.

And it was when he heard these words come from his own throat that he sensed something unpleasant lurking in himself of late. He was lonely without being able to admit he was lonely. He was melancholy without feeling he had any excuse to be melancholy. He was successful now, somehow, and he had forgotten how to enjoy success. The boy was understandably excited by the adventure at hand today. The question was why Andrew, at the far greater age of fifty-three, felt the same dumb thrill.

With caution they descended the stairs in silence, Andrew going first, carrying the box. They entered the basement of the courthouse. They found a pail. Andrew filled the pail with water, almost to the brim, a few inches left available for the process of displacement, and the boy said, Is this the . . . the proven treatment, Comptroller Green?

Proven? I have no idea.

Next he told the boy to stand back. Then he thought better of it, and sent the boy to hide in a cupboard twenty paces away.

The ridiculousness of all this! And yet wasn't this how so many citizens died each year—in absurdity? He removed his jacket, rolled up his sleeves, but what exactly would this achieve? He could hear the boy Samuel breathing hard beyond the cupboard door.

So very gently, so very slowly, shutting his eyes tight like a frightened child, Andrew plunged the package into the water and waited, hands cold, his mind fixed on a remembered baptism. His pulse was slow, which meant what?

He pressed the package all the way to the bottom of the pail. He opened his eyes to see it down there, made vague by the water, remote as a long-gone event.

Time passed in slow-formed thought. Then he heard a tentative knock on the cupboard door and was awoken from his musings. An angel's voice saying, Comptroller Green, are you alive?

Only now did he become aware of his heart beating fast. Alive, alive! It took a great effort to seem calm. The work, indeed, of a lifetime.

He said to Samuel, Come out, come out! And the boy came out.

Let us go back upstairs, he said. Let us leave the package here in the water awhile. We could have died, I suppose.

––––

Two hours later, as he led the boy back downstairs, he had calmed himself enough to see, more fully, the utter foolishness of having handled the package in the first place. There was nothing unserious about delivering such a bomb on Thanksgiving. The sender must have known it was one of the few days of the year when he would be one of the only men lonely enough to work. In fact, perhaps the timing even suggested a conscience? A desire to spare innocent victims.

And yet he, the intended victim, Andrew Haswell Green, had not even had the decency to properly protect this young messenger boy. He had only asked him to hide in a cupboard, as if that would have helped in the event of an explosion. What an act of selfishness, really. To want to show his bravery to the boy. To be his savior. To want, for once, to not be alone in an event. And now he had accidentally succeeded in making the boy bold and loyal. Young Samuel stood at his side, refused to leave him alone.

They stared at the package together. It looked paler now than it had two hours ago, immersed as it still was in this ludicrous pail of water.

Andrew rolled up his sleeves again. Reached down into the soft water.

The package felt weak and gentle at his fingertips. Malleable, vulnerable. It made no special signs of life as he lifted it—no click, no fizz, no violent blast of color.

The boy in his nervousness had started laughing, and soon Andrew started laughing too, in his case partly from fatigue, the fatigue of spending fifteen hours staring at numbers each day, and another five at night. They stood there, laughing, as the clipped newspaper characters that spelled out "ANDrEW GReeN" began, of their own accord, to peel away, a whole botched identity vanishing.

The package was a wet, dripping mess in Andrew's hands. The bells of the nearest church struck up beyond the window, but sounded sad. A strange atmosphere of disappointment descended as they fell into a fresh quiet.

He peeled the rest of the wet paper away as the boy watched. There were a dozen or so wet metallic cartridges inside. Most were upright, but three were lying on their sides, and there was a matchbox that was also wet, and several wet matches sticking out of that matchbox, and also sandpaper, coiled, soaked.

At one stage in its dry little life, this homemade bomb was probably a compact exercise in exactitude. Now some of the wildness of the world had got into it—water, air, elemental realities—and had revealed the whole thing for what it was, the product of crude engineering.

Every project, in its private making, achieves a kind of

perfection, Andrew thought now. It is only when the work goes out into the public sphere that stupidity creeps into it, or emerges from where it has been hiding all along. And what does it mean when there is a person out in the world who would like to see you dead? A person who feels something so strong toward you—a passion, a true passion—but a passion to see you *gone*?

Who might send you such a thing, the boy said.

And Andrew dug up a little line about being the Least Popular Man in New York, competing for this title only with Samuel Tilden. One of Tweed's men had probably sent it, he explained. It was incredible how you could plunder the public purse and still, with a foolish statement or two, hold on to people's hearts.

On his way out of the courthouse an hour later, Andrew nodded to Mr. Jones, who said, Would you like me to arrange transport, Mr. Comptroller? The streetcars today are comical.

He smiled at Jones and offered a wave. Wished him a happy Thanksgiving.

And then he turned back, dug in his pocket, and removed five crisp banknotes.

Would you see that Samuel, the messenger boy upstairs, receives this for his overtime?

Jones stared at the money as if appalled. But then he nodded.

It was now far too late to visit his sisters and their children. He would eat alone instead, a cheese sandwich of thanks back at his lodgings, and then spend a few hours studying numbers in bed. There would be time enough to send apologies in the morning, an offering to alleviate his guilt.

10

ARTISANS' GATE

The question of how Andrew first met Samuel Tilden, the man who would become his most beloved friend, is one still debated among the two or three historians who have consented to remain remotely interested in either of them. Some say they were introduced at a party in the late 1830s, thrown by a physician named Delafield, but that has the glitter of a doctored fact, for at this time in his life Andrew was not invited to a great many gatherings, and certainly not the kind of gatherings that upmarket men like Samuel Tilden flocked to.

As Andrew recalled it later in life, the story was this: they first met at the store.

Andrew was standing behind the counter at Hinsdale & Atkins when Samuel Tilden entered. Under the counter he had, in his hands, a book on engineering that he was secretly studying. The ordinariness of the store, its absolute absence of events, on this particular afternoon and on many other afternoons besides, conjured a sort of creative pressure that made the reading experience strangely intense. It took him a moment to hear the door, to look up, to stop blinking. He watched, stunned, as the new entrant smoothly removed his hat.

This was not the kind of customer to which he was accustomed. The gentleman seemed to be here by an act of pure caprice, a handsome and refined gift from the gods, an arrival to place a stay on the long thick boredom of a twelve-hour shift, or else to enliven it with fear. Questions.

Hello, the stranger said. How are you?

A smooth, warm voice. Almost hypnotic. The kind that carries forth the kind of smiling self-assurance a person can spend a whole life looking for, but which others have by birthright. Yet he looked a little overheated, this gentleman, and clearly he was, for he now took off his beautiful emerald-green coat, folded it casually, and slung it over his forearm as if it were something he'd just killed.

Andrew tried to offer his own smile, surely less steady, by way of reply. But his throat felt tight. He couldn't stop swallowing.

Failure—in the presidential race, in love, and in the effort to repair his unstable health—had not yet come for Samuel Tilden. It was all far in the future. He was six years older than Andrew. If his face was not always striking in repose, it was gorgeous always when animated by laughter, and Samuel, knowing this about himself, or perhaps not knowing it, would laugh often, easily, even on that first day in the store, despite or because of his serious nature. He was a budding lawyer heading to great places, turning his head toward high society as a flower does to the sun. Thin and erect. Smiling and flushed. Impeccably dressed. His eyes sat too big in their sockets, as if surprised by the home they had found, but in other respects he looked like a person beyond shock—one who sees and sees, very calmly, very clearly, into the distance. Here was a gentleman customer who was accustomed to moving through rich rooms, Andrew immediately thought. A person at ease under the thick scrollwork of beautiful ceilings, strolling amidst the hush of soft carpets, and now, somehow, here he was, brightening this dull place with his presence, searching for something. But what?

Andrew sensed, even now, in this first encounter, that here

was essentially a solitary man. That this was what they had in common. Perhaps *all* they had in common. A man with a hunger for study, a man of reading, but also a man who is clearly much better than me, Andrew thought, at adopting the guise of a social creature.

At this point Samuel Tilden held a clean palm up to Andrew and opened his beautiful mouth, clearly about to share some words of wisdom or advice. Andrew waited with tense excitement as Samuel said, Tomato?

Andrew's face must have shown confusion, for Samuel Tilden smiled.

Tomato pills, he clarified. Extract of tomato, that is what I am seeking!

Samuel's smile now turned uncertain in the silence, which was strange to see, and he looked more boyish than he had a moment ago. Perhaps you can, well, offer assistance . . . ?

Thoughts were fighting for supremacy in Andrew's head. But it seemed no clear winner wanted to emerge into speech. He felt sweat trickle down the collar of his shirt, damp already on account of his washing it last night. The lights in the store suddenly seemed too bright. Nothing ever dried here, it all stayed exactly the same.

And Samuel, as if unsure how to solve this awkwardness, or else seeking to ascertain if Andrew really was a mute, introduced himself, said his name for the first time, and Andrew thought: Dear God, another Samuel in my life. I am about to be bitten again.

Later in life Andrew would recall, within the privacy of his diaries, the strangely joyful fear that came over him when he tried to reply to the questions posed to him during this first encounter—like the excitement of a risky ride at a fair, he guessed, though having never taken such a ride, he really couldn't say for sure. Time itself seemed to stretch, an answer expressing itself in his head, then refusing somehow to form on his lips, because did Mr. Hinsdale stock tomato pills or not? Andrew had touched every bottle and box in the pharmaceuticals section of this store. He knew, but he did not *know*, and with this gentleman, more than with any other audience before, he wanted to make sure he did not make mistakes.

The silence gathered still more awkwardness, like a ball of dust that draws more dust, then more, and Samuel Tilden, blinking now, staring, smiling, seemed ready to dismiss Andrew as a natural fool, which was exactly what Andrew was desperate to avoid but also felt was fair. Samuel Tilden began to turn on his heel, gone forever, about to put his hat back on his head and his coat back on his body, but then—

Joy jumped in those overlarge eyes. In the wall of medicines, the handsome Samuel Tilden suddenly seemed to find what he wanted. He pointed, as if permission were required! Then Andrew watched him wander over. Saw him withdraw—yes, of course they were there—a bottle of tomato pills from the shelves.

Samuel Tilden held the bottle of pills delicately between his thumb and two of his long middle fingers, as if it were the beam of a balance. He smiled at the bottle. Then he said, Yes. I don't believe in these, exactly. But one must try a thing before one dismisses it, don't you think? So my brother always says. Always. He is very repetitive. Tediously so.

Andrew made a sound in response, one that was close to *Oh*. It was a start.

Then Samuel said, He does not much care for books, either.

For books?

Yes, my brother. He is an artisan, good with his hands, yet he will not hold a book!

With this, Samuel Tilden approached, extended himself on tiptoe, and peered over the counter, eyes now assessing Andrew's waist. He nodded to it—oh, to the book in Andrew's hands, the one on engineering—and he smiled and said, What elegant fingers. Are you a pianist? I imagine those hands could lend themselves to creation, but a different sort to my brother's. Is engineering not rather dry, for a dream . . . ?

Mouth dry, tongue thick. Andrew was feeling something he had not felt before. He barely got any chances, was the thing. He knew, with every second of dumb hesitation that accumulated within him, that he was wasting an opportunity which was all the more precious for being rare. It was a cruelty, really, that those people well practiced in the art of taking opportunities were the ones who had vastly more opportunities to rehearse the taking of them.

Andrew said, very carefully, I also have a brother, one who is interested in pursuing engineering.

Oh really? said Samuel Tilden. Then he yawned.

Life had prepared Andrew to meet a certain kind of face: one that hardened quickly into impatience. But no, Samuel Tilden's expression softened into boredom, and then into something akin to sympathy or guilt, which in some ways perhaps was worse? He licked his thin, lovely lips for a moment. There was perhaps, on reflection, something slightly sickly to the pallor of the skin.

What is your name? Samuel said, smiling.

Me? I? I am Andrew Green.

A fine name, Samuel said, gesturing to his own coat, which he had by now tossed on top of a decorative box for sale to the left of the counter. My favorite color. Though a name like Green does not quite suit your—

He was looking at Andrew's clothes.

But I can tell from your way of speaking, Samuel continued, looking as if he were about to laugh again, that you are no urchin. No, no.

His eyes, Andrew thought, suggested he was at home with the absurd.

You are descended, Andrew Green—the Lord strike me down if I am inventing—immediately from that stock of ancient half-savage Britons that Caesar could not conquer. Am I correct? Who exactly are your ancestors?

My ancestors?

You are not Welsh, are you, by any chance?

The Welsh, Samuel Tilden went on to claim, seeming to find his stride, but still clutching his bottle of tomato pills, for which he had not yet paid, because Andrew could not bring himself to ask him to pay, to cut short the moment or force it back into purely transactional territory, are a restless, fearnaught, go-ahead kind of clan, to be found almost anywhere these days, and always getting into trouble, both real and imagined. The Joneses. Thomases. Evanses. Enochs! Edwardses. Williamses! Jameses. Davises! Owenses. And oh, the fucking Cadwalladers. Don't even mention the Cadwalladers! Samuel Tilden said. Their feet all seem these days to meet our streets, but no, all Welsh extraction is easily announced, is it not, by a Christian name taken for a sir-name, and your name, Green—you did say your name is *Green*?—is not that way at all, no, so let us forget all that I have said. I have taken wine over lunch—with the Van Burens, do you know them? You have no Welsh in you after all, is my conclusion.

Samuel slapped the counter with the palm of his hand, as if it had been naughty.

This request, to forget what had been said—the name-dropping and the name-interrogating—did not, to Andrew's mind, seem easy to meet.

He felt himself drifting now. To his friend, the first Samuel, Sam Allen, their fight for intimacy on the grass, the silence which followed . . .

Samuel Tilden was taking a deep breath. Was holding it like a man about to dive. He looked on the verge of laughter again, a man trying to restrain a hilarity that only he fully understood.

You don't waste words, do you, Andrew Green? he said. But perhaps—he blinked—perhaps you like to read? Books other than books of engineering?

I do love to read, Andrew replied, trying to contain his own eagerness. It happens this, this book, is the only book I could find this week. But I believe . . .

Yes?

I believe that one can never be an elegant man without a taste for reading.

Hearing this last line, Samuel Tilden finally let all his hilarity out. He laughed hugely—but not altogether unkindly?— his mouth, his eyes, his brow, his whole slim and elegant and overpriced being swarming with common amusement. What a way to phrase the thing! he said. And then he apologized for his bad manners and added four words that caught Andrew with the twisted force of a riddle:

I like to collect.

Andrew swallowed. Made a guess. Books? he said. You like to collect books?

And as he said the word *books* again Andrew began thinking of the book he had been reading under the counter before Samuel Tilden entered, of a passage about the way bricks made with machinery are found to dry out with more difficulty than bricks made by hand, in consequence of the great pressure that has been made use of in their creation. The clay, being more compact, dries on the outside long before it dries in the center. And in consequence, the surface is apt to peel off and—

Yes, books, Samuel Tilden said, nodding and coming closer, his wrists resting on the counter now, so close to Andrew's hands, and his cologne uplifting the muskier scent of the other proximate mammal, the taxidermied raccoon on the counter. His tone of voice suggested the confession of a filthy thing. There was a confidential pout to his mouth now, the kind of look Andrew's father had liked to try to beat into a bruise.

Desire, Samuel Tilden whispered.

His expression told Andrew he was waiting.

Desire? said Andrew, trying to push away, through sheer willpower, the heat he felt flooding his cheeks.

Samuel nodded. He desired to buy a first edition of *Paradise Lost*, he said. Small quarto, gilt, London, 1669. A perfect copy, with a seventh title page, and bearing the autograph of Blakeway, the historian of Shrewsbury. He desired a sumptuous copy of *Cromwelliana*, also, the folio volume, extended and inlaid to five volumes. He desired Boswell's *Johnson*, Murray's royal octavo edition, extended to six volumes by the addition of a profusion of beautiful engravings illustrating the life and times of its subject. He desired Moore's life, letters, and the journals of Lord Byron: two volumes, quarto, extended to four by the insertion of choice plates. He wanted to collect many beautiful books to add to those he already owned.

I recently returned from Yale, he said. I did not like the food and the people there, he said. Both were too rich for his constitution, he explained. They weren't what he wanted at all—they were the whole cause of his present stomach trouble, very probably, the reason he needed the tomato pills in the first place, and really he was only here in New York to complete his law studies at the new university—but the books, the books at Yale, they had been fine! And by studying them, and starting on his path to becoming New York's most successful lawyer (he dropped this great ambition into the sentence like a random coin into a beggar's bowl) he would be able, eventually, to buy every rare book he desired.

Samuel did not blush as he announced his own future. When he eventually departed the store, the little bottle of tomato pills disappearing into his pocket like a secret they shared, leaving far too much money on the counter as recompense not only for the merchandise, he said, but for the fine conversation he had enjoyed, the time of Andrew's he felt sure he had wasted, Andrew felt somewhat faint and feverish, and also a little used, even before he noticed that Samuel had forgotten to take his lovely green coat home with him. He had never in his life met a man who spoke so openly of wants.

INVENTORS' GATE

Cornelius Williams is brought before the sergeant's desk. After being stripped naked and mocked for his appearance, he is re-dressed. Then he is made to suffer the high-pitched provocations of Acting Captain Daly, a man who tries to calm himself sometimes by putting scraps of paper in his mouth and chewing them, bits of notes and even warrants and records, some moist fragments falling into his big red beard and remaining there, hanging on for dear life, or else falling to their death on the table or floor whenever he yawns, all this happening as if he has not a care in the world, though in fact he cares deeply, or should, for this habit of chewing pages in fact works against him, as most of his habits lately do, because whenever one of his superiors is confronted with a suggestion that it might finally be time to promote Acting Captain Daly into, well, *non*-Acting Captain Daly, someone higher up says, Who, the paper eater? And then paperwork becomes the subject, an area in which he is weak.

Cornelius Williams tells Acting Captain Daly that he is forty-three years old. He gives his address as 256 West Twenty-Sixth Street. On his person, officers have already found a razor, a pocketbook containing five dollars, and a dispossess notice dated August 6 for premises at 426 West Fifty-Seventh Street. These items have by now been transferred from Acting Captain Daly's clammy custody into the cooler hands of Inspector McClusky. The dispossess notice, both men agree, may prove to be a key piece of evidence.

After a further beating of the kind nonwhite suspects are habitually subjected to—keeps their passions from acting up, Daly says—Cornelius Williams is finally given the opportunity to catch his breath and explain the crumpled dispossess notice: he once rented half a house with a woman of whom he is now no longer fond.

Mr. Green . . .

Go on, says Acting Captain Daly.

He'd been protecting her.

This woman?

Yes, sir. He made me do it, I had no choice.

At which point Acting Captain Daly, if the record of their interview is free from error, asks the prisoner if he has ever been admitted to an insane asylum.

I have been called foolish sometimes, Cornelius Williams replies, but never insane. I am not insane.

In his case notes, a mad scrawl of curlicues and aslant observations a modern reader might associate more readily with the hand of a medical professional, Daly writes, on the day after Andrew is killed, managing to smudge his ink a little (perhaps he is left-handed, perhaps he is in a rush), that as the alleged murderer makes this remark about not being insane, he is *twitching nervously at his mustache* while his eyes, which are *queer, roll continuously*.

A coroner's jury is swiftly drafted:

Alfred E. Marling, real estate, 47 West Forty-Seventh Street
Robert Walker, lawyer, 55 West Seventy-Fourth Street
Joseph L. Hilton, coachman, 27 East Fortieth Street

James Welton, retired, 52 East Forty-First Street
Walter G. White, lumber merchant, Murray Hill Hotel
Theodore T. Baylor, lawyer, Murray Hill Hotel
P. W. Radcliffe, undertaker, 316 West Nineteenth Street
Mornay Williams, lawyer, 315 West Eighty-Eighth Street
Thomas L. Farquhar, insurance, 159 Madison Avenue
Joseph S. Scofield, railroad agent, Murray Hill Hotel
William H. Haskins, MD, 42 East Forty-First Street

Each member of the jury knows the victim is a prominent man. Some of them have their own stories of him.
Everyone has walked through some part of his Central Park,
or crossed one of his bridges, or visited his Metropolitan
Museum of Art, or his American Museum of Natural History, or the New York Public Library that he founded when
executing the last will and testament of his great friend, the
governor and presidential candidate and obsessive book col-
lector Samuel Tilden. The jury live in the consolidated city
he has created; many of them have seen him in the street.
They reside in homes or workplaces close to the scene of
the crime. They have been chosen not for their good judgment, nor their good character, or sense of justice, but for
their proximity. It is a quality they all have in common. Like
being a man. And being white.

They read the notices in the newspapers to refresh their
memories. What an exciting case to be involved with, they
think at first. And then: What a pain, what a distraction
from the business of living!

Eighty-three years old. A lifetime of being a bachelor. This
extended life of aloneness might have an effect on a man's
character, might it not? Independence might have rusted
into obstinacy. What other explanation was there, some
suggested, for why Green did not fall at Cornelius Williams's
feet and beg forgiveness for whatever he had done, or hadn't

done, when the gun was pointed at him? Humility could surely have saved his life. Didn't have it in him? Or couldn't call it forth in time? Or wouldn't?

Did a weight of disappointment keep Andrew's heart at rest wherever it was placed? Did he fail to perceive the trouble he was in? Or was he simply too aloof and privileged at the age of eighty-three to believe he was in life-altering or life-ending danger? Pride before a fall.

The jury wondered, in particular, about these alleged words from Williams, overheard by a cab driver, and supposedly spoken just before the first shot was fired: *So you expected me to save you?*

Hard to know what this meant. Hard to imagine yourself into the half-gone context. The jury's distance from the key event, in terms of time, could still be counted in hours, yet already it was receding into unknowability.

Two errors, wrote Pascal, a thinker Andrew once admired. *One: to take everything literally. Two: to take everything spiritually.*

How do we picture the past? Does it become clearer as it drifts into the distance? Can it be seen from more angles, a better vantage, with finer instruments for optics, and more supporting documentation to draw from? Or has its essence already vanished, leaving space for lies to multiply and thrive, spreading across paperwork that is good for nothing except, perhaps, a nervous acting captain's next snack?

So you expected me to save you?

Perhaps Williams's final question before pulling the trigger was in fact a form of reply. Perhaps the words were offered in response to a statement by Andrew that went unheard, or unrecorded by history. Or perhaps Williams said something else, something similar, and was misheard, or misquoted, or misunderstood. It happens all the time.

12

SCHOLARS' GATE

To be a gentleman in New York, one needed an education. To obtain an education in New York, one needed money. To obtain money in New York, one needed to be a gentleman. The city formed its circles. This is what he thought as he stood before a mirror in the back room of the store wearing the expensive green coat Samuel had left behind. He looked different wearing it. From every angle, strange. Yet in this light it almost fit.

He felt he was edging closer to the future he wanted, a life that might exercise his brain and keep him fed, but how to gain any traction? Books, he thought. Books, books, books. Books to get him somewhere. Books to turn him into someone. Books to grab hold of on his way up. Books as a way to be alone without feeling so alone.

He took the coat off very carefully. The mirror was grubby with fingerprints that were not his. Beside the mirror, a horseshoe hung. He touched it, and tried to talk himself into being a person who would do anything to succeed. But then his focus was drawn again to the mirror's dirty fingerprints, the spoiled transparency, and his fledgling effort at superstition failed him.

Instead he gave in to a great inner compulsion to find a cloth and wipe the glass clean. As he passed Mr. Hinsdale's banisters, he touched the wood twice, then a third time, tap tap, tap. He was adding a rhythm and a neatness to the day. He did it almost every time he passed them, just as he almost always tugged five times on the corner of that bug-filled mattress before turning over to sleep.

He was not so tired and hungry now. Not like he had been during the first few months here. The stomach shrinks to its situation, accommodates its circumstances. The excess money Samuel Tilden had left for the tomato pills had funded a good reserve of milk and bread which he had used to supplement Mrs. Hinsdale's shad meals for a while. Slowly but surely he could turn his attention to other appetites.

His father had sent him away from Green Hill with only two volumes: the Bible and *The Elements of Bookkeeping*. To mark his progress in rereading the latter, Andrew was using pages fallen out of the former. Single and double entry. Bills of exchange. Arrangements to promote perspicuity. Genesis, Exodus, Leviticus, Numbers. Reading late into the night, every night, but wanting other material. And why should books be such elusive objects in this city? There did not seem to be a public library in New York. To be able to withdraw books from the Apprentices' Library, one had to make an initial payment of ten dollars. The Mercantile Library required one dollar up front, and then an annual tax of two dollars to be paid in quarterly installments. These sums placed too large a burden on his pathetic pocketbook.

He watched the door to the store every day. He waited, and waited, and waited.

And then Samuel Tilden came back—was passing by, he said, and suddenly remembered he might have left an old coat behind?—and the conversation turned once more to reading, and wants, and an extraordinary invitation was tabled.

———

The sun shone. The breeze was cool. First relief of fall. There was the sound of church bells in the air, an encouragement to faith, but the din of nearby business from Wall Street muffled the sound, made it human if unholy, and speculative men with restless faces charged south as if their futures depended on returning to their desks.

He and Samuel were standing before the New York Society Library, staring up at the facade. The building was made of brown freestone, with three-quarter Corinthian columns, resting on a projecting basement. Samuel was a member, it had transpired, and he was able to bring guests. Andrew knew the mathematics of what this meant. Must have paid the twenty-five-dollar price of shares, as well as the four-dollar annual dues. Even richer than ever suspected.

An ornamental iron balustrade formed a balcony. It was to this balcony that they retired after Samuel had given Andrew a tour of the library's elegant interior, the high walls of books in perfect alignment, knowledge collected and built into beautiful, insurmountable barriers that made him feel, instead of the curiosity he had expected, only a mix of awe and fear and dread. The smell of the books was the strangest thing. So many old volumes, each releasing its own scent, together formed a perfume that was new to him. Hints of grass, of dust. Of vanilla too. But also notes too bodily to be pleasant.

Out on the balcony the smell became flowers and smoke. Young gentlemen stood blinking slowly in the sun, carrying books to little chairs and tables in the open air, or else they stood at the precipice in order to enjoy the unobstructed scenery of the vicinity. Almost all of them paused to look at Andrew's shoes. In his childhood he had felt so often like nothing more than a spirit, a flimsy thing caught between the desire to stay and the desire to go, between self-expression and a need for silence. But these men? They were members. He was only a guest, even now. That was the difference—a difference he saw everywhere. They looked away from him with the quiet displeasure of people hoarding expensive secrets.

He had secrets too. He thought of them as he followed Samuel's flawless blue coat—did he possess an endless array of styles and colors?—to a shady area of the balcony. He was very quiet today, was Samuel. Perhaps he regretted this whole arrangement, the minutes already wasted on the tour? He shook his head rather coldly when asked if he was still feeling unwell.

Unwell?

The tomato pills, Andrew said, hoping to see that smile again.

Samuel nodded. The garden down there, he said. It belongs to a gentleman named Mr. Winter.

Dutifully Andrew peered over the balcony's edge. There were overhanging fruit trees below. A low Dutch church on the horizon. The delicious smell of apricots in the air. On this side of the building the sounds of commerce quieted and the city managed still to possess an atmosphere of repose that reminded him of home and made him long for more green space elsewhere. The air glowed. A bird sang badly but gladly. Life clung to some degree of rurality here, every house down below possessed of a private garden, and every private garden possessed of thick grass and aging trees, and the conversations of sparrows and wrens, and all this lifted Andrew's unease a little, reminding him of Green Hill, in an abstract and therefore painless way, making the unfamiliar familiar, and reminding him, too, that he did not really miss home so much now—only longed for it, which he supposed was a different thing?

Ah! someone cried.

A stranger had dropped a pile of books on the ground, it seemed. Andrew watched the man pick them up with flustered hands.

And then Samuel, with that way he had of moving into an utterly different mode within a heartbeat, seemed to become less blue. He began to offer forth an unstoppable torrent of talk out here in the balcony breeze, and Andrew began to think that what he had taken for sullenness a moment ago was in fact nothing more than the occasional shyness common to many seemingly very confident people. Like his uncles. Or his first friend, the other Samuel.

The young scholars and businessmen stared as Samuel took Andrew by the arm and pointed to the library's sunlit walls.

It was the initial intention of the library's trustees, he said, to have finished the principal hall of the library in an oval form.

Andrew nodded.

But realizing that a common mistake of library builders is to overextend themselves with no prudent thought for the expense . . .

Samuel made eye contact with a handsome boy carrying Boswell's *Johnson*, then explained, his attention drifting from Andrew often, that the trustees had decided to cut short the pattern of their ambition with this particular building. But now a new library location was planned, and the new library building would be larger, and rather more grand, one leaving more space on either side for the admission of light, a superstructure of Philadelphia brick and stone dressings—another very commonplace exterior, unfortunately, Samuel said, both in ensemble and detail.

But I do hope the present building meets your needs for now, Samuel said. If the expense of books continues to rise, Andrew, and every private establishment continues to shipwreck itself against the shoals of pecuniary disaster, there really should be a real public library in this city, as you suggested, no? You have made me think upon it—yes, you have.

Samuel paused to smoothly greet yet another young man carrying a book. Andrew waited to be introduced, and waited some more, then watched the stranger drift away.

There are so many accidents these days. I have a great interest in them. Do you?

Andrew wished to think about this, but Samuel's words marched on. His accent seemed elevated somehow, a little unnatural today, or even English, as if straining for effect in expectation of being overheard.

These swift mistakes and fated horrors, Andrew, that are dispatched in the papers each week, just as we Americans tend to dispatch almost everything, with the hurry of a breakfast roll! And they distract us from the need to plan for—for the—for the future, and a wider group of people, as it were. Murders, explosions, boats that sink, private collections that burn down and turn art to dust, events that bring a dozen people—without even the warning of a whistle!— into the land of the Dead. We take it all too quietly, don't you think, Andrew? We, the public, as if we are simply chewing our salad.

Samuel's face had succumbed to a faraway look, but that ended now as he leapt forward and squeezed Andrew's shoulder and said:

So, would you care for a doughnut, at all? There is a man named Mr. Redburn who has them near here at a penny each.

The feeling of that hand upon his shoulder. The intensity of Samuel's stare.

Breakfast roll. Salad. Doughnuts. Do nots. When Samuel spoke, Andrew's mind whirred to keep up—not with the meaning, but with the meanings behind the meaning. The physical closeness now, the sweet smell of Samuel's hair, made the day all the more feverish and confusing. People were staring at them, and only now did Samuel seem to remember his wider audience, stepping back and smoothing down that showy blue coat of his.

A place with more privacy, he said, smiling.

As they left the library behind, Samuel continued talking—about pursuing this doughnut seller named Mr. Redburn, about his hunger for public life, about how the study of law was only a means to an end. He held it to be necessary for every man to be acquainted generally with the laws under which he lived, he said, and thought it indispensable to know on what principles they were founded, and where they got their authority, and had Andrew thought of it too, at any point—of studying the law?

Andrew was suffering from a dull, warm headache. He was, on some level, he realized to his own surprise, bored. It was a strange liberation, finding this feeling within himself. I have not thought of the law, he said, trying to focus. But that does not mean I will not.

He waited for Samuel's reaction. There seemed to be no mockery in the eyes at all, no information and no misinformation, only a strange keenness for company. But it was a joke, surely—the idea that he, Andrew Green, could ever be a lawyer.

But then Andrew was surprised again. He was shocked, as he continued looking into those large and beautiful and now oddly earnest eyes, to find something he recognized: Samuel Tilden, like him, was in rehearsal for a different kind of life.

Here was a man who wanted someone to listen to his speeches. Who was training himself to be more impressive, more convincing, more *himself,* every day. A person who needed a sincere partner with whom to pursue his plans. Who did not care too much, perhaps, for that partner's background. As he descended the steps of the private library, Andrew felt, for the first time in his life, as if he might soon be part of a club.

13

HUNTERS' GATE (II)

I n their first year of taking walks together—once a
month, then twice, then whenever they could—Samuel
liked to say to Andrew that their childhoods hadn't
been so different, but the specifics he offered to support this
claim were never entirely convincing. It seemed to Andrew,
in his most insecure moments, as if Samuel were trying to
explain, to himself, why he would waste so much time on
a low-born boy he had met in a general store. And it was
fruitless, this method, Andrew thought; it was like trying
to explain a spark with a diagram. There was no satisfying
explanation for why Andrew and Samuel found themselves
falling into a friendship. It was simply a matter of attraction, and instinct, and need, as it always is. Those factors
and a hundred tiny, meaningless conversations that gradu-
ally accumulated into layers of familiarity. Conversations
such as—

Andrew, I have a present for you, to give to your
Mr. Hinsdale.

For me?

To give to your Mr. Hinsdale, yes.

He does not much like gifts, Andrew said, unless he can
sell them again at a profit.

Is his wife still unwell, Andrew?

Yes. She says she contracted matrimony in 1822 and has
been suffering the symptoms ever since.

Ah, indeed! Ah. Haha. But you must give your employer my gift. It's very special. It's—well, it's a buttock, actually. A *talking* buttock, from a faraway land.

A buttock?

One which talks, yes, and has much to discuss. Your man Mr. Hinsdale would enjoy conversing with it, I feel. An acquaintance of an acquaintance, Mr. Barnum's right-hand man at Niblo's, says he fished said buttock out of a distant ocean and should like very much to give me first option to acquire it . . .

—And how can you explain the familiarizing effect of foolish banter of this kind? The net of stupid safety it seems to create? How can you understand the spell it casts for a boy whose life contained no banter at all until now, only instructions, grunts, criticisms, and put-downs? Small talk was a luxury, a privilege, and Andrew began to enjoy bathing himself in it, even as he worried over his own ridiculousness, and sought to contain it behind a frown.

He knew Samuel might take all this away from him at any time. Samuel maintained, infuriatingly but at length, that he, like Andrew, was *a country boy at heart*—one who had never fully pulled up his roots. But Andrew knew his new friend followed fashions—those colorful, overengineered coats—and might move on to some new story at a whim, then pull in a fresh cast of characters to support it.

In Andrew's company Samuel generally chose to elide the parts of his own history that did not fit this country-boy narrative, but they had a way of leaking out: a childhood friendship with the Van Burens, the constant house visits from prominent politicians, the expensive education and refined apartment and access to country homes. And at other times, when it suited him, in the company of flashy friends such as John Bigelow, such leaks were not accidental, Andrew observed. Samuel turned on the faucet himself, his privilege becoming the center of the whole conversation. It drenched every topic it touched.

This was Samuel's way, Andrew could see. Adapt yourself to meet the needs of your particular audience. He was like a rose grower twisting the form of a flower to hint at a camellia or perhaps a peony, even the extravagant rotundity of your average savoy cabbage, intent on meeting the latest customer's subjective tastes in matters of shape and circumference. He was selling himself to whoever listened. He wanted public approval. He wanted to lead the world one day, he really did. He was searching always for the version of a story most likely to be remembered forever. He was clever, supple, hardworking, and prone to bouts of stomach pain and melancholy. He was considered idealistic by his peers, people who saw that in a few decades he might make a mark. He wanted better conditions for the working poor, as long as he didn't have to meet too many of them. And, bit by bit, he lifted Andrew up with him.

———

Around the time their closeness finally seemed to have been established for the long term—through the library visits they continued to make together, through the conversations about books Andrew had read on Samuel's recommendation, and through Andrew doing occasional paid tasks for Samuel, like fetching papers, or fixing a bookcase, or copying out a letter to be sent to fellow Democrats—Samuel invited him on a walk to the Battery, a piece of ground that Samuel insisted on calling *large*, and *free*, though it was enclosed by fences. Several walking routes existed here, small level paths, and Samuel said he wanted to wander and talk. That he wished to discuss Andrew's prospects.

Prospects. That one word made Andrew's blood buzz. He could already smell the salty air on the walk, the possibility of good news coming in on a breeze. In the privacy of his heavy shoes he flexed his toes, three times, five times, seven. A reward for the work he had done, surely? A full-time position, perhaps, in Samuel's newly created law office. A job that might allow Andrew to leave mercantile pursuits behind.

Yes, that was it, Andrew decided. He was going to be offered work assisting Samuel in the law. They would be—there would be the opportunity to be—closer. And what of the money such a position might enable him to send home to his father and siblings? He felt sick with excitement.

The day came. He walked alongside Samuel when the way was wide, then on narrow stretches behind him. From the largest curve of the first walking path they took they could see vessels in the harbor, and others still at the wharves, and still more skimming along with their white sails spread forth to the wind. The calm blue water stretched out until it became waves. All the while he waited for Samuel to deliver it, the good news, the discussion of prospects that had been promised, some indication of what might bring Andrew the next level of professional or personal happiness. He was beginning, finally, to feel a real expectation of success. He had started to think he deserved to be happy.

The Battery was a spot that had perfected a quality Andrew thought of often: *distance.* There was proximity to other people, but not too much. Strolling here was a way of being in company without having to suffer company's ordinary compromises—the need to stare across the table at someone for hours on end, trapped in position, knife and fork in hand, nodding and mumbling and chewing (and watching *others* chewing) while the rest of the world went about its business. Talking while walking provided a sense of forward momentum. Andrew had always felt this, even in the childhood years when he spoke out loud only to himself on adventures alone, and it was to Samuel's credit, as almost everything lately was, that he had chosen such a place to deliver whatever news he had in mind today. Yes, the paths were a little too manicured for Andrew's taste. The routes a little too structured. The whole area lacking the authentic wildness it must once have had. But he was getting used to the cultivations of the rich, and he was happy to hold his tongue.

Andrew wondered what his new title might be. Assistant to Samuel J. Tilden, lawyer? He was happy with how it sounded, but he reminded himself not to get his hopes up. Perhaps the work proposed would be menial, or perhaps the matters Samuel had in mind were not even related to work.

Samuel coughed. They both stopped to admire the view. Some of the vessels arriving now were surely coming from a great distance, carrying people from France and England and China and South America, far over the seas, ships loaded with people and with products, items to be eventually sold at Mr. Hinsdale's store or at the large wholesalers: teas, silks, cloths, calicoes, razors, penknives, ginghams. Steamboats were passing and repassing swiftly, carrying men and women leaving or returning to the busy city, yet the presence of the water all around, and the unobstructed view it offered, seemed to drench everything Andrew saw in a quiet slowness.

They stood side by side, breathing. Everything still was filtered through Andrew's fine, expectant mood. How easy to forget that there was beauty here at the edges of the noise and stink! See New Jersey. See Staten and Long Islands. Views of vessels of every description, from the Liverpool packet to the little market craft, and steamers arriving from every point. Prospects surely unbeaten by any view in the world.

Andrew sighed. Decided to try being bold. He felt his

own heartbeat rise in his throat as he put an arm, tentative, around his friend's shoulders. He said, It would be worth traveling one hundred miles out of one's way in a foreign country to see all this, would it not? And yet, having it under our noses, we hardly take this time to enjoy it.

Samuel nodded, but gently shrugged off Andrew's hand.

It was as if they were building their friendship stone by stone again. He wanted Samuel to tell him the news quickly, but part of him also wanted to respect any desire Samuel might have to draw it all out, to allow the possibility of savoring the taste. He told himself to relax.

There was so little that was delicious in New York. Andrew had by now learned to ignore the barely clothed children in the shadows of crowded streets. To ignore the old men seeking unstated pleasures. To ignore the dead bodies in the alleyway, pitted by a pall of flies. To ignore the dogs he once would have helped. To ignore the infested rookeries in churches and breweries, the half-collapsed wooden shacks, his father's voice present in letters and dreams and increasingly occasional visits, a thousand bodies brushing past you every minute, cursing at you, asking if you would like to become the Son of God, or perhaps meet a lovely Daughter of Eve. City Hall's elegant white marble facade was constructed to face south. Every day here life seemed to insist on surging north. He wanted to surge north, with Samuel. He needed a sense of direction in his life. And then, snapping out of his thoughts, he spotted some litter flying at his feet . . .

It was a single sheet of newspaper, and Andrew leapt at it. He pinned it down under his left foot, then picked it up, scrunched it, and pocketed it. All of this with no thought, only instinct. And only then did he notice Samuel's horrified expression.

What occurred just now? Samuel said.

The paper, Andrew replied after a pause. People drop these things, it ruins every view . . .

And as he said this he felt, under Samuel's gaze, a sense of rising shame that he wasn't sure he quite deserved.

Something seemed to harden in Samuel in that moment. Perhaps he was embarrassed by Andrew's low manners in picking up the trash, or perhaps he was ashamed that his own disapproval had shown through. Perhaps one discomfort was layered on top of the other. Whatever the truth was, Samuel now cleared his throat and began telling an anecdote about his grandfather. This story is small, he said, but it needs to be told.

My grandfather, many years ago, brought back from the capture of Louisbourg a French musket. Offered it to me—a grateful grandson—as a gift.

For sport? Andrew asked.

(Samuel's hand touched Andrew's elbow for a moment, then fell away.)

Yes, for sport. It had a flintlock, this musket, and a stock of French walnut. And it was a smoothbore, flaring at the muzzle, without any place for a bayonet.

(The clouds moved, the wind got up. Their shadows touched on the ground.)

This gun had become worn at the—what is the word, Andrew?—worn down where one held it, signs of other human hands, and it kicked badly at discharge. Oh, that musket kicked! It was nearly as dangerous to be behind that gun as to be in front of it!

Samuel wiped his eyes and smiled, as if the story were over.

Anyhow, Andrew, I learned a lesson of reckless behavior with it on one particular day in my youth. Under medical advice—my stomach again, and my breathing, all those days in bed with books!—I consented to an adventure with my younger brother, Henry, who was then just a little boy. I had always shrunk from killing harmless birds and animals for sport, but the possibility, with Henry present, seemed exciting. And so I took the musket with me. My first and last experience as a hunter and a sporting man, as it would turn out.

Henry was excited by guns. He carried the ammunition and the game. I wanted to impress him. We all want to impress our siblings, our younger selves, do we not? The habit starts very early, Andrew, though I see you disagree.

My first fire was at a flock of pigeons perched on a tree, Andrew. I brought one down, and I felt nothing—only the briefest thrill. It was too easy, you see. Far too easy, at first. So I coughed—I was always coughing then, even more than now—and prepared for a second fire at the flock.

This time I did not get a good rest against my shoulder. I was complacent, undoubtedly, Andrew. My character had been damaged by my first success, you might say, and my prospects of a steady aim had now been already spoiled. I had made the mistake of not thinking. Every thought is correct, I believe. It is the *absence* of thinking that is erroneous and gives rise to errors, Andrew. I had let my impulse take charge of me. I had been sure of my outcome, of my own power to create it and protect myself from unhappy accident, but on discharge the old pretty musket in my hands swept so violently back across my own nose that I dropped it on the ground, held my face between my hands, blood gushing out of my nostrils—and oh, the shame!

I tried to wipe away the shame, to make it gone. I tried to pretend it hadn't hurt. But my lips by now were wet with blood, and my nose was numb, and in the midst of all this a useless hope began to float within me: the hope that my younger brother, Henry, hadn't noticed, had been looking at a different flock elsewhere, and it was of great importance to me now that Henry should not have noticed, but was it really possible?

He was looking the other way now, Henry. Perhaps he always had been, or perhaps he was being kind. The young really can be kind sometimes, in ways that adults simply can't, although . . .

Here Samuel trailed off.

Andrew stared at the water, waiting for the ending. He was certain that poor little Henry was going to be shot to pieces. He was not yet worried about his own fate—about how the story might apply to him.

Then Samuel sighed and said, On the next fire, Andrew, I missed my aim. On the fire after that, I missed again. I stood on my honors as a sportsman, and have never picked up that musket again in the years that have followed, nor any other musket or weapon. I had forgotten that story, until lately. Power, and the desire to use it for pleasure, had made me into a fool, you see . . .

Silence. Samuel's lips—were they trembling a little? And Andrew felt tired, so very tired now, as if his body knew the punchline before his ears did.

Samuel clapped his hands, in a jovial way, as if there was no reason to interpret his remarks as anything other than an innocent anecdote. And then he said, his eyes glittering a little:

For the next few weeks, with great regret, I will be too busy to meet . . . I hope you understand.

Andrew stood there. Tried to focus on the weeds underfoot. On strangers' faces. On a body of water. Everything was beginning to blur, to turn. He thought that he might fall.

It was simply that people had been talking, Samuel said. One or two people. People at the library. Nobody of particular importance. About his friendship, *this* friendship, et cetera.

Samuel's family had powerful friends. They were every-where, he said. They expected him to be proper, always. To be perceived to be proper. Always.

Samuel rubbed his eyes, then shook Andrew's hand. His last words would echo on in Andrew's memory for a long time, mingling with other moments and voices, changing them, adapting the facts to fit the accompanying feeling: *Good luck, good luck, good luck.*

Dizzy and weak, he watched Samuel go. Then he took the crumpled sheet of newspaper out of his pocket—someone else's story—and threw it back upon the ground from which it came.

14

ARTISTS' GATE

A great lawyer is not only learned in the law, so that when the brief is laid before him he may place this fact with that. A great lawyer is also an artist. He is able to march into a land of untamed information and make it adhere to his own idea of order, creating a successful system where only chaos has hitherto reigned. In the mind of a great lawyer there exists a private tribunal of sense and feeling. He puts good with good, bad with bad, and resigns the false to the false. He strikes at vulnerable points in the evidence of others. He throws firm assertions into cloudy confusion. He finds the affinity that exists between actual events, connecting the everyday with the unexpected, and by weaving lines of testimony within and around the statements of strangers, through the most perplexing phases of fabrication, can bring the truth to light if it suits his client's case, or throw it into shadow if it doesn't. If he can master this art of light and dark, he can in the process become rather rich.

But it is not easy, thought Lawyer Kaffenburgh of the maddeningly mediocre firm of Howe & Hummel. He had aspired to greatness for many years and was just at the point of realizing he would forever fall short. He was a man of minor talent, was the truth. He knew it now, had accepted it, and the acceptance had brought with it a surprising sense of calm. Recent experience had taught him to cast any aspirations of history-making aside, and instead he wanted now only to live a reasonable life and feed his family well. He had decided lately to rely not on lofty dreams but upon two modest skills he had come to recognize in himself, assets that were far from starry but were also far from useless: a nose for opportunity and a willingness to swallow his pride.

Which made it all the more frustrating that, in the matter of the murder of Andrew Haswell Green, Lawyer Kaffenburgh's nose had, at first sniff, let him down. A man named Cornelius Williams had arrived at his office some weeks ago, in early October, before the killing. He had been seeking representation. He was smartly dressed, but he wore his clothes awkwardly, including the bowler hat that rested at a tilt on his head, and his speech seemed a little stilted, or scripted, as if this was a performance he'd been nervously preparing for.

Mr. Williams had sat in the client chair, which was more comfortable than Kaffenburgh's own allocated seat, and stated, without much recourse to specifics, that he wanted to pursue some kind of action against two people who had treated him unfairly of late, conspiring to turn him out of his home. One of these people was a Mr. Green, he said, and the other was a Miss Bessie Davis.

Kaffenburgh had listened patiently, and made notes, and then he had mentioned his fees. He was in the habit of making his fees very high at the beginning of each year, and reducing them slowly, by increments, as the seasons turned and his optimism shifted into desperation. It was a great shame, really, and one he could do nothing about, that the colored folk in this city could hardly ever meet the necessary price in January, and not in spring nor fall or summer nor early winter either. A discount is a discount. To discount it again would be to sell oneself short. He sent Williams away without hearing any further explanation of his grievance.

A man had to value himself highly. Kaffenburgh's mother had taught him that. She had married very well, though unhappily.

Kaffenburgh reached for his stick—he had walked with a heavy limp ever since a streetcar accident—and stroked his favorite flaw in the wood as he stared at the front page of the *Times*: *"Father of Greater New York" Shot in Front of His Home.*

Some mistakes come back to haunt you. This very man Williams, the one who had visited him, and whom he had turned away, was at the center of what would surely become the biggest murder case of the year. The kind of case that can make a competent lawyer's career seem exceptional, and a bad lawyer's career seem competent. Jesus fuck, Kaffenburgh said.

Daddy? his daughter asked.

He advised her to keep drinking her milk. Then, after spitting a mouthful of awful coffee into the sink, and a little, in truth, onto his pants in the process, Kaffenburgh rushed, without precedent, out of his house, leaving the *Times* on his table, and any plans of breakfast aside, kissing his small daughter on the forehead before departing fast in the direction of the police headquarters, which is where he assumed Williams was being held. The child was not alone—she would be in the care of Tony, the Irish setter, a magnificently loyal old dog of great athleticism but limited intellect who always chose to burrow under the fence rather than jumping over it, even though the barrier was only a foot high. Kaffenburgh's wife had died last year of a slow disease, and he had no one but the dog to take custody of his child outside the hours of eleven to four—and at present it was 9:45 a.m. He hoped his abandonment of Sue would be worth it and that the dog, in excitement at its appointment as guardian, would not spill all her milk.

And so: Picture the scene. Outside the police head-quarters, Lawyer Kaffenburgh finds a large unruly crowd calling for the death of the prisoner who murdered New York's famous creator. He has no way of getting to the front of this crowd with his life still intact. And he needs his life, his capacity to earn (very well in January, and less so now that the end of the year is near) to be preserved, because he needs to provide for his daughter. Is she fine at home, with the dog? Suddenly he feels the old regrets returning. Was she crying when he left? He cannot remember. He always used to feel it so keenly, her crying, and sometimes heard her weeping at night even if she was not, but that was before he took to crying himself. He waits in the cold November air. Inspects his own stained clothes. The faces in the crowd. The sound of present voices, and remembered ones. Then he has an idea.

His idea is simple but requires exertion: to rush around to the back of the police headquarters. Behind the build-ing he may find a lower density of restless souls. And what would *he* do, if he were driving the patrol wagon that would, at some point this morning, surely arrive to take Williams to the Criminal Courts building? He would bring it here, around back, away from the masses. He moves as fast as he can with this walking stick for company, wincing and pant-ing with pain.

As Kaffenburgh waits here, leaning his weight on his bet-ter leg, he rubs his forearms through his drab greatcoat and laments once more not signing Williams as a client when he had the chance. He also laments the lack of breakfast in his stomach. Coffee without food is worse than no coffee at all, and *bad* coffee without food is even worse than that, and why is it so difficult, in modern New York, for a not-altogether-unrespected professional to obtain a satisfactory breakfast? The city permits a man to lunch well in a great many places, according to his standard and his means, and he can also dine, of any given evening, through an embarrassing latitude of choice. But when a man rises and goes out to hunt for a breakfast on this island, sometimes with a small child on his shoulders, and a great dog on a lead? That is when his troubles truly begin.

Lawyer Kaffenburgh's experience as a breakfast seeker in this consolidated city has been one of universally perfunctory service. The waiter is almost always a probationer not deemed equal to the requirements of a luncheon service, and when not taking orders he is almost always coughing on fresh plates or noisily cleaning up last night's mess. The kitchen is relaxed, oh, very relaxed! An assistant to the chef presides at the range, shorthanded. The wait is tedious, the cooking is dubious, the coffee doubtful on one day and intolerable on the next, tasting in one cup like apples and in the next cup like cheese, and the fruit on the plate is without exception warm and wilted. A week of this sort of thing is enough to make an ostrich dyspeptic—and it goes on, of course, much longer than a week. It goes on for your whole damned life. The search for a breakfast free of the broom and mop and duster, cooked by an expert, served by a competent waiter, presented without a bafflement of accompanying flies, is, in this city, endless!

Kaffenburgh is reflecting on this entire sad state of affairs as a patrol wagon pulls up behind the police headquarters. The door to the building opens before he has entirely realized what has happened. A dozen officers rush out with a handcuffed man—the star performer, Cornelius Williams—and guide him toward the vehicle.

My client! Kaffenburgh shouts, waving his stick. That is my client! That is my possible client!

Williams's bottom lip is bleeding. The high smooth forehead also carries a cut. He looks thoroughly weak. But when his eyes rise up to meet Kaffenburgh's he says, like an old friend, not missing a beat: Oh, hello, Mr. Kaffenburgh. Why didn't you attend to that case after I came to see you?

And yes, Lawyer Kaffenburgh remembers now. The man had no money, but he talked like a gentleman. He dressed, very nearly, like a gentleman. And clearly he has a wonderful memory. It is as if Mr. Williams knows, has always known, deep down, under the surface mistakes, that he, Lawyer Kaffenburgh of the firm of Howe & Hummel, is a lawyer who can be relied upon.

A feeling of serenity mingles with unease in Kaffenburgh's breakfastless stomach. He shouts, I will be your counsel without cost, Mr. Williams! At very limited cost! Remember, do not talk! I will meet you in two hours at the Criminal Courts, after they have put you with the coroner!

Williams seems to nod as he enters the patrol wagon, but then again he might only be ducking to save his wounded forehead from a further blow.

Kaffenburgh stays standing for a few further seconds, stiller than he has been in several weeks, as he watches the patrol wagon turn its corner.

Then, with his bird heart fluttering fast, he retires to a nearby eating house, where he sits in front of a plate of wilted, fly-swarmed fruit, reading every newspaper in the proprietor's pile, his perfectly imperfect stick hanging from its handle on the edge of the table, and begins filling a notebook with any useful information about the case that he can find.

He reads that a Dr. E. B. Ramsdell has spoken to the press, a man who has declared himself the owner of 426 West Fifty-Seventh Street. This number 426 is, Kaffenburgh thinks, probably the building for which Williams received a dispossess notice—the one found on his person yesterday, at the time of the arrest, which was mentioned earlier in the *Times*.

This Dr. Ramsdell appears to be a member of the Forest Lake Association, according to the *Herald*. The association keeps a summer home at Forest Lake, near Masthope, located in Pennsylvania. Ramsdell had been staying at this home in the early part of August last, when, one sunny day, several concerned club members apparently came up to him as he was enjoying some quiet time by the lake. They told him a man had arrived and was asking to see him. An unexpected man, they said. A man who one would not usually *be welcome here*. This man had apparently claimed that he, Ramsdell, was his landlord.

Me? Ramsdell said to his friends. (We never expect the unexpected to apply to us.)

And the man at the door, when Ramsdell got up and went to see, was no less than Cornelius Williams.

According to the account in the *Times*, it takes a moment for Ramsdell to recognize him. Williams is not Ramsdell's most troublesome tenant, but certainly he is among their ranks, and if Ramsdell could be rid of them, all at once—if only white people wanted his rooms—well that would be a fine day indeed.

Cornelius Williams looks tired today, and distracted, and his hair is a mess—he seems changed, his earlier pride has gone, it's as if the city has begun to drive him mad. He now begins telling the doctor-landlord that he is unhappy about the dispossess notice he has received for number 426, which is, as Dr. Ramsdell puts it to the press, with aspirational phrasing and perhaps an eye on promotion, *a very nice row of houses, occupied by negroes of the better sort*.

The housekeeper, Ramsdell says. You talked incessantly to her of your obsessions, Mr. Williams. She said you—she said that you made a nuisance of yourself.

Lies, Williams says.

We have discussed this before, said Ramsdell.

No, Williams says. Not in detail, sir. And here he gives Ramsdell a small smile.

Yes, we have discussed it, Ramsdell says, and it became a question, if I recall, of whether you should go, or the house-keeper. She has been the reliable housekeeper there for many years, Mr. Williams. We decided—Agent Calhoun and myself—that you should go. That is our decision. How did you find me here? This is not a place for you . . .

At this point, according to Ramsdell, and according to the copy of the *Herald* Lawyer Kaffenburgh was perusing from the restaurant's pile, Williams begins a rambling story about a beautiful woman named Miss Bessie Davis, with whom he confesses he is still in love. He says a rich gentleman named Mr. Green befriended her, despite the difference in their skin color. Then this man Mr. Green proceeded to turn her against him.

I'll kill him, Williams says, if he will not let up.

Ramsdell pays attention to these words, as anyone would. He resolves that, when he is back in New York, he will go directly to this Mr. Green, whoever he is, and notify him of the threat that the tenant Cornelius Williams has made on his life. But then he becomes preoccupied with the ordinary mechanics of his own tidy existence, and the blister on his foot that needs piercing, and forgets all about the matter.

Well, thinks Kaffenburgh, writing down all these details and closing his notebook. The world is full of blunders and boat hooks.

He folds the newspapers and pushes his plate of fly-ridden fruit away. Then he pays the check—making sure to leave no tip—and rushes back to his daughter and his dog.

15

GATE OF ALL SAINTS (II)

Two days after his conversation with Samuel at the Battery, believing their connection to be thoroughly dead, Andrew took to bed. He was suffering from a great, dull pressure on his chest that would not relent. That sickening emptiness in his stomach too, the kind that follows an enormous defeat. He felt he had been flattened, and soon his breathing grew shallow. He was nauseous, hot, cold, helpless.

Lying upright on pillows, motionless, improved his situation slightly, but as morning slipped deliriously into afternoon he realized he could not get up. He thought of calling out, but he did not know, anymore, who in the world he would want to find him. Finally, in the early evening, as his voice began to grow as weak as his body was, he heard his landlady's key in his door. Seeing him, she made the sign of the cross on her chest. The next morning, two of his sisters came. Then his little brother Oliver, the one who had wet the bed for years back home. There is always someone weaker than you. Except: Andrew had helped Oliver hide this habit. Had washed the sheets, had hidden Oliver's weakness from their father, helping him to maintain his role as the sportsman sibling, the untouchable athlete. And now here was Oliver, striding into the house in his builder's clothes, solid-looking, sunburned, thick haired, wiser, his confident smile wavering only when he saw the pathetic state Andrew was in.

Are you all right, Andrew? Oliver said. As he spoke he clapped his hands together as if hoping to snap everyone out of a performance.

Andrew tried to smile but gave up on the effort. Oliver's features were wavering, his nose looked liquid, and he could not bear the thought of food or water or anything else his sisters or Oliver offered. He watched their fingers fussing at his bedsheets, their faces contorted with care, their eyes filmed with confusion as they peered at him through the rippling atmosphere of gloom his own skin seemed to release. One bitter-bright thought did break through the fog: So *this* is what it takes to make them visit.

The fever continued to rise. The shaking, the chills. And it surprised him, the fact his body was suffering so intently, with such tangible results, because he had wondered at first if the soul alone was hurt. He was drenched in sweat, twisting and turning out of time, dreaming of boats, and misfiring muskets, and angels in heaven. He overheard, while in this swamp, someone at the bedside asking if he had yet made a will.

He had wasted his two decades of life. He had achieved nothing that would last, he knew. If he survived this, if he could only take water again, if his stomach did not reject every attempt at sustenance . . . Yes, he thought of the ocean, of rebirth. He wondered if his father would come.

He was visited the next day by a human form who he later discovered went by the name of Dr. Washington, who after a long and unconvincing inspection declared there was a possible aneurism of the right artery.

Then he was visited by a Dr. Stevens, who said there was a nervous disorder of the glandular system, and that he would probably survive it, if he took enough alcohol to clean his system.

Then he was visited by a Dr. Edgehill, who determined that the cause of the illness was a shock of some sort, combined perhaps with overwork, and who extracted two good teeth from his mouth in an effort to reduce the fever. This sharpening of overall misery into a single screaming event— blood all over the bed, and the tools, and Andrew—did succeed, for a short amount of time, in providing the body and mind with a more precise point of distress.

His sisters kept encouraging him to take a bath, as if he could survive the movement. Oliver kept leaving glasses of whisky on the bedside table, and looked more and more saddened to return and find them untouched.

He slept fitfully all day, and at night he lay in bed, and then one morning he woke into a strange sense of refreshed equilibrium. He found that the fever had broken.

A priest was due to arrive that morning and say a prayer over the bed, and Andrew was strong enough to make his sisters turn this traveling salesman away. Then he asked them to bring him bread and honey and water, water, water. He ate and drank and this was bliss. Iced water! Bread! One and a half slices and he was gloriously full. He slept all afternoon.

Poetry. He asked his sister Lucy to bring him poetry as he regained his strength. Milton's sonnets. That was what he craved at first. The sonnet to Mr. Lawrence, and the one to Cyriac Skinner. And then, feeling a twinge of regret for his treatment of the priest, he asked for a Bible too.

Lucy offered to read to him, but that was not the point, not the point at all. He wanted now to hear *her* voice. To learn of her loves, her secrets, her dreams. To open the book of her life.

She taught in a school. She was a teacher, and a mother now, and she wanted him to have a child one day so that he could know this love too, she said—and also so that she could be an aunt, for she would be an excellent aunt, and she considered it to be the best of all roles in relation to children. Good hours, she said, smiling.

He had sent Lucy's daughter gifts these last few years. He had never heard anything back. He supposed that soon he would be well enough to visit—if work permitted. Make amends.

He stank, he was appalling. He loved her for mopping his brow, just as he loved Oliver for the useless liquor. He thought in this moment that he and Lucy and Oliver would be bonded for the rest of their lives by these days of care. But within a few years, of course, their correspondence would grow sparse again, as if that was how it should be.

The newspaper, he heard himself mutter as he drifted weakly toward sleep one night.

The newspaper? Lucy said.

Trash . . .

———

On the final morning, his sister knocked on his bedroom door again, and this time he heard her knocking clearly, understood the sound. She held a plate of eggs for him, and coffee, and she was wearing her coat. Her suitcase was on the floor at her feet. Oliver stood behind her, and he was wearing his coat too.

How did you sleep? she said.

Like the dead, Andrew replied.

His sister and brother smiled. Andrew nodded to the suitcase. Is it time? he said.

Yes, she said. I think it is time. You seem much better now.

If only you had drunk the whisky sooner, Oliver said. We

might not have had to sleep on your miserable floor for quite so long.

Andrew laughed, and his siblings laughed. For a moment they were all as loud and merry as bells at a family wedding.

He wanted to say, Don't go, but he still did not in truth know how. To open himself up to a hard, hurtful truth again seemed the very worst of all options. Some people are perhaps meant to live alone.

Thank you for coming, he said.

———

His city adventure had failed. His love for New York had gone unrequited. He had lost, during his period of sickness, his most recent employment at a cloth merchant. They had not been able to keep him on while he recovered, and now no one seemed to be hiring. The trade was depressed by some combination of greed, financial markets, and mulberry trees that he did not quite understand. The rent on his room was due. He could not pay it. He could take his chances on the streets or he could go back home again.

The first few days back on Green Hill were thick with attempts to avoid his father's gaze. Attempts also to avoid thinking of Samuel. Attempts to get the city smoke out of his lungs and regain his country constitution.

Andrew felt now that by pursuing a friendship with a man so clearly designed for greater things, he had neglected his own obligations, tricked himself into arrogance, and demonstrated the kind of ignorance of social status that his father had always assumed was within him. Yes, every conversation with Samuel had been a terrible error. Every attempt to rise above his own expectations had been foolhardy.

After several weeks on Green Hill, as his desperation for freedom increased, he made frequent visits to the library of Antiquarian Hall in Worcester. There he formed the acquaintance of a Mr. Elihu Burritt, who later became better known as the Learned Blacksmith. It was Burritt who eventually told Andrew of a potential opportunity abroad. A man named Mr. Burnley, Burritt said, was regularly recruiting fine young men to be supervisors on his sugar estate in Trinidad. Your family used to know the Burnleys, he said, though perhaps before your time?

At first Andrew thought this whole topic was a joke, a setup for something. Then he stared into Burritt's eyes and said, Where is Trinidad?

Burritt explained that by working in Trinidad for some brief months Andrew could make a reasonable wage while—and it seemed vaguely plausible, the way he phrased it—supporting the efforts of the Anti-Slavery Society in improving conditions of workers over there, who were *newly free*, and helping to cultivate a sense of independence in those accustomed, until recently, to suffering only cruelty and servile submission. And if he went to Trinidad, as Burritt thought he should, then he might also make sure to establish a Sunday school there. A place for the children of workers to be educated in the Christian faith. As Andrew was a man a faith, after all, was he not? The job would depend on nothing less.

Burritt was the kind of man who did not dance around an idea for long. Had Andrew perhaps ever met, during his time in New York, a reverend by the name of Ogilby? Did he feel well enough now to return to New York for a brief visit to that very same reverend? Such a visit, Burritt said, might be a prerequisite to obtaining the situation in Trinidad.

A few weeks later, on Andrew's twenty-first birthday, October 6, 1841, he added the following entry in his diary:

This morning at about half-past eight I was baptized by immersion, down at the Battery, by the Rev. Mr. Ogilby

(Prof. at the Theological Seminary in Twenty-First Street). Mr. J. W. Mitchell, Rev. Mr. Clare and wife stood sponsors . . .

It was a comic little scene, this baptism by immersion, though later it would recur in his mind with new resonances. We find, over time, the deepness of a thing. And if we fail to find it, then we invent it, to show ourselves we are not shallow.

A cold day, for October. Water that seemed to want to harden into ice. Wind snapping across its surface. Gray sky. Not a sound from the birds wheeling overhead. The Battery had already changed a great deal since that day he took a final walk here with Samuel. More vessels every week. The view growing less and less clear.

Now Reverend Ogilby was at the center of the scene, a nervous man with a thin nose and invisible lips, and a belly that seemed too big for his frame. He wore a long white gown and had put Andrew in a less fetching version of the same, snaked with old mud stains. Already sullied.

There is a debate, of course, the reverend said. He was eyeing the cold water with anxiety, Andrew thought.

A debate? Andrew said.

Yes, indeed, Mr. Green. Ah. As to whether or not—ah—the immersion method might . . . Whether it might have, as it were, ah, a natural tendency to produce a chill, as it were, which is the precursor of our most fatal diseases? Especially, I would say, in the case of delicate people dipped in with their, their clothes, during the winter season, or a frigid fall like this, and after a considerable illness producing already, in your recent past, I believe, a feverish state of the body?

Here the reverend paused and coughed. He looked

Andrew up and down. It was extremely disconcerting, his way of turning everything into a question, the intonation rising at the end of every sentence as if ascending into an unearned place in heaven.

There is the hazard of instant death, the reverend added rather more succinctly, and Andrew could not help but smile. Though—here the reverend, too, gave a little laugh— there are also those who say, ah, that for every six men that a good baptism may kill, it serves as a cure for a dozen others!

Andrew watched the boats going by. In the distance was a paddle-wheel steamer. It was not so different, Andrew assumed, from the one named *Erie* that had sailed in and out of the news in August. Full of Swiss and Germans hoping to start new lives in America, she had burst into flames in the night on her way from Buffalo westward. There was the explosion of some demijohns of oil and varnish that had been standing on the boiler deck, and within five minutes the whole boat from stem to stern was burning, and the passengers and crew forced overboard, or consumed by fire. At first 175 lives were thought to be lost, but the number had then grown greater every day, despite people across America's heartland saying, presumably, very regular prayers.

There is an idea, the reverend said now, glancing quickly at the sponsors, who also looked a little pale, that immersion may refresh the senses. But of course what we are discussing—he waved his Bible in the air, the latest stage in an ongoing battle with a butterfly that seemed to want to alight upon his head (yellow wings, white dots, an attractive unbidden thing that should nonetheless have migrated elsewhere by now)—what we are discussing is a single plunge! All must be dipped, Mr. Green. The whole of you. I myself have baptized many dozens of men and women, and some at all times of the year, in the bitter frost and snow, where ice was first broken, and women who were large with child or weak in constitution. I have never caused a death—that I know of? But modern physicians would not in their senses advise that such a procedure was without risk . . . ? Thus I felt I should raise the matter?

The reverend looked at Andrew, and Andrew began to wade out into the water.

I have limited time, he told the reverend. It sounded rather pompous even to his own ears.

But oh, how he enjoyed the feeling of freedom, wading through the cold water! Feeling the water take in his legs. Seeing the dampness rise up his gown, inch by inch, darkening the fabric, until the material floated around him like a little girl's dress.

And then the trembling reverend with him, touching his head, gently encouraging him under.

Those brief moments beneath the surface! Fragility. Transparency. The way every thought and feeling became bright and sharp and clear, when he had expected the only appropriate word to be *damp*!

He did not think of his mother. He did not want to think of his mother. He would not let them come for him, the lost souls, the saints and sinners, the already dead.

He asked to experience the immersion once again, and once more. Plunge, plunge, plunge. And the reverend in the end was breathless as a lover, giggling as he pushed Andrew under, both of them soaked through with cold—shaking, spitting, dripping with joy.

———

Eight days before traveling to Trinidad, he had another dream of dying, and remembered his nights of fever, and the later feeling of the freezing water washing away his sins, and the two memories merged to make him feel foolish again, but also afraid again, and some mix of these emotions conspired to occasion a hasty draft of a document he intended to operate as his last will and testament.

The document did not embarrass him during the writing, but it embarrassed him greatly when he read it afterward, for by then it had become external work, abandoned by the private heat that had helped the ink to flow.

Knowing not how long my life may be spared, and having for some time thought that I was not long to live here—God grant that it may be so long till my peace is made with Him through Jesus Christ—I have concluded here to give a statement of all my affairs and concerns that in the event of my decease may be attended to particularly and scrupulously by whoever may find his name at the top of this page to whom this is addressed, there being no person specified at the present date.

And oh, There being no person specified at the present date!

It hurt him to write these words, but more so to read them later, to be at a loss for a friend and so openly vulnerable in that loss. He thought of Samuel. He thought, and thought better.

In this first will of his, he set out all the small sums that he owed to everyone on earth. He hoped he could fully settle all debts during his first month in Trinidad; the salary would be handsome compared to what he had grown accustomed to. But it all depended on the success of his journey on the *Star.* He was increasingly convinced the brig would sink or burn or perhaps both, and survival in such circumstances seemed awfully unlikely. He approached the trip with a rueful resignation. He would get through it and succeed in Trinidad, or he would drown and die on the way. He had very little to lose. He would be in God's hands. It was intoxicating, suddenly, to think of a higher being, a force nullifying human will.

I owe to my sisters borrowed money on October 7, 1839, $2.70; paid $1.16.

The hardest lines to write were these:

To my father, who has been to me a kind and indulgent parent, I would say all that one can say: I wish him joy in this life and in the life to come, most earnestly wishing him to seek for rest in Heaven through Jesus Christ. May God reward him for his goodness to me

He did not include a period at the end of that final sentence. It seemed important not to add one. It was a tiny act of resistance, this seeming mistake, the way the line drifted off into space. A door left open to truth, should anyone in the future wish to walk through it.

16

WARRIORS' GATE

On November 15, 1903, Inspector McClusky, the man Mrs. Bray considered to be a brighter bulb than any of her other interviewers, visited various venues to avail himself of further facts pertaining to the case. And who was he, this inspector who slipped into Andrew Green's story? What qualities made him move?

History suggests that Inspector McClusky was a person built of oxygen, carbon, hydrogen, nitrogen, calcium, phosphorus, potassium, sulfur, sodium, chlorine, magnesium, pride, and shame. He was the same as any human, in other words—but perhaps with an extra dose of arrogance, and a corresponding excess of self-hate, which are both useful qualities for any professional trespasser to possess. If he were alive today, he might agree that what varies in all of us, on a case-by-case basis, is the proportions rather than the ingredients. He wanted the truth, this fool, and don't we all? When we're dreaming, that is. When we forget that we haven't the vaguest idea of how time comes to pass.

McClusky had served as head of the Detective Bureau for less than a year when he joined the investigation into Andrew Haswell Green's murder, and his presence on the team caused a stir within the ranks on account of his good looks, smooth talk, and certain incidents in the recent past. His reputation had first risen after a series of arrests he'd made, just before Saint Patrick's Day, in the Tenderloin district of New York, an area that had, over time, sprawled out beyond its original bounds, as all unchecked sites of vice tend to do, becoming a neighborhood that contained within its ever-changing limits a few well-kept hotels and famous churches, but mostly what Inspector McClusky considered to be the lowest and most degrading types of enterprises, saloons full of after-twelve drinking and fallen women, poolrooms and dancing rooms, policy shops and faro banks, bunco men, confidence operators, peddlers of green goods, men who play the races, actresses of the lower type, ambassadors of and attendees to a thousand forms of forbidden revelry.

Inspector McClusky had kept a patrol wagon in the Tenderloin at his beck and call for several days. Was he thinking of how to make his name? He would later admit that he was not *not* thinking of it. He traveled that week from one part of the precinct to another, again and again, traversing Broadway, creeping down side streets, stopping outside various dens of gambling and displeasure. When the mood took him—and it took him often—he charged inside such establishments, put likely suspects in handcuffs, and wrestled them back to the station for a slap-around.

It is usual, you know, the inspector said to the press after the Tenderloin arrests, *to round up crooks before a holiday. But that is not the special reason for this work. We decided to rid the city for good of all these people. We are sure it can be done. These rascals feed on persons with money. I am after all the creepers, wire tappers, and clever crooks of all kinds, the majority of whom keep in this part of the city, as there is more money spent here. It was a good time to make a start, just before a holiday, but I'll keep pounding them and pounding them. I'll hammer 'em until they get so sick of it they'll be glad to stay away. They hang around hotels and other places where money is spent, and watch every chance to work their games. But I'll drive 'em out and make Broadway as clean as a whistle, so to speak. They must know by now I am a warrior.*

On March 17, 1903, when the *New York Times* reported these words from Inspector McClusky, the paper followed the quote with news that Inspector McClusky's crusade, as word of it spread among the Tenderloin's community of petty criminals, had *resulted in a general exodus* from the city.

To the well-heeled residents of the city, McClusky was greeted as a hero, and soon he started to talk more like they did, swapping *'em* for *them*, opening up his vowels, and his colleagues did not like that at all, nor the showy way he had single-handedly dealt with so many criminals with whom some of them had, let us say, profitable arrangements.

So yes, the Tenderloin arrests made the inspector suspicious to many local policemen. No one likes a man of showy virtue. But it was, without doubt, the elephant incident that made McClusky truly unpopular with his contemporaries.

Topsy was the name of the beast. McClusky's distant colleagues, in Coney Island, wanted the entire force loudly to join in their demands that the creature be executed on account of recent behavior, but McClusky emerged instead as, in the heavy phrasing trumpeted by his critics, a lone *elephant-sympathizer* in the force.

The calls for the elephant's death had begun at noon on December 5. Frederick Ault, Topsy's keeper, had left Luna Park in an inebriated state astride the animal's neck. The elephant and its keeper *went lumbering along Surf Avenue,* the *New York Times* would report the next day, *the motion causing the mahout to become more dizzy.* The keeper turned pale as he rode his beast. He vomited to his right, and then to his left, and to his right again, taking great care not to sully Topsy's magnificent ears as he did so.

A crowd gathered and fell in behind the elephant and its rider. Soon, at every corner, this crowd's numbers were augmented.

After traveling nearly half a mile, the animal stopped and its keeper slid off. He began prodding the elephant's trunk and asking it why it would walk no farther. At this point an officer named Conlin arrived to arrest the keeper, where-upon the keeper, who seemed more inebriated by the minute, though there was no sign of a bottle about his person, threatened to turn the elephant loose upon the crowd. He'll stomp you, the keeper shouted. He'll stomp you all!

He was silenced only by the policeman drawing a revolver. After seeing the gun, both the keeper and Topsy, by this point seeming rather moody with each other, consented to continue on to the police station on West Eighth Street in order to answer some questions. Mr. Ault, the keeper, had only one demand before doing so, and that was that he should not be separated from his elephant, whatever might happen. A policeman was heard to agree to this.

But upon Topsy's arrival at said police station a few minutes later, neither she nor Ault seemed to understand that she was not permitted to follow her keeper inside—that every deal had its reasonable limits. She climbed the five broad granite steps leading into the building and became wedged in the door. This made her sad and frustrated, to say the least—and the least was hardly relevant, for everyone knows elephants are creatures of excess. As a dozen police officers tried frantically to remove her, Topsy commenced a terrific trumpeting and the crowd scattered in terror. Some of the police officers—the ones tasked with tugging the trunk, which the *Times* the next day would refer to as *the musical end*—sought safety in two of the cells that Coney Island officers generally kept available for the purpose of locking trouble in, rather than keeping elephants out.

When Inspector McClusky, who was nowhere near this incident, heard about the Coney Island officers locking themselves in cells, he made no secret of his distaste for their elephant-induced cowardice, and made a statement in the local press (he by now made a point of knowing local journalists by name, and supplying them with comments on all manner of matters, behind closed doors and in front of them too) to the effect that he believed Topsy was the only individual who had come out of the whole situation with any pride whatsoever. The way his Coney Island colleagues had treated the creature was already cruel, he argued, and now they wanted to execute it too, citing various other supposed moments of danger and disobedience, in order to turn their own embarrassment into action, and their weakness into seeming strength.

All this might in part account for why, months later, when it was announced that Inspector McClusky, under the urging of District Attorney Jerome, would be the man who would help bring the investigation of Andrew Haswell Green's murder toward a neat conclusion, the loudest words of dissent from within the police force came from Coney Island officers, who doubted that he had the necessary team spirit to unlock a murderer's motive in such a sprawling case, regardless of how many recent individual arrests he had made of criminals in the Tenderloin, and how extensively he had puffed about them in the press. Here was a man, in the stinging words of one Coney Island officer, who was, contrary to public appearances, *soft on crime and creatures*.

———

All this might have been on Inspector McClusky's mind when, two days after the shooting of Andrew Haswell Green, and shortly after conducting a further interview with Mrs. Bray, he made his way to 91 Park Avenue, the site of the crime. Feverish speculation surrounding Green's murder was spreading with increasing pace throughout the city, and the inspector's own theory of motive kept moving back and forth between various sticky yet insubstantial positions, like a sick boy trying to rest in a sweat-drenched bed. It was his job, McClusky felt, to put the story out of its misery. To deliver a definitive account in the coming weeks. But everything in New York was second- or thirdhand. You could rarely reach, with any speed, the source of talk. Whereas in DC, where McClusky had spent an earlier part of his career, chatter always came from the same one hundred men. The same restaurants. The same performances. Similar beards. It had been comforting, but also bland, like the Thanksgiving dinner they always served at headquarters.

That the killing of Green might have been caused by the conduct of its victim worried Inspector McClusky greatly. The president had already privately expressed his dissatisfaction at Mr. Green's death. Any scandal the murder investigation might now churn up—a great American civic hero of our time, associating with murderous negroes and their women, only to then be murdered by one!—could feasibly spread out and implicate the administration. One thing McClusky knew about scandals (and here the elephant incident weighed heavily upon him): they were always looking for ways to increase their mass. The president did not want to get his shoes covered in shit, and Inspector McClusky did not want to have to lick them clean.

He decided to travel to 91 Park Avenue the same way Andrew Haswell Green had traveled there on the day of his death. He took the streetcar, tried to ride inside the victim's mind.

By traveling on public transport, had the rich old man been trying to prove a point? Why else, McClusky asked himself as he looked around with a frown, would a famous figure in his eighties endure this daily press of bodies, the corrupt conductors and the pickpockets they seemed to be in league with, the slimy pole, the customers with a case of the itch, the ones who recognized your success and wanted your wallet while the driver whistling an ancient union tune, and swigging from some sort of special cocktail, pretended he did not know what was going on? The amount the streetcar drivers drank was cause for scientific study.

He was greatly relieved to get to the house. There Timothy R. Green, the victim's nephew, was waiting. Inspector McClusky followed him into the dining room, which was overflowing with flowers.

So many gifts of condolence, Inspector McClusky said. How lovely to see—so to speak.

Yes, Timothy said, his expression unreadable. People did not know him well.

They sat down opposite one another at a large maple table. There was a copy of the *Sun* laid out to McClusky's right, the front page providing one of the more salacious accounts of the crime, and Timothy looked at it with an expression of distaste, as if angry at whoever had put it there.

McClusky glanced around the room. He asked the preliminary questions, and tried to sound sure of himself, on the one hand, but in need of helpful information on the other. Police work, a balancing act: show your hand without showing your hand.

He asked Timothy whether his uncle could possibly ever have become mixed up with Cornelius Williams and this mysterious woman, Bessie Davis, that Williams was now talking about.

He asked Timothy if Williams was a person he, Timothy, had ever met before.

Then he asked Timothy if he had any idea who this Davis woman was, or where the police might find her.

Timothy Green looked very calm throughout these questions. The hair that sprouted from his nostrils and ears was the only unneat aspect of his character. Occasionally he smoothed down his shirt as he talked, though it was perfectly smooth already. Speaking on his murdered uncle's behalf, he reiterated what he had already said—rather unhelpfully, in Inspector McClusky's view—to a group of newspapermen swarming on the steps of City Hall: No, no, and no. The allegations of prior acquaintance between his uncle and Cornelius Williams were pure humbug and fiction from A to Z, he said. The *Sun*, he said, glancing bitterly at the paper, was correct in saying that there was no justification at all for the shooting, even if it had proved itself incapable of following other basic facts. Even his uncle's many detractors—all public-minded men attract detractors, Timothy said, truly enough—would surely find it difficult to summon the will to kill him at this late, defenseless stage of his life, when all his time was being spent, for no financial reward at all, on quiet public projects for the betterment of the city.

And your uncle had already done so much for us, Inspector McClusky said.

Timothy nodded, softening a little. The room's biggest window was half-open onto the street. The avenue was as busy as it always was. A cart was loudly passing by and this particular vehicle seemed to unsettle Timothy's smooth expression, McClusky noticed, sending his gaze briefly to the glass. Then he picked up the copy of the *Sun* from the table and held it up for display, as if McClusky had not already read it. As if he had not already read everything.

A. H. GREEN MURDERED

—

SHOT BY A NEGRO CRAZED OVER FANCIED WRONGS

—

Timothy Green stood up now, went over to the window, and closed it. Then he returned to his seat, looking somewhat more defeated than before. What bad luck, he said. And then, as if changing his mind, he added:

But I suppose, Inspector, that most murders in this city probably involve mistakes of identity to some degree?

The inspector could not help but frown at this. He waited for the nephew to elaborate.

I mean, said Timothy Green, that every murder must, by its very nature, involve some error of understanding or of judgment, a major missed connection or a series of minor missed connections, miscalculations, misconceptions, misstatements, mishearings, slips of the tongue, or of the hand, et cetera, so that *murder by mistaken identity* might, admittedly—here Timothy Green took a breath and, shockingly, almost seemed to smile—be a confusing phrase, a solution that is not really a solution, a judgment that raises more questions than answers, a category of mystery rather than a solution to one?

McClusky had nothing to counter this, so he merely reached for his water glass in silent disapproval. Then there was a tapping noise—the window. A man was waving enthusiastically at McClusky—no, at Timothy—while raising into view a thick-bottomed blue bucket.

Who is that? McClusky asked.

Fishmonger, said Timothy. He went over and drew the curtains, then turned and remained standing, his eyes going to the mantelpiece—the clock there, McClusky thought.

In the inspector's line of work, you never felt well lit.

Doubt darkened the edges of every shred of information. Worst-case scenarios ran through his blood. The philosophical aspects of his job were only interesting to other people. Civilians. Pedestrians. Relatives. He had to live *inside* the damned ideas. Once you did that, they weren't ideas anymore. They were just life—your life.

McClusky noted the strange almost-smile returning to Timothy Green's lips now, and he shifted in his chair. Was he being teased? It had been happening to him since childhood. The cabbage incident came to mind. The way his parents always made him prepare the cabbage. No other elements of a meal, only the cabbage. To chop up the cabbage. To shred the cabbage. To mix the cabbage, its appalling juices, with salt sometimes, so that it might begin to brine. The way the neighbors' children noticed the odor on his clothes. The way some nicknames are irremovable, like certain smells, or stains on your shirt.

Presumably, McClusky said, allowing his pen to hover over a page of his notebook, you will be a beneficiary of your uncle's death? So to speak.

Timothy's face became more appropriately respectful at that point. Inspector McClusky watched as the nephew left the room and returned with a file of press clippings. A breeze of present tense swept through the mind of McClusky: I am here, I am important, I am powerful, forget the cabbage years. And then a hand arrived in the doorway holding a much-needed pot of coffee.

Ah, Mrs. Bray, said Inspector McClusky.

Still here, she replied, with rapid singsong somberness. Still here, still here, still here.

You two are, Timothy said, already acquainted?

I am interviewing all the relevant witnesses, Inspector McClusky said. He watched as Mrs. Bray nodded to Timothy.

He was very good, she said.

Oh, McClusky said, I don't know about that . . .

Nonsense!

Well, thank you.

No, thank *you*! Mrs. Bray replied.

Timothy Green could be heard clearing his throat.

As the coffee was poured, McClusky noted the way Mrs. Bray stood on tiptoe to better see the papers Timothy was spreading out across the table. She smiled at him before leaving the room.

It is too horrible to think of, the mayor was quoted as saying in one of Timothy's clippings. *An unimaginable tragedy. I am deeply pained and shocked. He was one of the most respected and valuable citizens* . . .

Timothy reiterated to McClusky, as they both sipped from their steaming cups, that his uncle had never mentioned a woman named Bessie Davis. Indeed, he had hardly ever mentioned any women, except those to whom he was related. One exception was Mary Lindley Murray, a daughter of the American Revolution whom he had greatly admired, but she had died in 1782, and he had only ever read about her.

My uncle was like that, Timothy said. He enjoyed befriending the dead. He said they never let you down.

These last few weeks, before his death, his uncle had been trying to convince the mayor to honor Mrs. Murray's largely forgotten work with a plaque. And for similar reasons—a fear that good civic work, which deserved to be remembered, was nonetheless falling into forgetting in modern New York—he had, seven years ago, or was it eight, set up the American Scenic and Historic Preservation Society, which Timothy now said he and other family members planned to, well, *preserve*.

Then Timothy finally offered something revealing: that he had recently told his uncle over dinner that it was not too late to marry. Did he not want some company and care in his old age? Someone to talk to in the empty early-morning hours? Someone to preserve his memory in a personal way?

Inspector McClusky leaned forward. The chair creaked under him. The electric chandelier did not flicker, but it might as well have. He had learned over the years that it was a change of tone, rather than of content, that indicated when interesting information was coming, so to speak, down the pipe. There was a new lightness in Timothy's voice now. It presented a chance to press home an advantage: the fact Timothy seemed to want this interview over and done with.

What did your uncle say in response? McClusky said. When you encouraged him to marry, so late in life?

A long pause. Timothy looked a little offended, did he? But then he cleared his throat again and spoke:

My uncle said, Please pass the salt.

The salt? said Inspector McClusky.

Yes. If Timothy's memory was free from error, or at least was only as error-ridden as everyone else's, his uncle had ignored the question about marriage and had said, instead, Please pass the salt, Timothy.

And then?

And then, after the salt had been passed, they had both fallen into a discussion about the running of the first subway train in New York, Timothy said, and whether it would be a success, and how exactly the cars presently being built might be taken into the first tunnel.

Timothy had imagined that the cars might have to be hauled through the city streets and lowered by some laborious if not impossible process through a fresh hole to be made in the city's surface, but this was not the plan his uncle had sketched out in his notebooks and recommended at the relevant planning meetings. What his uncle had envisaged was that the cars would be transferred from the elevated railway tracks to floats. The floats would carry them up the Harlem River to the head of Lenox Avenue. There they would be run into the subway by way of an incline track, one built especially for the purpose. Although the east side branch of the tunnel would not be opened to traffic until the success of the main line had been established, it just so happened that the first car to enter the subway would traverse, by way of a test mission, the portion of that branch following Lenox Avenue, and would then continue under the northwest corner of the Central Park and across 104th Street to the junction with the main line at Broadway.

I will be alive to see it, Andrew had apparently said to Timothy, before proceeding to add salt to his food for a second time, with even greater vigor than before, perhaps because he was growing forgetful in his old age, or because his taste buds had begun to dim with each passing day, or because it was his set intention to preserve part of his portion of potatoes for the ages.

With that, Timothy Green walked over to the doorway leading onto the corridor. I am unfortunately late for an appointment, he said. One of my uncle's brothers is here from Chicago, to pay his respects, and amidst all this mourning and the constant questions I promised to show him some of the buildings Andrew was involved with establishing, the museums of natural history and art and so forth, the public library too. He has taken all this very badly, Oliver has, the poor old man. Though they never seemed to be particularly close in life.

May I stay awhile with these papers? McClusky said. I would not wish to keep you.

The nephew gave a reluctant nod.

When McClusky heard the front door close, he went in search of Mrs. Bray. He felt she might be open to giving him a full tour of the house, and perhaps even cooking him a meal, a bowl of warm food that might just soothe the boy-hood tickle that he, Cabbagehead McCabbage, now felt in his throat. After that sustenance he could turn his full attention again to locating Miss Bessie Davis, whoever she was. Another innocent housekeeper, most likely.

Out in the corridor he found a taxidermied raccoon sitting upon a strange little side table. He went to touch it, then withdrew his hand. Its fur was matted, greasy. One eye was missing. The tail was no longer fluffy. Not exactly a specimen deserving of the museum of natural history. Why would Green possess and retain such a dismal example of death?

Beside the raccoon was a very old book on accounting, the kind that has been opened and shut so many times over its decades of life that its spine has been almost destroyed. Inspector McClusky stared at it, walked on, and then . . . He turned back. The accounting book was resting on top of another enormous volume: a copy of the city directory.

17

FARMERS' GATE

What shone for him, toward the end of his life, were not the moments of public success. Those were already on the record, public work on public projects, and he assumed his contributions would survive into future centuries through the usual channels. What took up space in his mind as his seventies became his eighties were the transient private encounters of much earlier years, the events which he felt might vanish forever on account of existing only in his diaries, letters, and memories. Fading moments like the day on Green Hill in 1841, just after he had turned twenty-one years old and been baptized by immersion, when he built a sheep pen with his father.

Four sheep were to be sold for a desperate price. This was the final task before his departure for Trinidad. The sun low and lovely, the afternoon clear and smooth, the air warm as soil. A scene.

The creatures seemed to know the pen was for them. They bleated. They ran. Their pupils shrank into tiny rectangles in the shade, then blasted wide as they dashed into the light. Andrew watched them and thought of his impending travel on the brig. Of Samuel Tilden. Of why the friendship had vanished, the errors he must have made, too many signs of affection, or of desperation, neediness, the most appalling of all impressions to make on a fellow man. His only available course now was to put distance between his failures and his future, tighten the stranglehold on his feelings, and harden his heart protectively against the pain of further great mistakes. But at the same time he was thinking that perhaps he should not leave America after all, should not leave his rapidly weakening father, should not try to escape the roots of who he was, should just return here permanently, to the place where he was born, growing old at home even if it did not always feel like home. The idea of travel, though, was now already in his blood. There was something almost holy about the idea of putting goods and men on ships and sending these ships around the world. Vessels from unknown places, decks heavy with bags of foreign grain. The arrival of the *Albion*, a Swedish ship, seventy days from Göteborg. Schooners setting sail from New York for the East Indies. The advertisements in the papers back in New York, its population exploding, had been lit with lines that were shaped like prayers—*May fortune keep them afloat*. But were there not better things than fortune to place one's faith in? Timber and skill. Steam. Miracle of human hands. The fastenings of new engineering. And Trinidad had begun to represent these possibilities in Andrew's imagination. Somewhere, anywhere, new.

The dimensions of the sheep pen were established in silence. There was history here between Andrew and his father. Repetition, understanding. The cost of animals that die in passage was borne always by the seller. Six feet long, four feet wide, three and a half feet in height. Important to get every measurement right.

His father's forehead shone in the sunlight, more of it than ever before, a ruddy face busy with perspiration and the strenuous business of witness. Well-weathered skin hung loose in tan folds from his arms; it seemed muscle had suddenly retreated almost entirely from his aging frame. Andrew boarded the pen tightly on both ends, breathless at being watched. His father said nothing, wiped a fore-arm across his mouth, then saw a molehill by the tree and cursed it.

Less tightly on top, his father said.

A parent's aggravating attraction to expressing the obvi-ous. Andrew remembered, with a jolt to his settled perspec-tive upon her, that his mother had always done this too.

He did as he was told. Here on the grass he built a door through which to move the sheep in and out, and food in and out, and the drink they would need for the journey, in and out.

All the while the pigs roamed around. They thought their fate was the fate of the sheep. He wanted to cry out to them: Don't squeal! Father doesn't like squealing. Yours is a dif-ferent prison.

For the sides of the pen his father helped. They used slats an inch and a half wide, with three inches of separation, each slat smoothed at its better edges.

If you've forgotten how to saw, his father said, then give me the saw.

He had not forgotten. Sawed harder, coughing, getting angry now, and then stood back. Shielded his eyes from the brightness of the low light and his father's stare, and from the future, and from feelings, and he inspected the fledgling pen as his father inspected him, and as the pigs and sheep inspected it all.

Andrew assessed the angles. Made sure the protections he had constructed were secure. The pen was uncorrupt. He glanced at his father to see if he agreed.

His father looked back at him and said, with a small bitter smile, Only a dog wants for approval, Andrew.

Together they slatted the bottom, each slat four inches wide, and the intimacy of this work was lovely. Andrew used half an inch of separation from slat to slat, enough to let the urine and dung pass through, and at length he then ran—legs pumping, heart thudding, his lungs getting stronger and his legs seemingly longer since coming back here into the country air after his illness—and he caught a sheep, a healthy-looking one, but not too healthy, and his father said, not for the first time, but perhaps for the last time, at least to Andrew's ears: There is no department in the management of sheep so little understood as the nature and treatment of their diseases.

After a time, you start to read something into everything. They put the caught sheep in the pen, a test, his father saying nothing. They checked that the separation was not quite wide enough for its feet to pass through, his father saying nothing. The animal mewed as at last it was lowered by Andrew's hands, his father saying nothing, and then, with this test finished, Andrew let it go, and the sheep could not believe its luck. Its suspicions were well founded. Soon the rehearsal would give way to the real. Andrew looked at its little black eye as his father said, If you've forgotten how to grip a hammer, give me the hammer.

Three cleats his father nailed across the bottom now, refusing help, for he considered these to be the three most important cleats of the whole enterprise, the ones without which the entire structure would not hold.

The light was failing. The latest woman who was not Andrew's mother had opened the door to the house and was shouting out. She was saying, Bread is on the table, on the table, bread is on the table.

Yellow and blue stripes seen at a distance present a green mass.

Andrew had read, in the New York Society Library several months ago, before he fell sick, Johann Wolfgang von Goethe's *Theory of Colours*. It was one of those books that make very little impression on the reader while being read.

And yet afterward, you start to see colors everywhere—and differently. You start to observe, with a wonder that is just less than love, the tricks they are always playing.

The cleats would keep the bottom of the pen raised from the deck of the boat. The trouble with decks? They tended to get wet. Keeping dry was essential to the animals' health. For a traveling sheep to survive, its feet must not touch the floor.

Lash a bucket to the door, his father said, his blinking growing slow now, lids heavy with fatigue, less traction in the stare than usual. Lash it and we must eat. The food is ready.

So Andrew ran to the outhouse and returned with a bucket, not a common pail but a particular bucket designed for the task at hand, wider at the bottom than at the top, the sort that was less likely to spill when the ship rocked from side to side, and he lashed this bucket to the corner of the pen, because the sheep would need two pounds of good hay each day. His father was short of resources but still committed to living by a principle of excess, and he had always been kind to his animals, showed unexpected reserves of sentimentality with them, as if it were easier for him to see creatures, as opposed to people, in the hard light of justice—random, idiotic justice. So his father would pack twice the necessary amount, four pounds at least, and add two pints of good oats too. He groaned as he bent his back to do so. If everything is wasted, be wasteful. That seemed to be the idea. Fatigue had robbed him of many illusions, but this one seemed unwilling to flee.

The sight of his father struggling to tie the twine was what Andrew knew, even then, would linger in his mind during his own journey. The knowledge that all his remaining strength would soon leave his father. Look how worn they were, those hands. Look how they had shrunk! His shoulders too. Rolling inward, as if afraid. And the mouth had hardened, the chin was wasted to a point, the eyes were often unfocused. Notice how he no longer knew where to look in the moments when he was utterly alone.

Come here, the old man said with a tenderness Andrew had forgotten was possible. As if he had read all the worry, and regret, and longing in the air. As if he would use the lasting power of his approval to soften the ground between them.

The work had been done. They were about to walk over to the house for lunch. And his father, out of nowhere, like a capsized man grasping for something to keep him afloat, was drawing Andrew into an embrace.

Warm, precious. Andrew felt his own body relax just as it had in his boyhood, falling asleep on his mother's chest on frigid nights when the stock of firewood was low, and at times—was this true?—on his father's chest too. Memories of smallest youth, but the bones in his father's chest felt as delicate as the bones of birds these days. And then his father whispered something, a tickle in Andrew's ear, and it was this: You have shamed us, Andrew.

The shock of this moment. His thoughts hanging upside down.

You were to be my success, his father said. You were the cleverest, I sent you there, and now you have come back.

His father pointed across the field.

You have given up more easily than these sheep.

———

There had been good weeks, a few joyous mornings, clear moments on Green Hill when simplicity had still seemed the most precious thing one could strive for, when his dreams had gotten drowsy on long walks in fine weather, his worries pressed harmless like weeds underfoot, his chest feeling fine, his eyes stinging only on the days when strange seeds were sent his way by a sudden breeze. A single passing cloud or buzzing fly could, in such an atmosphere, seem transformative to the soul, but was it not all a lie? On a clear morning here, the world could seem but six days old, but he remembered treading through these fields as a child, and his childhood was already buried under entire years. His soles had touched every inch of this land now, surely. Old ground, getting older by the day. The impression of newness was a trick. There is never, in your most familiar places, any way to start again.

For a while perhaps his own brush with death had made him sentimental. But on four hours' sleep, the farming life, no man is sentimental. He sees things as they are. The true colors of a places or person.

So yes, he would go to Trinidad. He would become a sheep for shipping. He would put his ear at a great distance from his father's mouth.

18

MARINERS' GATE

The voyage on the brig lasts twenty-one days. The first fourteen are tempestuous. Passengers listing, fainting, vomiting, wailing.

The seasickness club is one he joins on the third day of the journey. Almost everyone else has already succumbed. The awful squeak of rope and wood. Roiling smell of strangers' bile mixed with his own. He thought he had his sea legs already, but no. He thought the trip might be exotic, but no. He thought if he was going to die aboard then the death would be dramatic, well lit, fire-filled, but no. The horrors are more mundane, yet they leave him begging to be thrown overboard. He is on his knees for hours at a time. His clothes are wet with his own vomit and sweat.

He is down in the cabin all the time with his face over a bucket, his insides trying to get out, the muscles of his stomach screaming as every aspect of who he is comes exploding out of his mouth. He tries to rehearse a few calming lines in his head to keep the seasickness at bay. Doesn't work. Vomits. Wails. Faints. The process cannot be stopped. Self-control he has lately decided to prize but here it is utterly absent, mocked and rocked. Doors burst open in the corridors. Strangers go crawling by, skin lacking color, eyeballs leaning into the floor, every one of them wet through with liquid from the stomach or the sea. How will he survive three weeks in this traveling hell? There is no way back.

The mineral chameleon, a name which has been given to an oxyde of manganese, may be considered, in its perfectly dry state, as a green powder. If we strew it in water . . .

He vomits.

If we, if we strew it with water . . .

He vomits yellow, green.

If the green colour displays itself very beautifully in the first moment of—of solution . . .

Oh, how he vomits, how he faints, how he aches!

. . . but it changes presently to the bright red opposite to green, without any apparent intermediate state.

Lame, sore, every muscle strained to actual pain, a finger-nail torn from gripping the bed's edge as he waits (what else is there to do but wait?) to be thrown against the wall.

And then: Calms come. Squalls. Like a man who comes through a plague, he can barely believe it.

His desperation has kept its depth but lost its diversity. He is interested only in one thing now: getting there, getting there, getting there.

Broken, empty, ready to be remade by anyone who promises him land, he can only faintly sense the extent of the new stillness, is lost still at times in the memory of motion, a person who is now all past, thinking that the brig continues to roll when the rolling is only in his head. If he dares look up he is convinced he will see again only blackness, pure blackness, in the porthole.

The captain, standing over him on day sixteen, laughs. Seasickness is influenced by the imagination, he says.

Andrew looks up at him briefly. You bastard, he thinks. Then he vomits on those shiny shoes and relaxes into a late, great moment of respite.

Intermediate state. Lies on deck, trembling, with all the other men possessed of imagination, a new solidarity forming among them, as if they were coming back from war. If the inside comes out, and out, and out again, then in the end what is left?

Other people. Their faces. Softest sunlight pushing in through his thin lids as he takes them in. New world trying to blind him, bring him a sense of being saved. Sea spray. Salt. Sun burning his bitter lips. But to be out here under a sky is beautiful. To be in the cabin was to be dead. He waits to be swept overboard by a very great wave—one which Nature, in its indifference, never brings.

Thus every colour, in order to be seen, must have a light within or behind it.

He arrives in Trinidad in November 1841, weaker than an infant, with Goethe, and letter paper, and six dollars in his bag. What he dreams of during his first night in his hut, sensing the land beneath him swaying, is bridges made of iron and bridges made of wood, bridges everywhere, stretching between great masses of land, presenting a chance to walk forever from one place to the next, endlessly, without fear, without riding any water, so that ships, brigs, every infernal boat that crosses this earth, would never again need to be boarded.

19

NATURALISTS' GATE

I n Trinidad he loses confidence in his own imagination. It is a much greener land than he ever envisaged. He had pictured the whole place coated in sugar, as if the product of the work would fairly bury the means, but at first it's as if he came all this way only to find himself back home.

In Trinidad he loses his sense of time. He loses a week's wages when he falls in the river. He loses his way as he walks back wet through the tamarind trees. He loses his understanding of the word *free,* for the newly freed still seem enslaved in all but name. He loses dignity, more dignity—a little in him still—as the workers in the eastern field raise their gaze to the sound of him squelching his way toward them in exactly the wrong shoes. He loses his ability to keep a straight face. He loses the respect of white workers when he speaks with the workers who are not white. He loses count of the sugarcane he cuts with his bill, the cutting he supervises, the cutting he imagines, lifting stalks to his lips to drink at the nectar that blasts away all fatigue.

He loses faith, for a while, in the collective. The *us*. The *we*. If he wants to make a success of himself in the years ahead, he will have to make it happen alone. His isolation here feels fitting. New York has sent him away so that he might become more like New York, self-sufficient, whale-lit, slick with its own swagger? He thinks of Emerson, a paper of his that he tried to study on Samuel's advice, in Samuel's library, a treatise with the title "Self-Reliance," and in his first few weeks here in Trinidad he loses, for a while, his instinctive distrust of that text. Loses his desire to ask if there is not a less selfish way to live one's life.

In Trinidad he loses the softer part of his youth. Lets a beard grow out. Lets his face become tan. Forearms, hands, neck. He takes great care of the way he holds his bill, how he slashes and cuts. He looks less skinny and gentle than a decade before, he thinks, the start of his farming life, a suggestion of experience added to the eyes now, a feeling of strength in his back and arms, his hair thick and almost curly here, growing and growing, a life of its own, licking about his ears, tickling him at night like the insects that want to crawl inside the whorls for warmth.

He loses a dream. He has it, and then it slips away—into the wider repetitions of the work in the fields. He loses some of his longing to own a home in New York one day, to be possessed of American property. He is happy in his little hut of nothingness here, eight feet by eight feet, sleeping surrounded by creatures and trees. There is no roof, only bare shingles placed across the eaves, frequently exposing him to the weather. But it means there is no space for vermin to establish themselves. A box of basic solitude, as at Hinsdale & Atkins, except this one is full of fresh air and light, and it is his, and at night the stars overhead suffer no noise.

In Trinidad he loses patience with Mr. Carlson, to whom he must report. The man who keeps calling him My Young American Naturalist. Who is amused by the fact Andrew knows the names of all the trees, the shape of their leaves, despite arriving only a few weeks ago.

He loses all capacity for conversation on Mr. Carlson's favorite topic, which is flies, and his second favorite, which is the workers. A man who is British-thin and British-tall, and British of voice, and British of demeanor, Carlson is smartly dressed but poor of posture, defeated and damp-looking, greatly interested in tales of local death and disease, for they must make him feel stronger in his own body. Self-reliant? Behind a pair of unsteady spectacles Carlson's eyes swim with indecision. He has the frowning inattentiveness of someone who had a thousand places he needs to be in the next ten minutes and who, having given up on the practicalities of reaching any of them, has still not quite rid himself of the taste of excitement that all grand plans—especially unachievable ones—tend to leave in the mouth. Carlson is the kind of man who will be murdered one day, Andrew thinks, his life lost while he's not looking, fate taking its revenge.

Mr. Carlson doesn't necessarily agree with workers who are free. Mr. Carlson doesn't necessarily like it when Andrew suggests paying them all a little more—for economic motivation, but also for fairness? Mr. Carlson uses the phrase *I do not necessarily* as a necessary part of almost all conversations.

Andrew loses his resolution not to think of New York and Samuel. He loses discipline over his own desires as he lies naked at night under a single sheet, trying to sleep. He loses his mind when a letter from Samuel arrives, containing a kind of apology that he reads once, and rips up, and throws in a fire, and then tries—too late—to rescue from the flames.

I feel we parted on

I regret the way we

If you were ever to return to . . .

He misremembers the lines. Reading a letter once is nothing like reading it twice; it is closer to the state of not receiving it at all. He loses three hats in storm season. He loses the tip of his left index finger while cutting a mango. He loses hope that it will heal. And when it starts to grow back, disproving his pessimism, skin growing on skin, flesh building on flesh, he remembers some simple knowledge he lost as a boy—the bland fact that bodies, people's bodies, hold miraculous power.

In Trinidad the weather fans him like a mother's skirt. The trousers Mr. Carlson provides him with rob his body of particularity. His broad-brimmed hat does not stop him sweating. He feels happy in his hut, and on the fields, and walking, walking, getting lost. He loses for a while his sense that what is happening here is not right.

In Trinidad he loses some, but not all, of his need for neatness. Loses the habit of brushing dust from his hat every minute, and from his shirt every other minute, and wiping parched soil from his cut and callused hands. He loses feeling in his hip after stooping in the fields too long, supervising the harvest but also joining in. He works on in silence, hours at a time. Wins some respect from all the lower workers that way. Only a dog wants for approval. He is careful to never ask anything of anyone that cannot be expressed with a nod or frown or smile.

In other territories, Mr. Green, these men might receive only twenty cents each day. And here? Fifty cents each task. And yet you say—

He loses sight of Mr. Carlson, pale-sweating, pale-proud, when the sun is too strong over the western field, a man touching his bloodred British lips as if nervous that all this talk about fair wages may have blistered them.

He loses his memory of why he came here. He loses faith in the idea that his employers want conditions to be fair. He loses his desire to speak up. He realizes he is part of the problem. It is a shock, really, to feel part of anything. He has saved enough money now to pay off most of his debts, so he will return to America next year, he decides, except it suddenly seems essential to save some more, to go back with enough assets to make a start on a business, or pay for classes, perhaps even a house, correcting the youthful errors in his education—in short, starting again. It might be possible. He has become aware of a flexibility in his thinking. If he is set a problem, he does not always quickly glimpse a clear solution, but he sees five ways to reach one, and knows what questions to ask to get there, and the next time a similar problem arises, his mind goes directly to the relevant precedent. The British supervisors listen to him now. He has changed the shift patterns, and the gathering process. Productivity has improved.

In Trinidad he loses track of the seasons. He loses his amazement at the swift blue violence of the November storms. He loses track of when the dry season will commence, and Mr. Carlson punishes him for this, makes a fool out of him in front of the women who wash the clothes and beat those clothes with stones and know exactly the dates on which every event in and around Tacarigua must take place.

He loses his surprise at the way workers kill a hog. They keep its head and feet and lose the rest. They clean the head and feet and boil them until soft in salt water. The meat is picked off the head and cut up into small pieces. It is placed with the feet in one of the copper vessels from the boiling houses. When the head is cold it is deposited in more salt water, and sufficient lime juice is added to acidulate it. Plenty of country peppers too. The meat, prepared this way, is kept good for two weeks at least. Nothing here that is inhuman is wasted. Lessons to learn, to remember.

He loses his notebook and then finds it in the dirt the next day. Three pages are missing, ripped out, and what was in those pages? Readings? Dreams? Simple little lists? He hopes it was only notes on pretty weeds and vines and fruits and herbs that thrive here, the granadillas, the watermelons, sweet cassava, lima beans, callaloo, tanias. Life is planted in old copper basins from the boiling-houses with scratches and stains and brief blisters of rust. Note them down. The quick comfort of exactitude. He starts his own garden and it thrives, yet his melons taste like turds.

He is losing memories of his mother all the time. He is losing memories of his mother, all the time.

Loss among forests containing the finest wood for ship-building. Loss among conspicuous red cedar and a great variety of palms.

Three workers lose their lives. Four workers. Five. Nutmeg has been introduced to the island. Cinnamon, clove. Outside agents which have proved they can flourish in this soil. The beauty of a sunrise, a cliché feeling fresh.

He loses a fraction of his embarrassment at seeing strangers' flesh. The women workers with baskets on their heads, the upper parts of their garments unbuttoned in the heat, Mr. Carlson's spectacles blazing with longing, and condescension, and greed, and there is something in that gaze that Andrew recognizes. He is losing himself to people he does not respect. He is taking their money, and the accumulation excites him, the thought of savings, of slow-growing security. He is losing sight of his old self, of whatever it was he wished to achieve. He tells himself he will not go to hell for getting rich. For deciding, only then, what else to do.

Cloth and sugar! Different worlds, I am afraid, Andrew! Your family farming experience, however, is proving . . .

He loses the ability to smile at Mr. Carlson's remarks. He loses the ability to separate, in the distance, shrieks of joy from shrieks of pain. He loses the ability to distinguish the sounds of the different breeds of sheep and birds, as if the reality of the place is intent on slowly undoing the study he felt had prepared him. He loses count of the number of prejudices Mr. Carlson cherishes in the dark and then brings out to light at grand dinners at Mr. Burnley's house, speaking and speaking and speaking.

Those dinners! The outdoor entertainments that precede them. Lamps positioned on tables and on areas of bare earth. Sunk daylight still lingering in the trees that border Burnley's idyllic garden. The coming night will be silver. With foresight, with guesswork. He loses every image of the New York night, every memory of the different shades of darkness that swirled around him as he stood on the roof of Hinsdale & Atkins just a few years ago, the sky up beyond Fourteenth Street becoming a purer black, a thing one ought to be able to touch or feel, a piece of coal or a length of slate, a field on Green Hill after burning.

———

Four women are singing in Mr. Burnley's garden. Three dancers are behind them, flourishing calabashes. The white expressionless supervisors sit and blink.

Fine wooden furniture out here shows signs of permanent exposure. Thin muslin, the general dress of the performers, is perfectly creaseless and clean, and trimmed with colored satin, with ribands and sashes of the same. Some of the musicians sport silk stockings. Some of them sport colored kid shoes. Gilt buckles gleam as they tap their feet, expected to entertain.

Andrew stands to the side and watches, a glass of water in his hand. He feels pity and shame and relief. He feels he has fully succumbed to a system. He feels an awful secret relief at not being the very lowest. At the end of the performance everyone claps and nods. Only the vigor varies.

Mr. Burnley's wife is standing at the door after the music stops, inviting *everyone*—she means the white people—to come inside the house for dinner.

That blindingly bland smile of hers. Its beauty lights up Andrew's inner world for half a second. Then her eyes go dead as they train themselves on the next person, the guest over his shoulder, and light up again, and go dim, a routine of rehearsed charisma. What would it be like to have *that* kind of power, to be the central point upon which a world turns, to be able to animate people with only a look, and yet to have to listen, at other times, to your husband pretending that you are nothing more than his ornament? Is Mr. Burnley ever intimate with her? And does she ever enjoy it? And what of Mr. Carlson's wife? These are questions Andrew will never get an answer to, just as he will never quite come to a theory as to why Mr. Burnley himself is barely ever seen.

The dinner unfolds according to a logic of decadence, the principle of excess. So many candlesticks, so many handsome shades, so many serving plates and bottles of wine that it quickly becomes impossible to fix your attention on any single thing, and this starts to seem like the point. The whole room is brilliant, therefore nothing is, and between courses bodies swim in and out of Andrew's field of vision, lost and found, and his panic, his sense of disorientation, sets in. The younger wives are always swapping seats, the impossibility of remembering all the names and faces becomes more impossible still, the difficulty of keeping others engaged with an idea stirs in his bones, the need to let the conversation fall into a smooth groove, his unease in this area, and it does not help that he has lost his copy of Charles Day's *Hints on Etiquette,* its advice on how to think ahead to the next linked comment or inquiry, shaping out a suitable topic with a stranger, because he loaned it to the latest arrival from America, the new-new boy, and people never do take care of other people's books, not unless they have had to fight for them. Proceeding as a gentleman might, he must try to remember what the book said about building a careful and satisfactory rapport, concealing any disappointment or anger or loss at a given comment from one's dining companions. The English here use different knives at different times. The rules are always changing.

Room smells sickly. Headwaiter announces that the substantials will now be served. Substantials! As if what has already been eaten is not enough to make a king sick.

Five platters of fish arrive. Roasted mutton. A boiled turkey. A ham! Two turtles dressed in their shells. This is how it goes, and out there beyond the windows the musicians wait in silence for a few loaves of bread to be passed their way.

He loses control of his ungrateful heart. It sinks further as his glass is emptied and refilled. Throat feels sore, brain swelling in skull, every waiter's left hand hidden in a white damask napkin, a method of precluding contact between fingers and plate, and by the time the stewed ducks and puddings and tarts have arrived, and the head cook has been fetched and forced to apologize for the apparent dryness of the pastry, and a sweet wobbling dish called the floating island has been settled on the table and highly commended and has sunk into individual stomachs that are already bloated with enough food to feed the whole world's poor, he feels in his body a yearning for expulsion that stirs up memories of his voyage on the brig.

He leaves the diners to their conversations. They are tedious, even for tedious people, and he is drunk, even for drunk. He is sure of that now, that he is further beyond self-control than he should be, than he has been, than he wants, but it's late, too late.

He finds himself ascending a staircase, an inch of brandy in his glass, eyes watering at the fumes. Thinking: Samuel, Samuel, Samuel.

He stands at a window in an upstairs bedroom, the walls swaying. No right to be here, no right at all, what on earth is he doing? Lost all sense of decorum, needed to be alone in quiet. Feels the nervy freedom of trespass sloshing soft in his veins. A fiddler is playing downstairs. Downstairs or outside. Sharps, flats. Samuel.

Perhaps for a moment he falls asleep standing up, for now he feels a break of waking terror: movement, footsteps. He can hear someone ascending the staircase.

No, he thinks. No. But where exactly to—to what is the word? Retreat.

He turns and sees, through the darkness of the doorway now, a female form disappearing into an adjoining bedroom.

The relief is immense, but then he hears further footsteps on the stairs. Creaking floorboard. Cough. He turns away, looks out the window, pretending to be unaware of this second stranger in the doorway, a person whose footsteps sound heavy with desire or similar drink.

He closes his eyes. And a moment later, as if in a dream, he feels hands on his hips. Warm breath on his neck.

A strange, lovely sense of not being alone.

The breath turns into a kiss just below his ear, and then—

What—what the? Green!

Andrew opens his eyes to see, standing there, just an inch or two away, then reeling back, frantically wiping his thin shining lips . . . Mr. Carlson.

I was looking for . . . , Carlson says. I have! I have a friend who . . . , Carlson says. I was checking on her . . . she was feeling rather . . . I must have the wrong, the wrong room, it seems.

———

Outside, fleeing the house, trying to take control of his heavy legs, running, falling, the ground so very soft under his soles, each step a fat exercise in trust, Andrew's brain feels full-bodied, his shadow moving faintly and freely in the moonlight as he stumbles toward the safety of his hut, unsure exactly what has happened or precisely how it came to pass. His mouth feels so very dry, and his stomach curiously empty. He could eat the whole dinner again. He is an amateur in the art of alcohol, he has reached new heights tonight, and in the morning, as he wakes, the crushing low will come.

These flies—we swat and still we swat, Andrew! The workers here barely notice them, just as they seem not to have noticed the end of solid contracts!

Carlson says nothing about the mistaken kiss. It does not seem to have touched the world of this man's prejudices and grudges. Several days pass in silence. Slowly, very slowly, he loses his fear that Carlson will ever mention the incident to anyone. And why would he, after all? He was responsible for it. Andrew merely stood at a window in the dark. A window where, admittedly, he had no business being.

They have a great prejudice against the spider, you know. They throw them at each other and then they scream. Have you noticed? Flies are of the race of Beelzebub, the prince of the devils, and Beelzebub had no children of less moral sense than all these black buzzing flies.

But as the silence extends across further days he realizes that he is, somehow, losing Carlson's respect. He is losing the discomforting company of Carlson's conversations, his chatter about us against them. He is losing his feeling of not being the very lowest. Carlson refuses to look at him directly now as they talk, and they talk much less. Redirects his opinions about flies and Beelzebub to the new American arrivals.

He loses patience with drawing down the stubborn wooden shutter in his hut. He loses his fear of light flooding in and finding him, half-naked, stirring. He loses his appetite on the one-mile walk for water each morning. He is losing time all the time. He is losing his memory of New York life and Green Hill life. What did his mother smell like at night? How warm was her skin in the mornings?

When he starts to lose awareness of the sentences he is reading by candlelight—four hours of reading each night, for self-betterment, but more and more pages beginning to pass without notice the later it gets—he takes the sugar jar down from the corner shelf in his hut, and lifts a small wooden spoon from his unlockable box of belongings, brushes off the ants, and tips a spoonful of sugar into his mouth. The sugar buzzes in his blood. Buys him more time before sleep. "Psalm of Life," to Webster on eloquence, to Pitt in reply to Walpole, several parts of *Endymion*, memorizing lines that he likes, sugar sugar sugar.

The cacao is indigenous. Its cultivation is extending.

In the eastern field, across an immense track of level land that is rich in alluvial soil, the planting season commences. Dews are regular and heavy. Want of moisture here is a rare complaint. Andrew pushes joints of sugarcane down into each precisely aligned hole he has made under the blinding sun.

Some afternoons, a great calm falls all across the land, every human eye watching the eyes of the immature canes, and it is as if nothing of value has been left behind in America. It is as if he has lost nothing at all.

20

WOMEN'S GATE

Bessie Davis, also known as Hannah Elias, the Witch, the Goddess, the Great Pleasurer, the Servicer of Church Bells and Gentleman Flapdoodles and Foozlers, the Monster, the Ratbag, Evil Whore, Glorious Queen, the Most Beautiful One, the Rich Negress, Cleopatra, the Hedge-Creeper, and various other names, all of which she found in certain moods amusing, logging them in the paperless recesses of her memory, each accusation or term of praise touching her only in the way that rain may touch a puddle, patterning the surface without ever greatly altering the whole, was suffering the company of her third customer of the day and by now quite looking forward to tea.

She stared up at the ceiling fan above her. It whipped the dry air, cut it into quarters, but the scent of the thrusting customer's cologne hung heavy nonetheless. He was presently on top of her, jiggling around, taking great heaving breaths. The fountain she had installed in the corner of her bedroom let out a steady trickling sound. This accompanied the creaking of the four-poster bed as it shifted beneath and around her. If he broke it, her new bed, she would in turn break him. Her expensive silken cushions had today not received any stains. This, at least, was cause for relief. It was a job, and not an easy or pleasant one, but she was hard to it by now. Harder than many of her customers.

Her first visitor of the day, the elderly senator, had left her a ten-dollar tip for services measuring that same amount. The second customer, one of the mayor's men, who liked noon appointments, had left ten dollars *in total*. She would make sure, next time, to be unavailable for the mayor's man, to pass him off on one of her other women, perhaps Jane, perhaps even Anastasia the Destroyer, and this would hurt his feelings, and the hurt would grow over time as he turned it over in his mind, wondering precisely why he had been spurned, and then regret would cause him to come back with a more appropriate gratuity next time. She was here to get rich and richer and then get out from under these men, not to accommodate mediocre mumbling coves. A man should be able to afford his own expulsions.

She had her eye on a fly buzzing around the ceiling fan. It was the season for them. The fans were a defense but not a solution. They were born, these baby flies, from the ceiling's wooden beams; they came out at night when the fire warmed the room to a certain level, and then it was the day's work to kill them.

She focused on this one particular surviving fly as she stroked the back of the customer gyrating on top of her, who could be abusive sometimes, meaning she could not allow the engagement to become prolonged; it was a question of decreasing risk. The fly above moved in seemingly pointless circles, much like her tired hips under the weight of this capacious, cologned, huffing-puffing so-called gentleman's so-called body, and yet it clearly had a plan, this fly, a design, a certain mindful or mindless dexterity, for it was never once struck by the blades of the fan. It moved in and out of danger. Around it. Through it. This fly knew exactly where it was going, even if where it was going was nowhere.

Urgh, said Mr. Hart into her ear now. Urgh. Oh. Oh. Oh.

The friction of his bulbous nose against her earlobe. That was the part that made her gag just a little. The appalling specificity of the sensation. Whereas his belly against hers? Not such an issue. A stomach meets a stomach and they simply say hello.

Did he even know he had those little fair hairs sticking out from his nose, from its most open pores? She would gift him a tweezer for Christmas.

She pressed her legs together now, tightened every muscle in her body, muttering sweet words of encouragement in his ear, and only then did she call him a name he loved, placing it in the context of a comment—reliable in its effect if not in its truth—on the size of his manhood. His speed and vigor increased. Oh, oh. It would only be ten or twelve thrusts now before he reached a conclusion.

Talking to a man who was in the throes of passion was much like talking to a tiny child. You needed a very limited vocabulary. Could draw upon the same few commands and encouragements. Parts of praise. Scraps of scorn. Her work was, in this way, and perhaps only in this way, easy.

Fill me up, Mr. Hart, she whispered.

He grunted wildly. His pace was somewhat impressive, in purely athletic terms. She thought of a Central Park scene she had witnessed not too long ago—a little dog trying to impregnate a pine tree.

She referred to this customer as Mr. Hart, while he referred to her as Bessie, Bessie, Bessie, and it was her chosen name for him for various reasons, not least because he reminded her of a now-deceased German gentleman named Mr. Härtwig, one of the very first customers who had come to see her here in this mansion, after she'd begun purchasing properties with all the money she'd saved from her work. These quiet reincarnations did happen, did they not? Life gave you a person who reminded you of another person, long gone. The present offered you the past, and in this way your memory of minor characters kept on refreshing itself. It was as if God only had access to a certain number of, what's the word. *Templates.* As if he occasionally sighed and said to his staff: Oh, I am tired today, let us simply make another Mr. H—. And then his assistants flooded to his side, fanning him, while the details of the creation were confirmed.

(She, too, did very much like to be fanned by employees.)

Oh! Oh! Bessie, Bessie!

Here it was. The time had come. Four, three, two, one. Mr. Hart finished with a strange little shimmy and whinny, the sigh of a horse, an almost-sneeze, a number of gestures combined in a kind of ball of becoming, one that bounced and unraveled, but held.

She rolled him, with great effort, onto the cool smooth expanse of bedsheets beside her, and then came the glorious feeling of limited liberation, that first delicious shade of almost-freedom one felt when the worst was over. The knowledge that his desire was gone and that soon he would follow it out the door.

She had no further customers today, and just as well. Her head ached, her body ached. Regret caught in her throat, disgust in her gut, but these emotions she could manage, they probably came with every profitable situation anyone on earth had ever held. There were days when the truths of her profession touched her in an awful way, yet she knew also that she was honest, less of a fraud than almost every client who walked through her great oak doors. How many people can say they have lived like a queen without ever telling a significant lie?

Old Mr. Härtwig, the original, had sadly died. It was his socks that had killed him. Unfortunate. One of the rarer ways she had lost a customer. Blood poisoning caused by the dye stuff from colored hose getting into an abrasion that a loose-fitting oxford had induced upon his heel. Dead from socks! What a mediocre conclusion! And the new Mr. Härtwig, Mr. Hart, the one lying beside her presently, naked, non-German, fully spent, panting, calming himself, his belly wobbling, his sweaty hand now reaching out to place itself upon her breast—she removed it swiftly, giving his knuckles a comforting pat, and then offering the very same comfort to his manhood, there there, my pet, there there, it will all be all right—Mr. Hart, too, was now watching the fly buzzing around the ceiling fan.

Circling me like a—a vulture, he said.

To be polite she let out a laugh. Customers often made strange jokes in the aftermath. It was, she thought, a way to compensate for the ridiculous whispered sincerities of all that had come before. Tragedy and then comedy. Comedy and then tragedy. In this way the days moved forward, through a competition of contraries, and it was true, too, and perhaps not unrelated to the seesawing emotions of the act of love itself, that some mornings she felt extremely happy, and then during the afternoon which followed she could feel very melancholy indeed, desirous even of cutting skin again, a thing she had not done for years, and then, come evening, the world would seem washed in a haze of acceptable mediocrity, grayness, middling and middling and middling, and she would count her money from the day and feel her work had been done. Elation, then melancholy, then something in the middle. It was a pattern she had come to recognize in herself, a sign perhaps that her soul was restless, that it needed to try on different costumes.

She moved to the very edge of the bed now. Slipped into her silk gown. It was important to get upright quickly.

Mr. Hart looked sad. He said, My wife says as much.

She coughed. Your wife says what, Mr. Hart?

That the vultures will soon circle me, he said. In my business, you see.

He looked up again at the ceiling, mournful, as if it represented a personal limit, but now seemed to struggle to find the fly that had been bothering him, and she too, following his gaze, wondered where it had gone, though she could still hear it. Perhaps it was riding the fan.

At the bank? she said, trying to sound sympathetic.

He nodded, and this was always a ridiculous sight—a man on his back, nodding.

I work very hard, he announced solemnly.

His face was still as death. They never did leave looking relieved. This was curious to her, because they kept coming back, almost all of them did, again and again and again and again, offering more money, the richest men in the city, and if a process did not offer you real relief, lasting comfort, why did you still go seeking it? The poor knew better. But she did not serve the poor, not anymore.

After the very first visit that any given man made to this mansion, it often took a few days or weeks for him to come back for a second turn. But then, sure enough, his need grew again, in silence, like a plant or a weed or a plan. Then he came knocking a second time, came skulking in with his small talk and his stories about power—about having a good deal of it, but not enough; or too much of it, but not the right kind—and once the second visitation of pleasure had passed, he seemed to have no hesitation about the third or fourth occasions, for by then he had learned that he could live with whatever had at first been holding him back (issues of money or of guilt, of self-disgust or lack of time). She did not hate her customers in the way some of the clever women she employed here did. She simply found them rather limited in their interests and their habits.

The doorbell to the mansion now rang, and rang again. The first surprise of the day.

She should feel grateful for it, probably. Transforming

herself from nothing into something had proved to be less exciting than it ought to be. And now, a stranger calls . . .

A nervous Mr. Hart reached out for his trousers as the doorbell rang yet again. Who is here? he said.

She heard footsteps out in the hall—those of her doorman, a muscular man, unmistakably heavy of tread—and then she discerned a barrage of not-quite-audible questions directed at said doorman from various voices. More than one stranger. A crowd at the door, by the sound of it. Which meant . . .

Well, she thought. Well well well. The journalists. They have finally found me.

Unfortunate. It had happened on other occasions, of course—before the murder of Mr. Green had even taken place. The press were terrible for business—you only had to look at Mr. Hart now to know that, dancing desperately into his trousers, his confidence destroyed, the special secrecy of the moment broken—but one could understand their interest. Some of the great men of the city came through these doors, and occasionally, though discretion was her game, a certain amount of information needed to be leaked to writers through that very same entrance, in the interests of peace, and also, though she would never admit it out loud, to generate the kind of quiet publicity that was essential to any successful provider of services.

Now she focused her attention entirely on sounds. The buzzing of the fly had ceased. Perhaps it was dead, or melancholy, or had departed through the mediocre crack from which it came. She heard, or imagined she heard, some of the questions at the door more clearly:

Does a Miss Bessie Davis live at this address?

Is it true she was acquainted with Cornelius Williams?

Did she know the deceased, Mr. Green, Mr. Andrew Haswell Green?

She was about to go out into the hall to tell her doorman

to shut the door on them, but then she heard it shutting anyway, and the voices became less loud. Yes, he was indomitable. She heard him calmly coughing. Yes yes, she was glad she had hired him. Very much so.

But soon enough the doorbell started up again. Rang and rang. Which became angering, frankly.

Mr. Hart was presently pulling his socks on. May I—may I use the rear exit? he said.

Not with me, she thought.

My boss at the bank, he said. He insists on a—a lack of scandal.

I thought you were the chief? she said. We have no rear exit. What dye went into those?

He looked down at his socks, bewildered. What dye? he said.

Be prudent, she said.

Slowly, in ignorance or awareness, he nodded gravely, as if she had spelled out his future. (They did, all of them, occasionally appreciate some wisdom. Times were changing. They saw that her instincts were sharp, that her mind was effective, that a well-formed body and face did not operate to exclude other assets.)

And tea. Sometimes Mr. Hart enjoyed tea after his exercise almost as much as she did. She had not planned to offer him any today, but it seemed appropriate now in the circumstances to do so—to drink tea together while waiting for the writers to get tired of ringing the bell.

Oh, Cornelius, you fool!

Men fell in love with her. It was unfortunate. You could not account for what they would do, what confusions love would send them falling into. It had been years, many years, since Cornelius had been able to afford her. But for some men, time is the thing that drives them mad. Their anxieties and obsessions flourish in the dark. If it is absence that makes the heart grow fonder, it is also absence that makes the mind grow weak, the impulses grow strong, and the line between reality and dreaming grow blurred. In her experience.

Her doorman now entered the bedroom, bare-chested as usual, and holding a hand fan. He did not need to explain with words—everything took place with a look and a twitch of those fantastical muscles. She nodded at him, wet her lips, and he sent in Charmion with the tea.

Mr. Hart, during this series of bedroom entries and exits, covered his face frantically with a jacket, then a cushion. This was endearing, really, but slowly, sip by sip, the itch to be rid of him became unbearable.

She had never felt lonely when alone. It was simply not a sensation she had ever in her life experienced. But the loneliness she felt in the presence of other people? That indeed was a force.

What shall I do? said Mr. Hart. His face was full and pink and smooth, the look of a man entirely lacking in ideas. His teacup was rattling in his hand.

She looked at the wall clock, its steady businesslike rhythms, tick tock, tick tock, in and out, over and done.

You should feel lucky, she said, smiling.

Lucky? he said.

You ceased paying for the privilege of my company two minutes ago.

A pause which could have signaled anger, but then Mr. Hart laughed. Customers like him interpreted every dead-eyed hurt she delivered as an effort at flirtation.

She stood up again, tightened her gown. She loved the way the silk caressed her skin. A cool, calm touch that nothing else, no one else, had provided in a good long while.

Where are you—where are you going? Mr. Hart said.

To rid myself of fools, she said. The doorbell rang, and rang, and rang.

She walked barefoot across thick crimson rugs, the color of kings—and queens. She passed her cabinets of sparkling jewels, the ones every visitor assumed were fake. Then she arrived at the door and opened it.

The journalists stood there, dumbfounded, blinking at her in the frosty sunlight. No faces she recognized from before. (The murder beat, she thought. It attracts a different type.)

We are looking for a Bessie Davis, one of them said. He removed his hat. Clapped his gloved hands, as if for emphasis, or else to keep them warm. Do you know her, this Miss Bessie Davis?

She decided to release a slow, deliberate sigh. She watched them all watching her. She felt, in this moment, that a career on the stage was still possible.

Gentlemen, she said. Your aim is true, but you have determined the wrong target.

The writers blinked. They looked at each other.

This is a house of pleasure, indeed, she said. But one designed for gentlemen to befriend other gentlemen, if you catch my hook . . .

Some eyes fell into a squint. Others went wide.

Come in, she said. I am merely the facilitator. We are delighted to have you join us for this specialized weekend!

A few of the pale-faced writers now began to back away. Terror had tightened their features, an effect which almost succeeded in making their bland faces appear engaging.

I believe there is a Miss Davis at number 99, she added.

Number 99? they said. Of what street?

A flurry of notebooks, of pens.

That I cannot tell you. You may need to try several here, though I warn you there are establishments full of roughs and rowdies.

With this, she closed the door, and the bell did not ring again that day. Poor Mr. Hart was able to make his escape, and she kissed him on the cheek to apologize for the professional discourtesy he had endured. One did not run a successful establishment such as this by providing a mediocre experience. This, as a banker, he probably knew.

———

The paper fans her servants held. Were *they* mediocre? This thought occurred as day became night. A few, certainly, had grown stained or torn. She decided that she would have every one of them replaced. The fans, not the servants, but perhaps some of them too. Mediocrity was her greatest fear, and she was drawn to stories of its avoidance.

For instance, a couple months ago her colleague Jane had come knocking on the bedroom door after the day's work was done. (They did not work at night, and in this way, their business distinguished itself from so many disreputable establishments nearby while also reducing certain risks.) And Jane, knowing that she was in the presence of someone who liked to hear a good story, had told one from the newspapers of the day. (Jane could read, an asset salvaged from her childhood. Rich father, et cetera. He'd hit her, touched her. Jane understood how the gentlemanly mind does work. She liked to hold a bottle of liquor always and swig from it as she spoke.)

The account that Jane relayed concerned the arrest in this city of a blind mendicant. The man had been hauled before the magistrate on a charge of vagrancy and violation of the city ordinances by soliciting alms on the public street.

The thing that amazed the magistrate was this: the blind man, at his hearing, said that begging was not necessary for his support.

Not necessary? the magistrate had apparently replied, stunned.

No, the blind beggar said. I am comfortably provided for by my brother, sir. Begging, for myself, is a recreation.

. A recreation? the magistrate said. But what satisfaction can be derived from such an employment?

To which the blind beggar, according to the story, tried his best to craft a careful reply. I only do it for pleasure, he said to the magistrate. I can't see like other people, and I would go mad if I sat in the house all the time. I do the begging to have something to keep me outdoors. Air. A sense of light. Conversation with other people.

Bessie had revisited this story in the weeks since Jane had told it to her. *A sense of light* was the phrase that stuck in her mind. The newspapers had focused on the idea that the blind man was perhaps a type of a very large class of New Yorkers, not all mendicants by any means, but all incapable of any other pleasure in life than that which comes from the close and often degrading pursuit of a gainful occupation after the strict necessity for concentrated toil has passed. There were in New York, the newspapers felt, some thousands of men who followed business for the same reason that the blind mendicant followed begging. Such citizens would not read a book, or think, or take pleasure in any form of intellectual recreation like other people, the newspapers speculated, and if compelled to sit idle all day would be at least profoundly unhappy, and perhaps worse than that. They perhaps had not the quality of brain to go mad in the conventional sense, or it may be that they were already insane—on the subject of acquisition—and were incapable of any other form of pleasure than that which was profitable in money returns. However this may be, the case of many a merchant and financier was, the newspapers said, very closely parallel to that of the blind beggar who had admitted he could not be content except in begging for more.

But, Bessie thought, had the newspapers not missed a crucial point?

The beggar had not spoken of a desire to be rich, at least

not in the version of the story she had heard. Perhaps he held such a desire within his breast, but even if so, could it not be a mere side effect of a greater need, the one he had spoken of with apparent honesty before the magistrate: to be in the presence of light, and air, and strangers? Opportunities? A sense of improving one's own situation, day to day? A sense of connection, even if that connection largely came about through misunderstandings and mistakes, a confusion between the beggar and his sponsors as to who he was and why he was here?

And yes, Bessie Davis, also known as Hannah Elias, the Witch, the Goddess, the Great Pleasurer, the Servicer of Church Bells and Gentleman Flapdoodles and Foozlers, the Monster, the Ratbag, the Evil Whore, the Glorious Queen, the Most Beautiful One, the Rich Negress, Cleopatra, the Hedge-Creeper, and various other names, had thought about this story a great deal in the weeks since she had first heard it. Could not stop thinking about it, in fact.

Beggars were commonly the objects of automatic sympathy, but what if that sympathy was in some cases misplaced, not to mention insulting? The begging blind man, given an opportunity to be heard by the establishment, had eaten that damned magistrate alive.

There were people who did things you never thought them capable of. Cornelius Williams, for example. He had clearly tired of being quiet, of living life lying down. Of being crushed under the thoughtless weight of rich white men.

She admired him just a little for taking control. He had found a gun and pulled the trigger. He had taken fate into his own hands. The press and the police wanted to know if his aim was true, if his target was well chosen, but such questions might miss the mark.

21

FARMERS' GATE (II)

The Sunday school Andrew had been building in his first months in Trinidad with his own callused hands was now ready to open its doors. He had no choice but to inform Mr. Carlson, who looked at him coldly.

It will not last long, he said, frowning at Andrew with a look of distaste that had, in the last few weeks, become general between them. Just another one of Burnley's . . .

Carlson narrowed his eyes as if to edit his view, then blinked to provide a period.

But I thought you were in favor, Mr. Carlson?

Andrew took a step toward him; Carlson took a step back.

Your shirt, Andrew added, holding out a hand.

Carlson looked down, brushed the beetle from his sleeve, and walked off.

Cockroaches, grasshoppers, sandflies, gadflies, wasps, woodlice, ants. Insect life was abundant and vigorous here, and Andrew was starting to suspect he too was just another bug ready to be squashed. He found himself hoping a chigoe would get in Carlson's foot. Sometimes these little fleas so thoroughly ate up a person's skin that a toe or two had to be cut off. Andrew prayed it would be a big toe that suffered this fate. Carlson's body could become as unbalanced as his beliefs. Future arrivals on the plantation would see what they were getting into.

The Sunday school brought hope and unexpected respite. From bitter thoughts, from panicked memories. The humiliations of the dinner party began to fade.

Andrew had been told again and again by Mr. Carlson, in the weeks before the incident at Mr. Burnley's dinner party had cast a silence, that the children in Tacarigua were all idolators. This proved to be one of many false British facts.

A show of hands on the first day, in the freshly painted little white-walled hut that served as his classroom, established that nearly everyone had been baptized, and those who had not been baptized felt the need to offer reasons why. There was no clergyman near their place of birth; as an infant they were too sickly to travel to a church; their mother died early, their mother died early, their mother did die very early.

Andrew found that every child in his class could explain clearly, and with less doubt in their voices than he himself swallowed down each day, that one God made the world, and one God created mankind, and that He was all-powerful and all-seeing. Most claimed to say their prayers morning and evening. Many described regular family prayer. Some boys of no more than six or seven years in age could happily repeat the Creed, and knew the sins of swearing and of pride. Knowledge of sins didn't necessarily stop them from sinning, of course—Sunday afternoons, after school, seemed to be the principal time for fighting, the boys butting heads, rolling on the grass, and the girls coolly standing by to assess which of these short-legged gladiators would win—but the same was surely true of all people everywhere. He thought again of his little brother Oliver, wetting the bed back home those years ago. He found he missed Oliver now. Missed him more than the others. People said he was a good builder and a fine engineer. Andrew believed this, felt proud. They had written to each other often in the months after Oliver had visited Andrew's sickbed—nearly two years ago now?—and in the last letter Oliver had written that he might soon take up a prestigious situation in Chicago. No signs of this future, none at all, in his childhood. Every time Oliver had helped to build a pen or fix a fence on Green Hill, it could be relied upon only to fail. But he had the style, had the thick arms and the torso, the sportsman's posture, the intent in his gaze. Yes, Oliver had looked the part and played it well, building up his body with exercise to shake off any chance at becoming known as the weakest of the brothers, and by the time the consequences of his incompetence on a given project had emerged for the whole family to see, Oliver had a wonderful story to tell— about a sudden great storm uprooting a post, or a bolt of lightning unsettling the ground—and these fantasies, perfected in the years when storytelling was all they expected from him, were delivered with a twinkling charisma that changed the weather of such conversations from heavy to breezy to bright. Oliver knew how to talk to people. Came into the world with an enviable ease—God-given, mothergiven, or, still later, whisky-driven.

As Andrew stood before his students he felt the nerves that rack any amateur hypocrite. To relax himself he tried to focus his own sweaty attention over the children's heads, on a rectangle of light at the far end of the hut, where the sun pushed some of its devastating heat in through the open door. Was there a posture he could assume up here, teaching them the Bible, that could eliminate any suspicions they might have that his own soul harbored doubts? He was landing on the conclusion that all of life was a question not of faith but of first impressions. It was all about how those impressions were planted, and farmed.

The girls all sat in the same way, their legs crossed before them, their backs perfectly straight. The boys alone were slack, some of them stretching their legs, yawning, leaning on elbows, and one of them lying down in the corner because he had been born with a broken back. It was a rule unstated but understood that the boilermen's children, every Sunday, could sit at the front if they wished.

Some of the mangoes the children brought to class during the second week were delicious. Others tasted like field carrots sprinkled entirely with turpentine. He accepted every gift. He smiled. He ate with them at the end. This Sunday school, more than his work in the fields, began to make him feel loved, and knowledgeable.

By the third week he was growing in confidence. He paced the floor before them and said, When I was a child, I spake as a child. I understood as a child. I thought as a child. But when I became a man, I put away childish things.

He blinked. Paused. What do you believe these lines to mean? he asked.

They stared at him with the blank intensity of the truly innocent. Then their answers came, and a fresh breeze came in through the door, as if his freezing baptism at the Battery last year had buried in his bones a secret capacity for coolness which, if only he believed in himself sufficiently, would keep him safe from the worst of the heat forever more.

He would not reply to Samuel's letter. Weeks had passed, months. The idea was almost gone.

———

He had seventeen pupils in his class on the fourth Sunday, a record high. Then twenty the next week—word was spreading. Parents nodded to him on the pathways, smiled at him in the fields. It took him a moment to put his finger on what he was experiencing. Then he found the word: respect.

It was around this time that he heard news of another Saturday dinner at Mr. Burnley's house. Andrew for some reason was not invited this time. This seemed like it might be an oversight, so gently he inquired, but his inquiry was met with silence.

The Sunday after this party, which apparently was full of hilarity, only twelve children came to his Sunday school. He reasoned that their parents were tired from performing music, or cooking, or serving food.

Next week there were ten, and then eight, and then six.

On the eleventh Sunday school class that Andrew held, one boy in the back began whispering something, and Andrew heard, among many words he could not discern, Mr. Carlson's name. But it was not until the next week that he caught two of the children acting out a performance outside the little whitewashed hut, a few minutes before class was due to start.

A little crowd had gathered. A joke was being played out for the entertainment of the others.

The joke went like this: The bigger boy hugging his smaller friend, hands roaming over this other boy's back. All while saying, in a voice high and British, Oh Mr. Green! Mr. Green!

He stormed inside. He stumbled through the lesson. Was he imagining their smirks? Was his face as red as it felt?

A mother approached him in the field on the following Monday morning. She said, Every massa needs a wife.

Three students the next week. Then two. Two! One of them was the boy with the bad back. Andrew suspected he was there only to enjoy the shade.

Once the last of the boilermen's children had chosen not

to come to class, the rest of the children seemed to know, with that cruel eye for weakness the young always have, that the game was as good as over. They could play in the fields instead, and they would go unpunished.

How had it come to this?

When he raised the matter with Mr. Carlson, barely able to conceal his own anger, Mr. Carlson's pale eyes took on a sheen of satisfaction and he said, Well, one's reputation, Mr. Green . . .

Yes? Andrew said.

It is like a fly struck with a newspaper, is it not? Once it is gone . . .

He lay awake at night, overheating. Dark thoughts came to him, they strangled sleep. All the warmth in his bones was boiling him now. He was a child again. He spoke as a child and thought as a child. It was . . . it was all simply so . . . so very *unfair*.

The familiar, sinking feeling of failure again, just as he had begun to cool his own indulgent thoughts on loss.

The farce with Mr. Carlson. How had it bitten him so, after all those weeks of silence had passed! And how had Mr. Carlson, the instigator, suffered no damage at all! What had been said at the second dinner? What lies had been spread? What viciousness was at play?

That ridiculous, ugly, accidental kiss . . . The foolish consumption of alcohol . . . The mistake of climbing those stairs, seeking quiet. And why does accident always reveal instinct? Why can it not simply be content to be *only* accident?

With the classes collapsing, he felt helpless. His week had no end point and no start. He found he could not read, he could not pray, could not focus. He threw himself even more ferociously into working the fields. There was nothing more he could do.

———

Weeding the young canes succeeds the planting. It occurs when a height of twenty inches is reached. For this tedious work, the labor of seven- and eight- and nine-year-olds is preferred, for their feet are small, less likely to tread down young plants.

Andrew supervised the careful choreography of this process for the eastern field until a thick day came when he lost his ability to ignore a fact: His own presence here was poisonous. The workers would no longer work well for him. The other supervisors would not even meet his eye.

He wrote a long version of a letter. Burned it. Rewrote it. Destroyed it. Settled, in the end, for only half a page.

Dear Samuel,
I plan to return to
I am due to
I intend . . .

Stripping the stalks is the next operation. Every joint as it grows throws out two long leaves. The leaves are dried out by the labors of the sun, ready to drop and wither on the ground, and then the stalks, in their naked length and strength, are free to drink all available light, to ripen and tighten and lift in time.

Trash. That was the word for leaves that are stripped or lost. The lighter leaves blew about like thistledown until they found a feature upstanding.

Next week a British ship named the *Hummingbird* would be taking sugar to New York City. On the Sunday before it docked, and before a single soul had a chance to arrive or not arrive at the door to his school hut, Andrew produced a sign on a piece of wood, engraving words in its surface, like a mason tasked with cutting a memorial into stone, fearful of making any small mistake but also energized by the possibility of permanence, of leaving something behind.

~ CLASS TOMORROW CANCELED ~

Underneath this message, he scratched his name, spitting on the wood to make it easier to harm, thinking that he would never again allow his own recklessness to besmirch it, this name, his name, any name, and in the space between ANDREW and GREEN he added, as an afterthought that stuck, the wound of his middle initial.

22

WARRIORS' GATE (11)

Five fatal shootings occurred on the streets of New York on the day Inspector McClusky finally closed in on Miss Bessie Davis. Two stabbings, also. One hanging. A poisoning. Thanksgiving season was descending upon the city, a time for family connections, appreciating the common Father, and determining on a case-by-case basis the specific limits of one's gratitude.

The inspector on this crucial afternoon felt fully unwell. Suspected he had a fever. Had not, in truth, slept much all week. It was not only the stress of wrapping up the investigation into the murder of one of the city's most respected men before the holidays began in earnest—though the pressure from the mayor's office, and the president's extended circle, to find a quick and clean solution to the mystery of motive was increasing by the day. No, there were other elements he was battling and would be thankful to be rid of. Night sweats. A tightness in his chest. Symptoms that seemed to go beyond mere mental fatigue. He felt he was getting thinner, also, unless his eyes and his belt buckle were somehow conspiring to deceive him, and although weight loss did not seem the worst side effect to succumb to (one needed a lot of guts in his profession, and they seemed to expand almost every day), there was always the possibility, ever present in the mind of anyone who investigates murders for a living, that his thinning body was at work on a secret plan to disappear entirely. His father had died young, his grandfather also. The most prominent social evil in Manhattan was gambling, and the second was optimism, and not frequently did Inspector McClusky feel like an idiot for remembering only the first part of this rule. Why had he ever believed he would have whole decades ahead of him in which to prove himself, then retire early, and become the teacher he had always meant to be? Why had he allowed a damned elephant, and his own sentimentality, to squash his reputation in the force? The time was now. He had to prove himself with the Andrew H. Green case or else he would descend into nothingness, his name would go cold, he would become the next Acting Captain Daly, he was sure of it. He prayed to God to take his current sickness away. He wanted an actual Thanksgiving this year, a sit-down meal with his wife outside of police premises. Perhaps there was still hope. Her radishes, her broiled pompano. A Philadelphia turkey, chestnut-stuffed. The day was frigid but his clothes were soaked with sweat. He asked himself, Is this a trick of the mind or am I really dying?

Faster than everyone else in this city, he meant.

The house he stood before now, the one which he believed might contain the woman who had wronged Cornelius Williams and caused him to kill Green, was a splendid mansion at 236 Central Park West, one of the finest addresses on the map.

He had heard rumors that Miss Davis was a servant here and he had followed those rumors to this very door. A street boy had tipped him off this morning, and that same boy had helped him find the building just now, services for which McClusky had given him a nickel, paid in advance, an act of faith backed up by the guarantee that if the boy was lying he would end up in a cell with his brain all over the walls, the sort of fate that Cornelius Williams might experience soon in the Tombs.

But the boy had been right—about knowing the fastest route to this house, at least—and now, standing at the grand doors to the premises, Inspector McClusky waited for the lingering boy to leave.

Presumably seeking a further payment, McClusky thought. Terms of which had not been discussed, let alone agreed upon.

McClusky wiped his hot brow with a handkerchief, then blew his nose with the very same item, and before speaking further, he praised himself for having the good sense to pat his pockets to check that, in the course of their walk here, nothing had been stolen from him by the rascal.

Boy, he said. How old are you?

The boy offered a freckled grin. Almost eight, he said.

McClusky nodded. So you are seven.

The boy shrugged and put a finger up his nose. Began excavating for treasure and emerged with a winner that he now wiped upon his pants. His clothes were tatty, his face was dirty, he was missing at least two teeth.

And you consider it good practice, do you, said McClusky in the healthiest voice he could muster, to set a price for services rendered, so to speak, and agree upon that price, only to then ask a gentleman inspector such as myself for an additional sum at a later stage?

The boy considered this a while. Then he said, I did not know you were an inspector of gentlemen, sir, when I agreed upon the price.

There. Inspector McClusky clipped the boy around the ear. You are, he said, without a doubt, the ugliest seven-year-old that ever did frighten himself in a mirror.

He waited for the boy's reaction. If it was a smile,

McClusky would give him the additional nickel. If the boy took offense, he would receive nothing more.

The boy's face remained entirely neutral as he rubbed his ear and delivered these words: Mirrors, Inspector, cost money.

And so, when Inspector McClusky knocked on the door to the mansion at 236 Central Park West a few moments later, he was even lighter of head and pocket than he had been before. He watched as the boy, wearing his intelligence lightly, skipped away down the street. It was hard not to find joy in the sight of a delighted child. Their sense of momentum was as infectious as whatever he himself was suffering from currently. His wife said it was simply a case of the kind of flu that men, perhaps, feel more keenly than women. But he knew she was wrong. She was often wrong. Whereas he was only ever *misled*.

He heard nothing from inside the mansion.

Knocked again.

Then he stood back—police work, after all, sometimes required a little distance—and looked up. In a high window he saw a curtain flickering like a soul in the last darkness of its life.

Eventually a man full of muscles came to the door. Opened it without ceremony. Without any sign of surprise in his eyes at all, this burly man, who wore a vest over a bare chest—no shirt at all—left McClusky in the doorway to wait.

I am looking for a servant named Davis, Inspector McClusky called after him. Bessie Davis is her full name, I believe . . .

The man did not hear, or was not interested. It was an effort not to stare at his shining shoulders as he disappeared from view. Was a vest over naked flesh some new fashion that had somehow passed McClusky by? He wondered if he might be hallucinating.

Soon the man returned with a woman who, when she poked her head around the door, McClusky at first took to be a maid on account of the color of her skin. But she did not appear particularly appreciative of being called away from whatever it was she had been doing—was in fact more blunt in her attitude than any maid he had ever encountered before—and then when she stepped into the light, shivering, he saw her strange attire.

When it came to clothes, jewelry, and other female furnishings, Inspector McClusky was even more out of his depth than when assessing a new male trend in vests, and yet his initial feeling about the silky item Miss Davis was clothed in presently, the neckline that now plunged as she picked up a feather from the doormat, arrived with its own rare undertow of conviction: it was, he knew, an item better suited to attendance at a gala than to dealing with cleaning, or cooking, or tidying—whatever the owners of this mansion might reasonably expect from an employee such as her. This confused him, and he could not stop looking, on a purely professional basis, at her ample bosom.

She allowed him to step in through the door. The hallway of the house itself was scarcely less ridiculous than the exterior, but the air smelled of delicious fruits, a scent that cut through the blocked passages of his nose and afforded him a moment's relief. He took it all in now through the delaying haze of his own unwellness. The part of the mansion he was standing in seemed to be decorated in the style of—what, exactly? Ancient Egypt?—and some of the other servants he caught glimpses of, who seemed strangely deferential to Miss Davis as they passed, as if she were a higher form of staff, perhaps even the head servant, if that were possible, carried, as they walked, large long-handled feather fans in their hands of the kind one sometimes saw in exotic paintings hanging in Mr. Green's Metropolitan

Museum of Art—if one had the time to contemplate such things.

In cabinets made of old rich wood to the left of this woman, through their sparkling glass windows, he now noticed displays of diamonds and furs.

Inspector McClusky felt her looking him up and down. A few hints of possible panic in her features, yes? But they soon erased themselves. As she bowed for him, her attractive face, weathered by a certain degree of worldly experience that the inspector couldn't help but be excited by, broke into a smile that then opened into a laugh and ended with an odd remark:

I knew you would come! One of you, or two.

He thought for a moment. Could not help but blink.

Are you, he said, Miss Bessie Davis, so to speak?

The room was swimming a little. His throat was raw at every swallow.

She blinked and offered him a strange smile. Then she said, That is one of my names. Would you like to come inside?

———

Lifting a cup of tea from the aggressively shiny surface of a tiny table, Miss Davis sat back and said, I have been slandered, it is true. The press have already been here, you know.

Inspector McClusky leaned forward in the chair he had been allocated opposite her. It was lower slung than hers, quite noticeably so.

The press? he said. How did they . . . ?

He tried to crawl back inside the present moment. To focus, focus, focus.

Everything that has been said about me is a tissue of lies! she said.

The word *lies* heartened him—somehow it always did—but he succumbed to another urge to cough.

Miss Bessie Davis tightened her gown around her waist. This gesture toward modesty, if that was what it was, had the side effect of causing the silk to slip a little way down her left shoulder.

She said, Perhaps you would like some apples, Officer?

Apples? he said. And then, regaining his composure, he instructed her in the proper address: Inspector, not Officer.

She clapped her slender hands in delight. Inspector Apples!

Inspector *McClusky*, he corrected.

How confusing, she replied.

It seemed it was his professional fate to be caught up, forever, in odd conversations with strangers. People who did not quite appreciate the gravity of his work. And did she already know somehow that he was sensitive when it came to being nicknamed after foodstuffs? Was she simply acting on instinct? Or had the household, expecting him, conducted some form of research?

Perhaps I should speak with the gentleman of the house, Inspector McClusky said, aiming for a new brusqueness of tone. I will need a few minutes of your time—he sneezed into his hands—perhaps even an hour.

Ooh, she said. An hour?

I should not wish to get you in trouble with him, when he realizes you, that you are—another sneeze came—gone.

That will not be possible, Bessie Davis crisply replied.

Not possible? Inspector McClusky said.

Not possible, she repeated. Such a gentleman of the house does not exist, you see. Unfortunate. There are many men here from time to time, sir, do not misunderstand me, but none of them are gentlemen, and there is no—her voice went high-pitched for the phrase to follow—*gentleman of the house*.

Then I shall speak with the *lady* of the house, Inspector McClusky said, coughing.

She paused. Laughed. Looked at him with a strange-seeming wisdom and said, The lady of the house, Inspector Apples? That would be myself.

He was hot, he was cold. He was lost, he was found. What on God's earth was she talking about? A woman of black skin in a silky gown, owning a mansion such as this! He rubbed his eyes.

Sleep. Sleep. Sleep. It would be a fine and delicious thing, after a night of none, to succumb to the urge for uncon- sciousness. But the mayor wanted answers. The president. The judges . . .

There are places all over here patronized by roughs and rowdies, Bessie Davis continued, scratching her left breast through the silk, forcing him to look away in shame, his skin growing hotter, and hotter still, at which point he was con- fronted with her reflection in a distant mirror—no escape.

And some of the houses of pleasure 'round here claim to be run by ladies, Inspector Apples, but really, it is only me who can call myself that. A lady. There are, in these other establishments, which try to resemble mine, but do not resemble mine, men who turn their shirts wrong side out when the other side is dirty, and look for a fight with a girl on the town, who after all wants only to be loved, as my girls here do. They'll give you more detail than you'd ever in the world want, these wrong-sided men-customers, and I can see, Inspector, that you are not—oh no—one of them. More story of why they're with you than you'd care to know of anyone. Oh, I married wrong! Oh, my needs are specialized! That's how you know them, Inspector Apples— the specialized needs and the wrong-sided shirts—and that is not a fine gentleman such as yourself, a romance seeker, a refined eater, a professional professional, oh no it is not, so perhaps you should tell me how I can *really* help you, and be resolving all this business in the papers spread by Mr. Cornelius Williams, an old love of mine, I will admit, and in time an old tenant too, who, like many of the men of my acquaintance, has transpired to be insane. I believe he lived with me in 1895. I have not seen him since. Insane, I tell you, like the rest of them—meaning men.

She had leaned forward and settled her hand on his wrist during this speech. This unthinkable act of impudence he had not got the strength to counter, so the hand remained there. He felt new under her fingertips, that was the secret thing.

Inspector, she said softly. Are you feeling unwell?

Against his better nature he felt the floodgates of inner feeling open, and thanksgiving come pouring out. Yes! he thought. Yes, I am unwell, and someone has finally noticed, someone has cared to ask! Slowly other thoughts staggered through the rooms of his mind, the astonishing evidence of his situation. He was here with Bessie Davis. She wasn't a servant in this absurd mansion. She owned the entire thing, and she knew Cornelius Williams, and she was admitting it.

And has Mr. Green ever been here, he asked, returning by a strange route to the place he had in mind. By the look of this mansion, it seemed Bessie—he thought of her already on first-name terms—might have had a great many powerful clients visiting here in the years since Cornelius Williams and his kind had lost her business.

She looked at him, frowning. I've no idea, she said.

No idea?

He gathered himself. Cleared his throat. Said, Mr. Williams says you wronged him. Did you wrong him?

I am sure I did, she replied.

Her voice was flat. Her eyes were fair and amused. She looked around, seemed to catch herself in the mirror, then caught herself in the door glass too. I have wronged a great many men, she sighed, just as a great many men have wronged me. And yet I like to think . . .

Yes?

That overall I have come out on top.

Inspector McClusky mopped his brow with his handkerchief again. He marshaled all of his remaining resources against her irresistible smile. He said, Mr. Williams, the murderer, he claims that Andrew Haswell Green was protecting you, and that is why he was, was—excuse me—shot?

All his hours of preparation, of carefully envisaged inquiries, and this is how it came out! A sentence broken by yet another fucking sneeze! This, this whole encounter, which should have been a highlight of his professional career, would feel, for years to come, like a humiliation.

Bless you, she said. Then: A friend did read me aloud a mediocre version of the events you speak of. But I can say, truthfully, I am not sure I ever met an Andrew Green, nor recognize his picture. I have dealt with many of his sort, of course, but never him, I believe. Probably.

And why would the murderer be mistaken in this?

In response to this question, another smile, but tighter, slighter. She seemed to have one for every occasion.

I would say he is mistaken in a number of things. Would you not agree, Inspector Apples?

A white man entered the room now, holding another giant fan, and wearing only small golden shorts. The inspector tried not to stare. Tried to focus on how quickly he could shut this evil establishment down.

Do you need anything? the man asked.

She waved him away.

Inspector McClusky closed his eyes for a moment.

What other names do you use? he managed to ask.

Other names? She sighed, looked at the ceiling. She was known to some as Hannah Elias, she said. She used Davis only for work—this kind of work. She produced the word *work* as if it were a toy she had licked clean and returned to a child.

He stared at her, and at the luxury all around her, the muscular butler lingering in the doorway. The excess. The lace. The jewels. A vast mansion of grotesquely expensive disrepute. He didn't know for sure, not yet, how she'd made all this money, but it was his firm belief that it wasn't through selling cakes at a family fair.

And all this? he said.

She sighed. You like my little house? I like it too. I own several places like this. One client calls me the richest negress in America, and perhaps it is time the public should know, so that I may be an example to others? It has not been easy, I will say. I have found myself here through a certain amount of . . . of creativity, and willful deafness. People who look like me did not force our way into your country, Inspector. We came here by emphatic invitation. And we now have a colored population in the United States nearly equal to the entire population of Mexico. Things are changing, yet this is a city still full of whites who . . .

Here she trailed off into a smile. A rather determined, unsettling one.

There needs to be a growth in education and intelligence, she concluded.

You seem, Inspector McClusky managed to say, not uneducated.

I was not talking about me, she explained.

He scratched his head. He wanted to go back to his office. He wanted to bring her with him. But what would his colleagues say, if he walked in with a woman like this? The newspapermen were still swarming outside the station. He would have to think it through. He would have to blow his nose. He would need to drink a lot of water, a great deal of it, perhaps with gin. Whatever he could find. Why was she talking about Mexico?

He wanted to open the top drawer of the desk back in his office. Take out his four-percent solution of cocaine, inhale it up his left nostril for immediate relief. It made him sick to think some people used the very same medicine for improper purposes. He alone needed it. He would feel his airways open up. He needed it. His thoughts would start thinning, cooling. He would be able to decide what to do next, if he had the cocaine here to inhale. He would feel sharp, razor sharp, as sharp as a razor that had been sharpened beyond its usual sharpness. He would cut her flirtations into tiny pieces and brush them away. His penis was hard, currently. It was always hard when he was unwell, it was where the unwellness went, but especially so now, curiously. It throbbed. Throbbed. He needed a diagnosis. A cure.

Inspector, Miss Davis said. Would you like to lie down in the next room?

It was so very easy, and yet impossible, to read her expression.

She seemed to live several lives at once. Other mansions like this, she was saying? Other houses of sin? Owned by this Bessie Davis, who was also known as Hannah Elias, and who knows what other names?

The sweat on his forehead was slowly cooling. She stood up and came closer, around the table, kneeling at his side; her breath washed him clean like a corpse. She took a small fan from under the table. She fanned herself. She fanned him. She reminded him of the beautiful young woman who had cared for him as a child, the one let go by his mother for suspected stealing, and the way he had carried within him all these years, from childhood to now, the shame of knowing it was not her, the fired woman, who had taken the money. It was him. It had always been him. He had wanted to save to buy the wooden car he had been denied at Christmas. But he never did get that car. After she was let go, he had buried the stolen dollar in the garden with the worst parts of his nature, a treasure he had never since had the courage to dig up, and committed himself to a more moral life. A life lived cleanly, with momentum. And yet it had turned out to be a life of temptation, too—of interviewing resourceful, whispering geniuses like Bessie Davis.

One day, if he ever recovered from this city flu, he would return to the garden of his youth and dig. Dig up that dollar. Dig up everything.

You need to rest, she said.

Well, he replied. I do feel a little . . .

Of course, she said, taking his arm. Of course you must lie down. Unfortunate. You look so very tired.

I am feeling, he said, somewhat . . .

Of course, she said. Yes, of course. You have been working too hard, poor man, far too hard.

In his feverish state he followed her through to the back of the building, thinking that just a little rest was required, a period of relief from who he was, a kind of vacation. A chance to receive thanks.

23

GATE OF ALL SAINTS (III)

A journey to Green-Wood Cemetery, soon after his return from Trinidad. Every time the driver sneezed up front, Samuel winced. A great terror of contagion seemed to lie at the center of his character now, and perhaps the tomato pills, long ago, had provided the first clue? Fear could itself be contagious, Andrew thought, as the carriage jolted them back and forth. Spread to other bodies, other minds, or within oneself as the years began to pass. As if all of humanity were part of the same single susceptible mass.

Samuel was afraid, he confided on the ride, that he would be returned to the sickbed of his youth. His admission was short, it was followed by silence, but Andrew could piece together the rest from earlier conversations. He feared the delirium of childhood fevers, the doctors who looked like painted clowns, the throat that often seemed to want to close on him. He was afraid his constitution was weakening again, that he would become a child again—speaking like a child, Andrew thought; thinking like a child—strange shadows beating under the bedroom door. All this brought back to Andrew his own memories of the one illness in his life that had tried to kill him so far—the fever that had left him bedridden before Trinidad, the fever without which he might never have left America.

But he did have money now. Clothes. Much better shoes.

Reasonable lodgings. He had come back to a kind of power—and he was finding that this power created, by the day, more power still, like an asset that after the initial effort of purchase keeps rising, beyond reason, in value. He had first returned from Trinidad not with confidence but with the ability to feign it—and it had transpired that this pretended version was almost as good as the real thing. Feigned confidence had been his friend on his first reunion with Samuel, back at the library he knew Samuel still attended. Andrew was handing over his first payment for membership when Samuel came up, aghast, and then overflowing with smiles.

Oh! Andrew—Andrew Green! How are you? How was . . .

Oh, it was wonderful.

Trinidad, yes? It was wonderful?

Absolutely, Andrew had told him. A wonderful place, a wonderful year.

Well we must—

Yes.

I'd love to—

Absolutely, said Andrew. If we can find a time.

As he paid his first membership dues to the man at the desk, no longer a mere visitor here, he had made sure to show the whole library how full his wallet was, and to make a mental note of the way Samuel was staring with admiration at his shoes.

The carriage rumbled on and the driver sneezed again. They had come to a stop to allow some pigs to cross the path. Samuel now leaned forward in the carriage and said:

Extraordinary amount of illness of late, driver. I hope you have not succumbed?

The horse snorted. The carriage carried them forward, the wheels creaking again, but also rocked them sideways, into each other, and away. The driver had not heard Samuel's question, or did not want to hear, or else felt it was a truth too self-evident to state out loud—yes, people were indeed much sicker than one ever imagined.

But at least, Samuel continued—for, like most budding politicians, he never knew when to drop a subject—we are dealing only with American illness. My friend Andrew here is back from great travels overseas, you know, during which time he no doubt saw much worse, if only he would speak his secrets!

The driver looked back at them both. He said, Yes sir, I see. Then in a casual tone that seemed lit by wit he added: The big disease is expected soon, sir, as I understand it.

Samuel swallowed hard, his Adam's apple doing a dance, and his hand briefly reached for Andrew's knee. Limited intimacy, as if by accident. A person who loved to hide behind the possibility that a deliberate gesture was an innocent error. Andrew watched as the hand was withdrawn. Watched, too, his own knee tremble just a little in the aftermath. He still had a sense sometimes, so sharp it almost hurt, of his own body as being beyond the fringes of his control. As if it were a ghost which both was and was not him, following its own inclinations toward appearance and disturbance.

The big disease, Samuel whispered, as if trying to come to terms with the idea. He was taking from his pocket a handkerchief, a kind of comfort blanket, and as he did so, a piece of paper fluttered out.

Andrew picked it up. It might be an intimate note from Samuel's friend John Bigelow, a man mentioned almost every day since Andrew returned.

But no. His stomach relaxed. The paper bore an unfamiliar name. It held no hint of cologne. The number 16 was written upon it. A case note, perhaps. A scrawl Samuel had made, a point for court?

Samuel must have read the guesswork in the air, for he

explained now, as he retrieved the piece of paper from Andrew's hands, that it was a note he had made during a card party he had played for various stakes last month.

Toward the end of this card party, Samuel said, a young father, becoming dead broke as well as dead drunk, had offered to stake his feverish infant child against a dollar on the issue of another game. The other players laughed. The child was sleeping with its mother in the very next room. But then all eyes settled on the man's principal opponent, who everyone knew was the husband to a childless wife. She had been driven half-mad, it was said, by her own inability to bear a life.

The game was played. The childless man won.

The soft and sleepy infant was retrieved from its mother's arms, Samuel said. At first this occurred with no apparent protest, only the flickering eyes of the other ashamed players. But then the mother realized what was happening. Her confusion turned to screams of fear. She threw herself at the man who now held her child. She bit his arm. He screamed, and she screamed, and she tried to wrestle the baby back, then started to beat her inebriated husband around the head. The new custodian of the infant left his cards on the table. He ran out of the house with the eight-month-old girl pressed to his chest.

For a while, after this story had ended, Andrew could not speak. He realized his hands were shaking, so he sat on them, and tried to think gray thoughts. Tried to put mothers out of his mind.

Lately the idea of studying law had taken a definite hold in him. He had—speaking of grayness—begun reading Blackstone. He was surprised to find that he could pick his way through its pages quickly and cleanly, relying often on intuition rather than experience, and perhaps the fact that recently—for a few years now, in fact—he had been reading a great variety of literature every night and every morning. If he did not understand a legal term, he looked at its context, the information at the fringes, the trimmings of a given phrase or sentence or paragraph, and found a way to dance into the central meaning.

He had written Mr. Hallett of the Superior Court to find out about the requirements for entering the bar in the state of New York, which it transpired were even more rigid than suspected. It seemed, though, that with affidavits from Mr. Folsom evidencing the fact he had done well in his evening classes in the classics, and a further affidavit from Samuel testifying that he would help Andrew through his legal studies, it was possible to curtail, quite dramatically, the seven years of study that was generally required in order to become an attorney. Even so, a world of work lay ahead. How to convince Samuel to support him through it?

Andrew knew no other lawyers. Samuel—Samuel's law office, which lately had been left half-abandoned by its proprietor's frequent trips to Albany—was Andrew's entire hope. He was, once again, like a fool in the throes of addiction, gambling everything he had on a single friendship. But this time he knew better than to reveal his hand. The face he wore was newly cool.

The carriage squeaked onward. It took them from South Brooklyn along the margin of the bay, soft sea breezes refreshing the air, then a comical gust full of newly cut grass pushed them into the pleasant village of Gowanus. At a corner bearing a memorial of a bloody battle in the Revolutionary War they stopped for the horse to take water. Samuel murmured a conviction that the path ahead was too thin to pass through, but Andrew suspected this assessment was wrong, and the driver, who would not even discuss their doubts, had reverted to feigning deafness again.

Andrew said, And what does the number sixteen mean?

Samuel squinted at him, as if the question were purely philosophical.

On the piece of paper, Andrew added.

So Samuel explained that the man named on the piece of paper, the one which had just dropped to the floor of the carriage, owed him sixteen dollars from the night of cards just described. But the debtor was a friend of the man who had made off with the babe at the end of the game, and neither of them had been heard from since, probably because they feared the birth mother would pursue them and steal back their new child, as would be quite just, or because the father might—as no doubt he had—have regretted his own heartlessness and sought out some violent revenge. Men sunk in regret are capable of anything, Samuel said. So, although it was not the saddest part of the story, not the least of it, the sixteen dollars would never be paid back to Samuel. That was his small portion of this night of loss, and he had written the amount down to remind himself never to play cards again.

They reached the main gate of Green-Wood. Heavy footsteps. A guide climbed into the carriage, a man with a huge shock of blond hair and a very tiny mustache, his face inflating with the effort of ascension. When he spoke it was in a low, nasal tone.

My name is Bill Harding, he said.

You are the third Billy of my acquaintance! Samuel said, his face bright with the instant smile he saved for strangers.

Bill, corrected Bill Harding.

Soon Bill the guide began lecturing them on enclosures. On iron railings. On vaults. On shrubbery. On the objectionable nature of posts and chains that were now coming into view. They were liable to rust, Bill Harding said, stroking his chin, and on account of this they should, in his opinion, be entirely eliminated. He was trying to instigate a change in the regulations, protecting the dead from trespass, from the reckless ornaments installed in this cemetery by the living. It should be only trees here, and stone, he said. And grieving people like yourselves, if that indeed is what you are here for. Stone—it can remain forever!

Like corruption, Samuel said.

(Like uncertainty, Andrew thought.)

Like whores! Bill Harding said.

Silence.

Are you here to visit a corpse? Bill Harding said.

Not at all, Samuel told him. My friend here has been complaining of a lack of leisure space in New York, missing the free green fields of his youth. We understood you might show us the places to walk.

Bill Harding sighed and went on to complain that his work here at Green-Wood was placed under great daily strain by children who would often play on the chains of memorials, using them as seats and swings. If he had his way, they would pay for this.

They passed through land shut in by low, rude hedges, and shaded by forest trees and brushwood. As their guide began to expand upon his love of marble, of stone composed of layers like the leaves of a book, and spoke too of his belief in the need to avoid placing headstones in positions that expose them unfavorably to the action of the frost, Andrew looked left and saw that the landscape had changed yet again. Rich fields of grain now, and corn, and then the first views of forest and streamlets, the guide saying that the foundations of monuments should be laid strongly in cement, and naturally be not less than six feet deep, and that the stone of which any memorial structure is made should always be free from visible defects, flaws, errors, although some people seem to *like* such things, he said—to believe (the fools!) that there is honesty in imperfection.

Andrew was still thinking of the baby girl. The girl's mother, the girl's father, her new family. Lives changed at a foolish card party at which Samuel somehow lost a significant sum. And he was thinking too of his voyage back from Trinidad on the *Hummingbird,* a British ship bound for Baltimore, and the two men he had seen embracing on deck. He had not been seasick at all on this return journey, though the weather had been just as bad as in going.

He spoke a thought out loud now, without quite knowing why:

I can collect it for you. The debt of sixteen dollars.

Their Green-Wood guide looked baffled by this interjection, but Samuel laughed.

You do not even know the thief's face! he said. All manner of people have been looking for him on my behalf, Andrew— you know how I hate to waste money on fools—and none of them have had any luck. And you, Andrew Green, returned from Trinidad, reinventing yourself with fresh clothes overnight, calling yourself Andrew *Haswell* Green, think you can fix everything?

One minute they were lost in a further mass of trees, and in another they arrived into smooth lawns of the deepest green, the lane taking their carriage up to meet the wooded brow of a steep declivity before sweeping them down to the margin of a silent little lake. The creak, the rattle. The friction of travel. Andrew began to feel more alive than he had felt for weeks. Pleasantly insubstantial, here in the fresh air, surrounded by the dead.

He said, long after Samuel must have felt the subject had lapsed, You can give me half of the sixteen dollars as a finding fee, should I manage somehow to recover it.

The words came a little blunter than he had intended, but Samuel laughed again, nodded. Very well, he said, yawning.

Andrew looked down at his own shoes, soon to be muddy.

It was true he looked different these days, changed from the bottom to the top. Elegant soles. Good leather. Reasonable laces. Excellent socks, well-made trousers, a fine white shirt. He had been sent to Samuel's tailor, and had spent a good part of the Trinidad savings on refreshing his appearance, and a further sum on the library membership, and private classes to remake his mind. Whatever failures he had encountered while trying to cultivate sugar and faith, the time on the plantation had given him a new hunger—a desire to attack New York, its exclusivity, with renewed vigor. He wanted to work his way into its heart, and he felt such a thing might be possible now. He wanted to create work for himself that might fill him with pride instead of shame. Something relating to public space, perhaps. He remembered his mother, locked away from freedom long before she died, cooking and cleaning, cooking and cleaning, tolerating her husband's outbursts of violence and the house's atmosphere of ingratitude, working indoors all day and then sleeping for an hour or two, until one or another of her children woke in the night. She had spoken sometimes, holding him close after a bad dream, of wishing she could join him for his walks in the open air. And in New York, there was so little open air beyond graveyards like this.

There was a high point to which Green-Wood Cemetery rose, and they climbed toward it now, a summit to allow the living to witness a wide view of the City of New York in its perpetual haze. A hundred spires, a forest of masts upon water. The East River with its slow show of commerce.

Bill Harding pointed them toward a walking route and accepted, with a frown, their insistence on leaving him behind to wait with the carriage.

They walked between the few gravestones scattered sparsely across the hillside. They strolled down into a vale that felt untouched by any moment in real time. Andrew tried to imagine this cemetery a few years or decades from now, marble monuments crowding every hillside, a future metropolis of the dead, a thousand more memorials pressing against every existing one he could presently see, each of them competing for space, for respect, for the kinds of cut flowers which for a while he had laid upon his mother's grave back home before tiring of the idea of killing them, of laying death upon death. One reliable prediction in New York statistics: More people will die here every year. More acres will be covered with the dust and bones and stones of new and old arrivals. And to Andrew's surprise the future scene he pictured now—human corpses and their ornate stone signifiers, covering all of nature—made him feel unaccountably annoyed, for what right did the departed have to use up all this space in one's world? The living were merely looking for new ways to mark their mourning. It was the dead who had let everybody down.

Here you are, Samuel said. The closest thing to a great public park we have. Stand here and you can hear the ghosts of Brooklyn saying all the things they never spoke of in life.

———

A week later, he sat down in Samuel's law office, as arranged. Here Samuel asked whether he, Andrew Haswell Green, honestly felt that a former farm boy had the skills necessary for the law. He was clever, clearly. He had learned quickly. But was he hungry enough for the actual work, or only for the possibility of further improving his lot in life?

He resisted the urge to punch Samuel in the face. Instead he told him, by way of reply, that he had, speaking quite honestly, not yet entirely made up his mind to relinquish all mercantile pursuits. But for now, while mercantile affairs looked so dull in the world, and given he had not yet thought of any more useful way to serve society, he had resolved to take the path of the law. He had come to realize, from time spent with Samuel—time he felt very fortunate to have had, both as a friend and as a student—that it was necessary for every man to be acquainted generally with the laws under which he lived, and that it was indispensable to know on what principles such laws were founded, and from where they got their authority. Familiarity with these general principles, at any rate, would be highly useful in any profession in the coming years. His father, for example . . .

Yes? Samuel said.

My aim, Andrew said, deciding to change course, would be to deal fairly and candidly with all clients, never urging them to maintain controversy for the sake of obtaining costs, and to make myself a master of the history of important laws—their rise, advancement, and influence—so that I might find out if the secrets to winning a case for a client might lie, sometimes, in lessons in the past. I will try to take an enlarged view of the workings of law in all ages of the world, Samuel. I will not confine myself to the mere pettifogging (Samuel liked to hear and use that word, *pettifogging;* to echo it was to offer a compliment and a confession of reliance all at once) routine of daily court life.

He looked at Samuel. Waited. It had felt like the longest and most ridiculous speech of his life. He only hoped that the rather formal tone had been well judged, in the circumstances. And then he spotted a pen on the rug, to the right of the desk. He moved to pick it up, then checked himself. Left it where it lay.

Samuel said he would commit to think on the matter further, and this too was intensely aggravating, because what else did he need to hear? How many more years of talk and experience were required before Samuel would consider him near enough to an equal?

Twenty minutes later, as they tensely discussed other subjects, there came a knock on the door.

Samuel looked stunned by the prospect of a guest. He had been in preparation for a case for the last nine days and nights, and was surrounded by paper and books and ink, and case boxes covered by a great winding sheet. He held up his hands as if in surrender.

Andrew hurried to the door and opened it. Closed his eyes so as not to give anything away, and stepped back.

When he looked again Samuel was staring at the woman who had entered the space as if she were an utter lunatic.

The woman was Mrs. Bray, a young cleaner whose acquaintance Andrew had recently made, but Samuel knew none of this.

Mrs. Bray took a breath. The wait was unbearable. Then she said, finally, Sir, you are Mr. Samuel J. Tilden, are you not?

Samuel nodded. I am he.

I have sixteen dollars for you, sir, she said.

Samuel blinked. His forehead was doing something strange. Andrew tried to act naturally, but it was difficult, for the natural response in this situation was to seem as unnaturally shocked as Samuel was.

This is what my brother owed you, Mrs. Bray went on, ignoring Andrew entirely. A card game, I believe. His debt to you.

Samuel looked at Andrew. His mouth fell open, then closed.

Your associate here, Mrs. Bray said, pointing at Andrew now. This Mr. Green, sitting here. He did a better job of finding my brother than I have and convinced him somehow, through a strange power of persuasion in words, to repay his debt he owed you, and recover his conscience, or a part of it, one or both, I do pray. So my brother, after Mr. Green's eloquent and convincing speech to him, has sent me here to repay his debt. He hangs his head in shame, gentlemen. I only wish I could say the same of his friend, the one who stole the child.

It was a reasonable performance. Andrew was not sorry he had cast her.

She offered forth the sixteen dollars. Samuel took it and said, By God. Then he said it again. Well, by God, by God.

In reality the money had come from under Andrew's bed. He had been frugal until this point. The sixteen dollars was half of the surviving savings he had brought back from the world of sugar, the portion not already spent on education and clothing and lodgings. And he would get half of this half-of-savings back from Samuel, of course—the agreed-upon eight-dollar finder's fee—so his net loss, viewed from that perspective, was only a quarter of his prior overall savings, which did not seem so bad, for a lawyer, if hired as such, could earn that amount in a day. Mrs. Bray would need to be paid for taking the stage, of course, but that would be in kind, a favor owed.

Mrs. Bray now turned and lingered at the door. She said, Gentlemen, I would add—though you may not trust me, on account of my brother—that I am looking for work. I clean well. I work hard. Should a situation arise, please consider me. That man—my brother, I mean—he has destroyed my family's prospects!

This had not been part of the script, and neither was the next line from Samuel, who was rubbing his eyes, stunned, thoughtful, staring at the dollars on his desk:

Will your brother's friend ever give the child back?

Mrs. Bray blinked and let a long pause pass. That remains to be seen, she said.

Samuel had seemed to conclude, on this day, that if Andrew was capable of collecting such a distant debt, and had the tact, moreover, not to reveal his methods in the excited aftermath of success, he was a worthy worker to always have at hand, and should be offered a full-time position in the law business. Years of poorly paid tasks gave way to years of fairly paid tasks, which then segued, finally, into the opportunity to secure the last of the professional qualifications necessary to become—the New York dream—overpaid instead.

It was January 19, 1846, when Andrew was finally sworn in as attorney and counselor of the Supreme Court with Samuel's support. Ten days later, he was sworn in at the Court of Common Pleas, and soon afterward a business agreement with Samuel was signed. He had graduated in a little over a decade from the position of apprentice in the general store of Hinsdale & Atkins to a partnership with one of the most distinguished lawyers in the land.

His father greeted this transformation in fortunes with ordinary, unvarying silence, and the very same silence was employed in response to Andrew's decision to pay off, in the years that followed, all of his father's debts. And his decision to buy the entire Green Hill farm, to save it from creditors. And his decision to meet all necessary expenses for repairs and upkeep of the property, indefinitely. And his decision to renovate his father's favorite rooms to ensure he could be comfortable for whatever time he might have left in life.

He did eventually make one decision that he knew would hurt his father: to cut the old Green Hill house in two, from side to side, moving back the rear portion and putting a fine mansion between it and the maintained facade, so that the old face of history could be preserved while a modern central space was created. But what could the old man really say? Their roles had finally been reversed.

You wake up one day and realize you are a different person. That seems to be how life happens, how it establishes its patterns. The adult becomes a stranger to the boy he used to be. You become distant from everybody, especially yourself, even if, in the secrecy of your heart, you feel mostly unchanged.

24

WOODMAN'S GATE

I n the early years of the firm of Tilden and Green, Mrs. Bray and her dustpan were a regular presence. She had only recently married, but was already sarcastic. Andrew was intrigued by her gentle mockery of superiors, the shrewdness of her gaze, and the ease with which she had helped him commit the card-game trick on Samuel. Like him, she had turned that trick into an opportunity, and the opportunity into a job. Only rarely did it occur to Andrew that in admiring her savviness he was really finding a way to compliment his own. Even less often did he consider that in failing to hold her accountable for her muddy ethics, he might be establishing a convenient and proximate precedent for keeping his own conscience clean. Mrs. Bray had, at this point in her life, that most attractive of all qualities: self-assurance. If its value doubles in an age of doom, it multiplies without limit in a gold rush.

The idea that he now worked only with paper and people and books still filled him with an awe that he suspected he might never be able to process and disperse. He wondered afresh each morning what he had done to deserve such an easy year, and then two years, and then three. He was working all day, six days a week, and most of the nights too, but it was work of the mind; it bore no comparison to farming in all weather or standing bored behind the counter of a general store with only a stuffed raccoon for company.

And then, come midnight, as he fell asleep among more paper, volumes and notes and letters everywhere, he sank into panicked dreams that it would all be taken away from him soon, that his appointment as a lawyer had been a great mistake, his salary too, his comfortable lodgings, which had good windows, and good water, and good light. He felt sure he would be back to work in the mercantile trade tomorrow, or the very next day, found out as the fraud he suspected he was, once again sweeping floors of stores with an obses- siveness which somehow did not match, even in results, the elegance of Mrs. Bray's approach to cleaning.

Samuel seemed to have little time for her, he rarely engaged with her stories, but he did appear to enjoy recall- ing how Andrew had majestically initiated the recovery of the card-game debt. The lies supporting his version of events therefore had to be renewed and rebuilt every few months, whenever some new client was forced to endure, as Andrew sat blushing in small shame at the opposite desk, Samuel's description of how their young maid had first arrived. And Andrew, as he watched Mrs. Bray smiling and nodding through these false recollections, was seized by a conviction that she had an unusual grasp on the instabilities of history. She seemed to realize what he himself had only lately come to see: that one's past was as much a work of imagination as the future. Perhaps if one relaxed fully into this truth it was possible to feel secure.

Mrs. Bray had a head of soft red curls that the less imagi- native clients compared to fire, and the more imaginative ones related to certain cheeses. She was possessed of dark eyes that seemed full of secrets, and a box of codfish balls was often at her side, these being her preferred luncheon items. The first and most important thing to be remem- bered, she liked to tell him, speaking specifically in respect of such balls, was the virtue of planning ahead. Put your codfish to soak a day and a half, Mr. Green, and then boil until tender.

———

One Monday Mrs. Bray enters the law office holding only an umbrella. This is presumably her way of announcing that rain is coming. That she alone will remain dry as a bone. She often claims to experience auguries in relation to weather, but also food, and matters concerning the happiness of dogs and cats.

Andrew, seated behind his desk, where he has been since five in the morning, asks Mrs. Bray whether she has enjoyed a pleasant Sunday. He feels, after the mental exercise of the early-morning shift, calm and happy in his own body.

She smiles at him as if seeing this. Takes a breath. Then she glances over at Samuel, who arrived at ten thirty, as if to make sure she has his attention too.

Well thank you for asking, Mr. Green, she eventually says. But I am rather tired out, in truth. It is my very strong impression that this building here is entirely haunted. I did not see you over the weekend, or I would have told you then. If you ask about my Sunday, my yesterday, I tell you, first, that it was full of work, making this place clean for the start of your week, and secondly that it was—let us say—philosophical.

Samuel gifts Andrew a quick, slight smile. Do tell us, Mrs. Bray, he says.

Well, Mrs. Bray says, exhaling heavily, as if fighting her way past her own reluctance in order to begin. Friday, late at night, as I continued cleaning, past my usual hours, as I often do, the whole strange case began. I heard a noise from on high that was not dissimilar to the macabre music made by a rolling cannonball. Then, a few minutes later, arriving after church to clean an additional few things I had not had time earlier to do, and hoping to establish a certain standard of neatness for the week ahead—as I do!—I encountered a different shock.

Mrs. Bray saw, she says, gesturing now with her hands, the brush-room door fall open before her, and the dustpan fall to the floor with suspicious slowness, as if its passage through the air had been interfered with by a being.

A being?

A being of vapory dimensions.

These proofs would not in themselves be enough to worry her, Mrs. Bray is at pains to emphasize—sweeping her hand across the room now to include the office cat, Milton, in her assessment—but when combined with the recurrent and perhaps related sound of someone walking back and forth in the unoccupied attic upstairs? At a leisurely pace? And then the sound also of wood being chopped up there? As if the invisible woodchopper had a good deal of time to spare, and was contemplating ways to waste it, for example by climbing inside a young woman's soul and canceling out her character, such things not being unheard of? Well, the overall effect on her health is proving dreadful, she says. So very dreadful, in fact, that Mrs. Bray regrets that it is now difficult to contemplate continuing her duties here without . . .

(Here the room holds its breath.)

. . . a small increase in salary, to account for her long hours, and dedication, but also for her forbearance of the ghost in the attic, who she has established is probably a Mr. Focutt—

Focutt?

Focutt. He died forty-six years previously, upstairs or nearby, after having chopped wood for a local family for years, presumably among several less loud tasks.

Well, Samuel says. Focutt. I see.

Andrew watches him lean forward in his chair and add: Mrs. Bray, you seem rather young for a spiritualist?

With three fingers prematurely crooked from cleaning, and full lips alive with delight, the lovely Mrs. Bray now makes a sign of the cross—forehead, stomach, shoulders, amen—and says that most of all she considers herself to be a talented eradicator of filth.

Samuel now asks if the flying dustpan has returned itself to its proper place after its little adventure. At this, Mrs. Bray raises a finger and shakes her head in disappointment.

Mr. Tilden, she says, you are a man of experience, but you have made a mistake that Mr. Green here, your partner, would never make. For I ask you, did I ever say that the dustpan was *flying*? I did not. No, no. I said it was *falling to the floor with suspicious slowness*. A different act indeed, if you consult the laws of gravity.

Samuel seems to reflect with satisfaction on this. Then he says, The ghost should have a raison d'être, Mrs. Bray. If it did, your stories could be even more effective.

My *stories*? she says. Her eyes are wide with false surprise. It takes Andrew a great effort not to laugh.

Tales, Samuel says. For example, the ghost which walked the battlements at Elsinore had a purpose well defined, and our esteem for him was therefore much higher than if he went pottering about in a cloud of vagueness for no assignable end. A clarity of purpose, when it comes to ghosts, and also often to the living, can create, would you not agree, Mrs. Bray, an exceptional esteem for them—for the ghosts—as we have seen over the last half century in London, where almost every house in the heart of the city has been said to be haunted to one degree or another, as you probably know from your relatives there, or indeed in Ireland?

A small, tight smile arrives on Mrs. Bray's face.

But the presence of such ghosts, even the purposeful ones—the cannonball-rolling variety, the dustpan-flying spirits—can be rather irritating for those who wish to get on with their bland daily work, Samuel continues, especially during these blooded and quite finite days through which Andrew and I, mere mortals, must still steadily tread, and earn a living. Do you understand my point?

I understand some of your points, replies Mrs. Bray, though I wonder when they might adhere into a conclusion.

The presence of ghosts indeed, Samuel goes on, a strain of irritation showing now in his face, and high on his neck, the part that always reddens first in exertion, and where a quantity of wrinkles has arrived in the last year or so, can cost a great amount of money, Mrs. Bray, to a small firm such as this, a business that Mr. Green here, during my recent absences in Albany for political matters, has made a great success of. Many haunted offices fall into a state of wretched dilapidation, and the loss of rent upon them can be equal to enormous sums, not to mention the cost of the time which, if not lost to ghost discussions like this one, might have been spent on client work. I wish to set that upon the record.

Andrew watches and thinks, She has beaten him. She really has.

Which means I can beat him too.

The warping of love with rivalry, of innocence with advantage. The twisted perfection of the relationships that form our lives.

Samuel stands up and puts his hands in his pockets. It seems appropriate, he says, given everything we have discussed, that I should increase your weekly wage by one dollar, Mrs. Bray. That seems, does it not, a good mark for the knife?

A handshake.

A swept floor.

The clink of crockery as Mrs. Bray, several minutes later,

returns with a bright beaming smile and a hot pot of unre-
quested tea.

———

He has learned things about Samuel since they went into
business together. He has learned that Samuel is talented but restless. That he is fearless in following his own
instincts, but always cautious of imagined opposition. That
he is more circumspect on paper than he is in person. That
he, too, sees the law as a stepping-stone, but not one he will
ever let himself slip upon. That he is more concise in his
opening arguments than in his political speeches. That he
is at his most devastating when responding on his feet to
another lawyer's stated case. That in the social sphere these
days he shows sparkle and wit to every stranger he meets,
regardless of their seeming standing, as if one never knows
in this changing city who might be called to give the cast-
ing vote upon one's character. That people meet him and
are impressed. That he knows how to convince a judge to
say yes.

He has also learned that, when Samuel has solved a problem that will result in a win, he is like a schoolboy on a Friday afternoon, unbearably glib, fleeing the gates with glee
for somewhere ruleless and new, sometimes returning the
next morning to finish the task, but more often, of late, giving Andrew the job of seeing things through to the finish.
That he can be a bore. That he can be a snob.

He has learned that Samuel gives more money to charity
than he can reasonably afford, but expects a large show of
gratitude in return, and that if beggars ask him for a penny
in the street he never gives them so much as a glance. He
has learned that Samuel never takes a full day of rest when
he is interested in a thing, and never a full day of work when

he is bored. He has learned that Samuel often tries to do too many things at once. He has learned that Samuel still suffers often from an awful stomach, reduced to his bed every few weeks, alternating his appetite for rich foods—he loves the small birds, Italian-style, a polite collection of tiny bones given shape by a comma of sauce—with bouts of absolute abstinence from everything. And he has learned that one of Samuel's favorite tactics is deflection—how are *your* eyes today, Andrew? How are your lungs? How, indeed, are your spirits?

He has learned, too, that Samuel despises slick thieves entrenched in power. That nonetheless, as he receives his own first portions of political power, he looks to entrench himself within it. That he is careful always to earn a profit. That he is surprisingly careless at times—card games, heart games—in how that profit is spent. That he has a mind full of quotations, not all of them cited, and a city full of powerful friends. That he has a tendency sometimes, when he is trying to hail down a cart, to harbor behind those large but delicate eyes a small resentment, never in the world to be expressed, that someone else—Andrew?—has not run out first to hail it for him. That he has finally given up on claiming that he and Andrew are both men from equally simple backgrounds. That he loves the hush of heavy furniture and the gleam of elegant antiques. That he wants to cover these gorgeous, creaky old wooden floors in the office with thick and tastelessly expensive carpets. That he will never get around to unpacking the last box from his previous office. That his elegant hands are often in motion during a conversation, but have never thrown or caught a ball, never whittled a stick or pulled an oar, could never build a pen for sheep to be shipped, nor twist a chicken's neck. That there is a supremacy Samuel hopes to exercise in all conversations, an ascendancy it is in his nature to gain, whether the matter in question is the toasting of an English muffin or a point of law, and that if he is ever out of his depth he grows moody as a goose set for slaughter.

————

You know, Samuel said one other afternoon as they sat among the wasted and unwasted words. That girl, Miss Heller. I had the impression she was one of the few who had made any particular impression on you. That you might, in the end, think to marry her?

And Mrs. Bray, who was on her hands and knees in the hallway at this moment, cleaning the floorboards, the final task of her day—her commitment to what could not be put in proof, to eradicating dust that was too sparse to see— sighed very softly, and looked over to Andrew, and for a second seemed to smile.

No, Andrew said. I do not think I will ever be married. But I imagine *you* should consider it, Samuel, if you are still planning to be president one day?

He watched Samuel blush. The deflector deflected. Watched, too, as Mrs. Bray went about her work. Those covered shoulders, those lovely scuffed knuckles, the pale expression of someone who understands. The floor, under her attention, gave up a lifeless gleam that Andrew found less amicable, sometimes, than the dirt she had erased.

25

ENGINEERS' GATE (II)

Three years before his death, Andrew traveled to Chicago by train. He was visiting a sibling who had not yet sunk into soil: Oliver Bourne Green, his brother.

Oliver had asked Andrew a question thirteen years before: *You're still mourning your special friend?* These were the words exactly as they had been spoken, or exactly as Andrew heard them or remembered hearing them, and the mocking tone in which they had been delivered, especially in that emphasis on the *still*, had caused Andrew such pain that he had, ever since, evaded all invitations from Oliver—birthdays, Christmas, Thanksgiving. He wrote the words out now in the notebook in his lap, circling and underlining the phrase *special friend* to try to better understand it, as he rode the train to Chicago, a newly gigantic city, the fifth- or sixth-largest in the world, a modern symbol of renewal, like the sprinkling of water used to be, a sign in the Scriptures of forgiveness of past sins. Bicycle boom. Paved roads leading out into the countryside. The new Sanitary and Ship Canal had required an earth-moving operation even larger than for the Central Park. The system reversed the flow of the Chicago River and all its years of waste.

Oliver was a civil engineer by profession. He had obtained his early experience while in charge of tunnel construction for the Baltimore and Ohio, and had also been engaged in the first surveys of the Mississippi Central Railroad. All this before moving to Chicago and rising to prominence through his canal work. He was an expert in safe harbors, but also in the art of dredging, and had only recently retired entirely from active business.

A shared interest in architecture might build a bridge between them now, in old age? That was Andrew's current hope, and the real purpose of his voyage, though he was pretending to be in Chicago partly on a business matter. Turning eighty this year could not help but put him in mind of beginnings and endings. Shared some of Andrew's hunger for involvement in massive undertakings, did Oliver, works of unavoidable scope that might stand the test of time, and the amusing thought came, as the train tried to lull Andrew into sleep, that he and his brother had spent their whole adult lives building places and spaces that their dead father might have approved of, had he been a person who had approval in him. Andrew remembered again how when Oliver was small and had suffered that habit of wetting the bed, Andrew in secret had cleaned the sheets on his little brother's behalf, before their father saw, for he knew what shame felt like in that house. Had a bond not been created then, one which seemed set to last forever? But the few tolerable pieces of correspondence between Andrew and Oliver during the last decade of the recently closed century had been of the kind two civil but distant strangers might engage in when stumbling upon a subject about which both of them cared. Letters about the extension of railroad lines, the improvement of highways and waterways, the increasing application of steel and reinforced concrete to construction work, and enhancements to water power and irrigation projects. When they talked about work, they were sometimes friends. In all other instances they were family, and they failed as families fail.

When Andrew arrived he needed a nap. But he could not tell Oliver he needed a nap. This would grant Oliver a victory.

Hello there! said Oliver, waving an umbrella in a crowd.

Hello, Oliver. How are you, how is the family?

His extraordinary eyebrows had grown even more wild, but his beard was as well cut as his coat. No whisky was on his breath.

They shook hands, and in the cold air Andrew coughed.

A mistake indeed, that cough! From the moment they met on the platform to the moment they arrived at the house, Oliver wouldn't stop asking Andrew about his lungs, the cough's tenure and tone, and kept extending this specific chest infection Andrew had been suffering from of late into more general questions of health, expressing his great concern, which might have been real, within a structure of sympathy that seemed engineered, with no little expertise, to imply that Andrew was an old dog about to die and that Oliver was, by contrast, a jumping spring chicken. This method had been in play for decades. Such banter from a younger brother quickly becomes fatiguing, but the really cunning part is that the fatigue it provokes—its signs and symbols, Andrew's yawns and eye luggage, his paling skin— all had the effect of supporting Oliver's point, justifying his cause for concern.

In the days that followed, they visited buildings of interest. Oliver was always walking at full speed, happy to risk a fatal fall in pursuit of proving his greater pace and power. Andrew's breath caught in his throat as he tried to keep up. Further coughing fits. Several times he had to stop and spit. The first few minutes at any architectural site were passed in heaving wordlessness, both of them recovering without wanting recovery to seem a thing they might need to seek. Then they would talk about the walls, the type of stone, the efforts made to accommodate the surrounding mood of the neighborhood, local businesses, families.

On the third day of the stay, on the corner of a frozen street, Oliver said through his scarf, without warning: The Bible.

Andrew stared at him and loosened his own scarf. What of it?

Oliver nodded. Do you not remember? he said. The words from the Bible father printed out and adhered to the walls of the house. Do you not recall the Rules to Live By?

Andrew met Oliver's smile with a smile of his own. Arrived unbidden, like night thoughts.

Do everything at its proper time, Andrew said.

Use everything for its proper use, said Oliver.

Put everything in its proper place.

Be punctual!

Be regular!

Be clean!

Rise early!

Without meaning to laugh, they were laughing. Bystanders stared, and this made them laugh more. Like friends. Like lovers. The years fell away from their faces. They became the children that in their souls they knew they were still on nodding terms with.

Then Oliver casually mentioned that the handsome building across the street was one he had been the engineer for. This was Andrew's cue. He was in the kind of rare ebullient mood that left a man eager to take it. He asked Oliver about enclosing walls, interior columns and bearing partitions, floors, roofs, and the spacing of beams. Andrew asked him about fireproof materials, terra-cotta roof arches, column coverings, attempts to prevent the corrosion of steel, fire-resisting woods, beam plates and anchors and separators, flanges and web splices, trussed stringers, caissons, grillages, and cantilevers. He asked Oliver about laws and specifications for construction in Chicago. He asked about the calculation of stresses.

And then, eventually, for the afternoon seemed wide open now, and he was due to travel back to New York tomorrow, he asked the question that had been on his mind for years:

Why did you say what you said, Oliver? The question, last time, with that awful smirk on your face, just after Samuel had died: *You're still mourning your special friend?*

Oliver blinked. Frowned.

As if, Andrew almost added, the friendship was ugly. As if it should not be mourned. As if—that word *still*!—a single year was long enough to grieve.

Oliver shook his head. He looked, for once, speechless. Then he claimed he did not remember the form of words at all.

About Samuel, Andrew said, the old throbbing pain becoming sharp again.

Samuel Tilden?

Of course Samuel Tilden!

Oliver shook his head yet again. He seemed bewildered, and now it dawned on Andrew—an awful sinking feeling— that the bewilderment was real.

It was Oliver's turn to look hurt. Is that why you have not returned my more intimate letters? he said.

Of course not, Andrew lied.

Is that why you have not visited for so long?

Do not be ridiculous, Andrew said.

Oliver looked up at the building he had helped create. Something in his expression changed. At the funeral, our sister's funeral. Is that the conversation you are referring to?

Andrew nodded. Waited. His throat felt tight now. He had in his bones an urge—old, long buried, a thing of the past—to touch a solid object once, twice, then three times;

not so much a superstition as the comfort of a safe little habit.

Oliver said, taking off his hat, Then I was speaking of—I remember the moment now—of the first Samuel, Sam Allen, your best friend in childhood, who we had been discussing as we walked out of the church. I said he had recently been married there, in that same church, do you recall? And a blank look came over your face, Andrew, perhaps simply because you had not thought of old Sam Allen for years. But I thought it something more, so I asked you—and not with a smirk!—whether you still mourned the loss of that friendship, which father had ended so ruthlessly. I knew how it had hurt you. I was inviting you to speak!

———

Andrew left the next morning. He was very tired.

There may be mistakes in the choice of means to attain an end. But success or failure also involves much that lies beyond our power. We are not responsible for the inevitable, nor for a knowledge that is beyond our reach. Solely the ends, honestly chosen, and consistently sought, determine the moral quality of a life.

But how had he misunderstood his brother so gravely? How had he let that misunderstanding flourish in darkness and silence, like a monk, or a secret under a bed?

His first instinct was to think that Oliver, who could be good at stories, had thought one up on the spot to excuse his cruelty thirteen years previously. But that was not the kind of storyteller Oliver was. He admired improvisation, but it was never part of his tool kit.

Andrew told himself he had tried, tried to get closer to his brother. He told himself he had worked hard to that end. So why did he feel so awful? Why did he sense he would never see Oliver again? How had so many years been wasted away? And why did those wasted years, now gone, seem to demand that still more time, the future, would be wasted still? Oliver's eyes had been so cold when they had shaken hands an hour ago on the platform. As if he could not believe, would not ever forgive, Andrew's lack of faith in him. As if Andrew's whole character, its flaws, had suddenly come into the light, explaining everything.

On the train journey back to New York—present city, pastless—Andrew remembered a few moments from their youth. Swimming in the rain, climbing in the sunlight, throwing frogs into the eastern pond. He fell into his own embellishment of the old shattered facts. He wished he had found a way to express to his brother the intensity of his love for him, but it was too late now, it was all too late. Everything has its limit.

They stopped at a station where a woman now boarded. She was helping a frail man. He was adrift in his nineties, it seemed, a rare feat indeed, and the woman announced that this man was her father, and would Andrew mind if she put him in the seat opposite?

Her father would be traveling on to New York, yes. This was where he was going, this address on this piece of paper here—she held it out, a number 16 followed by a street name—and if Andrew could in any way find it in his heart to remind her father where exactly he was going, for he was greatly forgetful, that would be so very appreciated.

Then she hesitated, seemed to have second thoughts. Does she recognize my face? Andrew wondered. Is that what was causing her to falter?

He was about to put her at ease, to let her know in some small proud and stupid way that she wasn't alone, that strangers in fact approached him all the time, that they said, Father of Greater New York, you are a genius among men! Or they said, Father, you are a first-class fool.

But before he could tell the woman that he was indeed the person he thought she thought he was—perhaps she had attended one of his speeches, perhaps they had even met once before at a charity event—she said, with the tonelessness of a total stranger, How old might *you* be, sir?

He, Andrew Haswell Green, did not dignify this with an answer.

I only ask, she said, because I hope you will help him, my father here—he is prone to forgetting, you see, as I say. But if you, too, are . . .

I am not, he said.

She nodded and hopped off the train.

On the remainder of the journey, it transpired that this old Chicago man sitting opposite Andrew, all wrinkles and bone, all wise eyes and smiles, clutching a large umbrella like his life depended on it, was prone not so much to forgetting as to memorializing. His problem wasn't an absence of the past but the absence of a present with which to frame it. He believed himself to be living through 1873, this man, it seemed—a year which was by now nearly three decades in the past. It was written on the piece of paper his daughter had handed over, under the address—*He believes it is Thanksgiving, 1873*—and, miraculously, it seemed to be true. The old man's mind was trapped in the year—the very month!—when Andrew, as comptroller of the city, had received a letter bomb from one of William Tweed's men.

Of course, this stranger had no idea of the bomb that long ago might have ended Andrew's life. His past, like everyone else's, was personal. As the train picked up speed for the final time the old man said he was thankful he still lived in Chicago, instead of St. Louis or Cincinnati. He said he was thankful that navigation would be closed awhile and that those damn bridges wouldn't be able to swing every time he tried to cross the river. He said he was thankful that he had received a good deal of advice this year, and that he hadn't followed any of it. He said he was thankful that the hog trade was better than ever. He said he was thankful that there wouldn't be a war with Spain. He said he was thankful the idiot running his neighborhood would soon retire to fry sirloins and sausages—though even that sport was too good for him. He said he was thankful that the streetcar seats had been carpeted and the floors strewn with hay to keep his little granddaughter warm during winter rides. He said he was thankful that, though times were hard, they could be harder still. He said he was thankful that since everyone was pretty hard up in Chicago this year, no one would expect too many Christmas presents. He said he was thankful that Italian opera had never come to Chicago, for it was pretentious, despicable. He said he was thankful that prices of simple goods were finally falling, like an inebriated New York politician on the steps of City Hall. He said he was thankful the panic was slowly going away, and that the woman he had loved from afar for most of his life, never gathering the courage to say as such, was still happy with her ancient husband, or seemed to be, and that his own dear wife—he made a sign of the cross on his frail chest—was still warm under the weight of God's good soil, and had been for two years now. He was thankful that his granddaughter had cut twelve teeth so far, saving the family the expense of a false set, and her the pain of installation. He was thankful that when he dreamed of his wife's death, which was often, and woke to realize that indeed it was true, that she was gone, had left him alone, the next thing he heard was often the sound of his little granddaughter crying or coughing in her cot in the hallway, and in this way life kept rearriving, inter-rupting any plummet into melancholy. Duty and family, he said, saved a man from reflection.

Andrew sat very still, listening to all this, and when the

old man's speech was finally over, he heard someone in the carriage weeping, and it took much longer than it reasonably should to realize that this person was in fact him. He could not remember the last time he had cried, and perhaps never like this. Tears soaked his cheeks. He could not wipe them away with sufficient speed. He was shaking, rocking back and forth. He thought of his mother in bed, lying still. He thought of Samuel. He closed his eyes and colors danced.

The old man nodded, as if weeping was the response he had expected all along. Then, with sadness and sympathy in his eyes, he offered Andrew his umbrella, held it out with a smile, as if as a gift or solution.

Do you know my brother Oliver? Andrew said through his tears. Oliver Bourne Green, of your Chicago? A fine civil engineer. A fine man, a good brother. We had a misunderstanding, you see, about my greatest friend, Samuel Tilden, whose name you probably know, I am sure, I am certain, for he achieved a great many things, in New York and beyond, was almost president, but had it stolen from him, but will be remembered . . .

For a moment the old gentleman seemed like he might reply. Then the train came into the station.

26

BOYS' GATE (II)

He was in bed with Samuel. It did happen, sometimes, when they were not quite young and not quite old, though not often, not really. Only if they were working late together on a speech or a public project, or an idea that seemed too intimate to discuss within range of strangers. They would work into the night by the fire, then fall asleep here on the daybed, fully clothed, in a swarm of blankets, side by side, because Samuel said the staff had not made up the guest bed, or that the bed was broken and being replaced, or too creaky for a great friend, a close friend, to try to sleep upon. Sometimes their hands would touch. Sometimes, they would fall asleep with fingers interlocked. Not always, though. Not always.

They celebrated Andrew's birthday by eating ice cream on a clear fall afternoon outside City Hall, discussing what adventures a person's thirties should hold. Afterward they returned to Samuel's house again, worked a few hours, lay side by side upstairs to talk. The word on his mind, as he had watched Samuel's political career begin to flourish, was accessibility. *The walls of my imagined park should be low*, he wrote in his diary. Bodies on the grass, men lying in the sun.

I disagree, Samuel said. If you are seeking out a public project, the Board of Education needs a sensible man. I will make an introduction. Do not concern yourself with grass. A park is a park. Very few people would use one in the center of our island. A Green is drawn to greenery, green hills, the spacious walks of his youth, I do understand, but this middle park of yours is—forgive me—it is a poor, sentimental idea, and one which . . .

The creak of a floorboard was enough to stop him talking. A reminder that he, too, was afraid. That fear would never leave them.

Probably it was one of Samuel's staff moving through the darkest corridors of the house, or a small creature scurrying up in the attic. In these intervals, all Andrew could hear was breathing—his own, Samuel's, their bodies moving in time. Only in time.

Perhaps, Samuel whispered, looking up at the ceiling, It is a ghost with a cannonball?

Was it not an ax? Andrew said.

Your dear Mrs. Bray, Samuel sighed. I have a feeling she will be with you forever.

They lay together very still. They listened for signs of movement from the living. Then Samuel asked a question he had started to ask often. This time it was shaped like this:

Do you think it would be different between us, Andrew, if we did not have to think always of our work? Of our, *reputation*?

And Andrew said nothing.

If we did not always have to be on tiptoe, to need to be needful, looking over each other's shoulders, ensuring we make no missteps?

And Andrew said nothing, nothing at all. Could feel anger rising up within him, in fact. What a time, after all these years, to keep reopening, month by month, this particular wound.

It is my birthday, Andrew said, nonsensically.

And that closed Samuel's mouth, his talk of missteps, for a moment or two.

Missteps. Andrew imagined them stumbling down a dark path together, then up uneven steps, passing through a wild part of the park he now spent so much of his time imagining, trying to find a way home from one of John Bigelow's parties perhaps, or escaping Mr. Carlson in a foreign land, falling sometimes, grazing their knees, yet rising again, pressing onward, and in the end perhaps reaching somewhere splendid. Through missteps.

You know what I mean, said Samuel. You know exactly what I mean. If we were not ambitious . . . If we did not care what other people thought . . . If we did not want to, to change America . . .

Andrew laughed, for at this time it still seemed to him rather grand, to talk about changing anything. And this laughter upset Samuel, just as it had been intended to.

Samuel's hand touching his hand. A sense of shame came, it always did in Andrew, a sudden influx of more-than-ordinary terror, a reflex to counter that other reflex, the one toward closeness and warmth. If Andrew could have blown out the flame of his own fear as easily as the flame of his own desire, he would have done so on these nights with all his might, wouldn't he? He did imagine a different kind of life.

But then he thought, in spite of everything, of his father's words. *Hold the ax like a man.*

Or he thought of that absurd mistaken encounter with Mr. Carlson upstairs at Mr. Burnley's house.

Or he thought of young Sam Allen in the field on that summer night, Sam's mother watching at the window.

Or he thought of the client of the law firm who kept trying to take him out for dinners full of drink.

Or he thought of how his father's impulsive decisions—to

become a farmer, to marry and marry and marry—had taken the family from prosperity into near poverty in the space of little more than a decade. It was very easy to achieve nothing in life if one succumbed always to whims—the whim of the moment, the whim of the day, the whim of the season, the whim of the year. Whims had consequences. They came at a cost.

It was too late to abandon himself to that which he could not control. He would not roll around in the dirt of the past. He would not climb up drunk into rooms built for other people's pleasure, and risk an accidental kiss at the window, a kiss that would ruin everything, that would necessitate a great escape. He would not risk being banished from a life in which he was now starting to succeed, absurdly, inexplicably, in building public projects on a massive scale. The law had opened up a door onto important civic work. Jobs, mostly unpaid, that few real gentlemen seemed to want to do.

His mother had wanted space. Open air. But his father had crushed that need, and some shadow of that crushing had passed down. It was time to open up the city for study while keeping himself closed.

Restraint. That is the key to a dignified life, Andrew. Restraint, restraint, restraint.

———

Later, much later, in the years before Samuel became governor of New York, and before the attentions of the press became focused on whether the governor would finally make a proposal of marriage to one of the lovely young women who threw themselves at his feet, Andrew kept trying to convince Samuel to take an afternoon off work—one single afternoon in a span of months—so that they might take some exercise together in the Central Park, the park that Andrew had somehow made real despite extensive opposition, and then kept alive before and during the war, while all the Irish laborers, desperate to avoid the draft, knocked and screamed at the door to his cabin each week, begging for employment, for any task at all. How he had needed to turn most of them away, every day, looking into the eyes of men who wanted only work, and women with their hair hidden under hats, and apprentice children with mud shadowing their jaws, creating an inconsistent, shifting impression of age.

So much of a life happens offstage, in silence. You suspect this in your forties, but you know it in your fifties. You know it every day. And it was the idea of an afternoon in the wintered park with Samuel—the hope of it—that had preoccupied his selfish, entitled mind for months as the last parkland squatters were evicted, whole families left homeless to make his perfect vision of New York possible. The city had presented many of them with new buildings, but most did not want to go, wanted instead to be free, and that idea was strange to him now—freedom. It brought him back, with dissatisfaction, to memories of his time in Trinidad. He would pay for it all one day, he thought.

In his perfect, sentimental vision of the park in winter, he and Samuel would be bundled in furs, sledding, snapping the whip and feeling the horses go faster, the two of them drawn through the thrill of the snow, the air freezing their faces along with their sense of selves. Utter whiteness. Birds in blue sky. The energy of friendship, of union, in land protected and repaired by all that snow. He had a strange idea that if they could make themselves sufficiently cold, become men made entirely of ice, everything else between them would have to break or thaw. They would be able to start again with whatever kind of friendship they wished for, instead of what they had at the moment, in almost all moments, which was a friendship built on years and years of each of them wanting different things at different times, the timings of their wants never coinciding, their terrors see-sawing too, one man's fear up when the other's had abated.

Reality refused them the moment. They didn't go during Samuel's first year as governor. They didn't go sledding when his name arose as a candidate for the presidential nomination. They didn't go after the convention, after fighting off Broadhead and Parker and Hendricks, and Hancock, and William Allen, and Thomas F. Bayard, and Joel Parker, and Allen G. Thurman. They didn't go after Samuel had the presidency stolen from him by a series of frauds and mistakes.

And they did not go before Samuel died in Greystone, the mansion he held beyond the city, on August 4, 1886. Each passing year it seemed there would be time. But the final realization of life is that there isn't time. There isn't time. It is slipping from us with every smile.

Had he died of disappointment? Would he have lived longer if he had been elected president by something more than the popular vote?

Samuel should have married. He would have won, if he had been married, would he? And what he would have lost in doing so, he had lost anyway.

He had not been there to hold Samuel's hand. He had been too busy back in the city with work. He had arrived a few hours after the dying had finished. By then the obituary writers had arrived at the door, and Andrew had asked each of them calmly, one by one, how many lines they required.

———

Andrew's last appointed role for Samuel was executor. He stayed awhile in Samuel's house during the fattest nights of mourning. He filled notebooks. He muttered truths to himself, half-truths, nonsense. The march of the American people westward. The march of businesses and residences up the island. He struggled to picture the first version of the metropolis he had encountered, as a boy working at Hinsdale & Atkins, a city confined below Fourteenth, one you could get your whole imagination around. Can you kill someone, or some part of them, by neglect?

He fell asleep on Samuel's cold floor, with his maps and books, thinking of losses, and of Trinidad too, and after a few weeks of this, so many such nights, he began to wake before dawn with an argument forming behind his stinging eyes.

The most powerful people in New York saw the rivers and waterways as barriers, as separating forces, but this was a mistake, surely, a way of misreading nature. It was a perversion of policy to regard a bond of union as a symbol of division. He longed to tell Samuel his plans, but Samuel wasn't alive to hear them.

Samuel had been there with him during the park years, though, and he told himself this was something to try to be thankful for. The years when Andrew's thoughts in any given situation would turn a corner, suddenly, and the Central Park would open up in his mind yet again, as if he were seeing it from the sky, a site of created nature, a kind of captured paradise, an obsession, a series of composed views that felt more real than the surrounding urban world. But what he pictured most often when falling into the fitful sleep of middle age were not the glories of summer days wandering through the park's great spaces. What came to him instead were the numbers. The figures that fell in the shadows of grandiose ideas. The battles with budgets. The administration behind the beauty was, to him, as attractive as the trees. And was it so bad, really, to be plagued by regret? Might our private loneliness, our most crushing inner fears, push us outward, at times, into greater public good? The building of bridges, of open spaces, of consolidated places where others might feel less alone? Is such an idea too ridiculous to form the foundation of action, or inaction?

Pythagoras was lonely, and Socrates, and Jesus, and Luther, and Copernicus, and Galileo, and Newton, and probably Mary Lindley Murray too. *To be great is to be misunderstood.* This was what he told himself often, quoting a thinker he still secretly thought of as a fool. He repeated this thought in the mirror most mornings for years, searching for conviction in his voice, and then he began to grow out his beard—to keep his throat warm in winter, he told himself. A side benefit was that he would not have to see quite so much of his own face each day, the regret to be read between its lines.

And yes, those evenings spent on the daybed together, Samuel sleeping against his shoulder, bodies covered by the blankets. The memories of these moments could not be taken away, especially on the days when one wanted them gone.

This space between action and inaction. The inability to swallow. The dream of cutting through all thought and fear and doubt as the blade of a plow slices earth.

27

CHILDREN'S GATE (II)

Mr. Sinclair presents the application of the School Officers of the Sixth Ward, for an appropriation to make
alterations in School House No. 24.

ORDERED, That said application be referred to the Committee on Repairs.

Mr. Davenport presents the application of the School
Officers of the Twenty-First Ward, for an appropriation
to fit up and furnish School House No. 49.

ORDERED, That said application be referred to the Committee on School Furniture.

Mr. Phillips lays before the Board a communication
from Thomas Fisher, relative to a new work of Mathematics.

ORDERED, That said communication be referred to the
Committee on School Books and Course of Studies.

Mr. Smith lays before the Board a communication
from the School Officers of the Twentieth Ward, in relation to the payment of the salary of Prince Loveridge,
teacher of Colored School No. 6, asking the adoption of
a resolution:

RESOLVED, That the President and Clerk be autho-
rized to sign a warrant in favor of Prince Loveridge for
fifty dollars in full for his services as teacher of Colored
School No. 6, up to the 1st day of July; it being understood that he is not to be employed as a teacher after

that date, unless he receives a certificate from the City Superintendent of Schools.

Andrew H. Green, the new President of the city's Board of Education, lays before the Board a communication from Peter B. Mead, Secretary of The New York Horticultural Society, inviting the Board of Education to visit the Society's next exhibition of fruits and flowers at Clinton Hall, Astor Place, and enclosing twelve tickets together with a promise to gladly furnish more if necessary.

ORDERED, That while the Board of Education is engaged in cultivating the minds of our youths, and forming them for usefulness in after life, The New York Horticultural Society is engaged in a pursuit scarcely less lovely and important—the development of public space and of Nature herself, as a tool of education. The visit shall be arranged and the thanks of the Board tendered to the Society.

OTHER BUSINESS:

President Green's speech to the city's Board of Commissioners, to be delivered at the end of the month, was presented in draft form. President Green read from the speech and distributed copies, recommending the services of his local printer as he did so. The speech emphasized that each dollar of requested funding would be justified to the penny. It was emphasized that any received funds would, firstly, correct the effects of the corruption that come from having allowed private donors to control the management of our public schools. They will, secondly, allow the Board to ensure that teachers are properly paid. They will, thirdly, allow the Board to ensure the proper management of schools in the city going forward, which President Green believes should be public not only in name. Such schools shall be run by the state, and supervised by the Board, and open to private donations but not to private influence, Mr. Green's speech emphasized. Many children currently are left to educate themselves as circumstances press at them. Much depends on how fortunate they are in their family connections. Much depends on chance encounters upon which they may fall or rise. Do we wish to entrust our children's education to questions of luck? Do we not believe that an educated citizenry will in the end contribute to the future greatness of our city? When a father cannot afford a basic education for his young family, should the city not intervene to secure that education for its children and for its own future good? Those who believe in municipal betterment and the notion of stewardship should agree with these points, President Green maintained, and if they are too selfish or corrupt to do so, they should be convinced by other arguments, such as the supremacy of the commerce that they seem to value so very highly.

ORDERED, That President Green's speech is candid, very candid, and that a less candid version should perhaps be tendered by him at the next meeting of the Board.

———

Inspector McClusky reviewed these minutes, and other minutes, minutes from hundreds of meetings.

He looked at Green's diaries. Sniffed. Saw certain letters. Coughed. Read all the published speeches. Tried to take a nap under his desk. He examined a cache of documents pertaining to the Central Park, many hundreds of pages his team had managed to assemble.

They were the kinds of papers that are supposed to offer clues to a life, but he found nothing particularly useful in them. Somewhere in Andrew Haswell Green's existence there might be an explanation of his death, but often it was the other way around, he had found. The manner of death could be the clue from which the heart of a life could be reached.

Many people across the ages had known this, he thought. Take the popularity of death masks. If you see a face fixed in its final expression, so to speak, you glimpse your subject in a moment when all attempts at performance have fled. The dead have stopped pretending.

His wife liked them. Death masks. It was the sort of creepy obsession that had drawn him to her. That and her magnificent elbows. The unblinking gaze that he also saw in Bessie Davis.

Inspector McClusky had discovered, in his second and third so-to-speak *interviews* with Bessie, or Hannah, or whoever she was on a given day, that she had been born in Philadelphia in 1865. A woman implausibly rich now, so much richer than he was, a great many properties in her name, and all from playing hostess to the supposed gentlemen of this city—including some, it seemed, who had sat on the city's Board of Education long ago.

But no clues indicated Green, no real evidence to date led to the victim directly. At best there was a sensation of almostness, of quietly tantalizing *potential* connections, slight ideas that created the prospect of finding, through a network of meandering paths, down across a wild garden of downtrodden Could Be plants, and flourishing Possibilities and Perhapses, a few sunlit facts in the grass. The key that could unlock the gate. He was getting carried away by his own ideas.

What a patchwork life an investigator leads! Those we investigate, McClusky thought. They fill us with shame. They remind us of our limitations. Of our own smallness and stillness. Their worlds seem swollen with emotion, struck by attentive light. They become more real than we are as we watch them. They hollow us out. They encourage us toward overblown imagery. They grow while we shrink. We are getting smaller with every part of our dreams that we gift them, every effort we make at understanding. Disappearing into other people's stories, stepping into their shoes, so to speak, is supposed to make us into bigger people, but Inspector McClusky did not feel big, not anymore. His feet were sore and weary, he was an urban explorer on the edge of collapse, he wanted shoes that fit, that belonged only to him. Fine shoes. Good shoes. Fancy ones. We stare at a death mask for so long that we ourselves start to die.

The mother of Bessie was, he had discovered yesterday, a negress herself. Her father seemed to have been an Indian. He had located now the family's first address. From what he knew of the area, Bessie had probably been born into squalor—a rough part of the negro quarter of the Quaker City.

Records suggested that at the age of fourteen she was sent out to make a living on the streets. She had once married a railroad porter named Davis, by whom she'd had a child. One arrest—one only—had occurred in her past, as far as he could see.

It appeared that when she was just a girl, Bessie had stolen a gown. It had belonged to her mistress. She had been sent to prison for this act, despite apparently wanting the property for only one day, more a loan than a theft, McClusky was tempted to say. She had worn the gown to her sister's wedding and then been caught the next morning while trying to return it. She became an inmate of an almshouse, and then was released, and then came the gaps in the facts—whole years unaccounted for—and now she owned vast mansions, had two dozen servants working for her, fanning her, and he had even thought for one sinful instant, or two, of fanning her himself. Presumably at some point in her history she had grown tired of having nothing and being treated as nothing.

To help him through his current congestion Inspector McClusky now lifted his cocaine spray from its drawer, and blasted another shot of secret mist up his right nostril. It was breathtaking, really, how a clear nose led to a clear mind, so to speak, and how a clear mind then led to a clear—

Knock on the door.

He put his nasal spray back in the drawer, and fumbled for the lamp, but not in time. The door creaked open.

Acting Captain Daly stood in the doorway. He said, Is it not very dark in here, Mac?

Daly's voice belonged to a mouse, his body to an elephant. And Inspector McClusky, as previously established, no longer enjoyed contemplating elephants.

Yes? McClusky said.

He watched as Daly took five quick steps forward, a newspaper under his arm, and then hesitated.

I looked back through the murderer's possessions, Mac, for a city directory. And the answer is yes—there was one there. It's on my desk if—

I shall collect it from you later, McClusky said. He felt an annoyance prickling within him. This awful flu, or whatever it was, was forcing him to rely upon the likes of Daly more than usual.

Daly nodded. In addition, Mac, I was wondering—I was only wondering, Mac, if I should review, once more—a second time—the records you managed to extract—so superbly, Mac—from Bessie Davis's mansion?

Tomorrow, McClusky said.

Sure, Mac. Tomorrow . . . But the pressure is, of course, increasing. The mayor's office has been making waves again.

I know this.

The president's circle too.

I am very much alert to this, *Acting* Captain.

Not to mention the writers, Mac. Those writers never stop. They're doggy.

Dogged, McClusky corrected.

Doggy diggers.

Dogg*ed* diggers.

They're always digging, Mac. Like dogs. Want my handkerchief? We can put that animal Williams in a cage forever, based on the evidence already gathered, justice served, but without a motive we'll never cleanly close the, the uh, *case*, and I for one am hoping—

Tomorrow, McClusky said again, sniffing.

The records from Bessie's mansion, her old client ledgers, were at his home. He wanted them at his home. If McClusky's wife for any reason wished to know the nature of his relationship with that woman, he would be able to point to the files stacked upon his desk and say: There, that is my relationship. Professional. Rigorous. He might even let her review some of the papers. When he was working late every night his wife liked to feel involved. Her ideas were seldom helpful, her detective work primitive, but he made sure to pretend to listen.

Now Daly took another step forward. I was wondering, Mac, he said, if there is anything in *names*.

Inspector McClusky stared at him. Names?

You know, said Daly. As they apply to—in—the ledgers. Obviously this Bessie is keen on making up names for herself. And you mentioned there was a record of a client named, what was it, I think you said—

What is that under your arm? Inspector McClusky asked, unable to contain his impatience any longer.

So Daly removed the newspaper. Placed it flat on

McClusky's desk. He frowned as if offended, and started to chew something.

The newspaper was the *New York American*. A corner of the first page was missing, but it was clear that the lead article pertained to his case.

What is this? he said, glancing up, but by then Acting Captain Daly had departed.

———

McClusky sat reading in the half dark of his office. The writer for the *New York American* had not only discovered that Bessie Davis was Hannah Elias, he had managed to get an exclusive interview with someone claiming to be her intimate friend. The more he read, the more McClusky felt the joy seep out of him, and his fever peaking again, a desire for darkness and silence, perhaps even the obliterations of liquor, rising up from under the panic of knowing his investigation had been thwarted by the press.

He switched on the lamp he had reached for before. The pages before him went bright with light and the pain in his eyes grew sharp.

The *New York American*'s interview was with a Mrs. Belle Marshall, a white woman who had been Hannah Elias's housekeeper for three years.

Elias had, this Mrs. Marshall claimed, extracted vast sums of money from powerful men over the years.

She was a sort of Cleopatra, Mrs. Marshall had told the journalist. Where she ever got the Cleopatra idea was hard to understand, Marshall indicated, but the fact that her hold over white men caused them to give her unlimited supplies of money probably furnished the basis for the notion.

The interview confirmed several things McClusky already knew. That Elias had almost no education. That she had gotten rich from a wisdom that was all her own. *She could read after a fashion,* Mrs. Marshall had told the journalist, *but she couldn't read with anything of facility literature that was above the dime novel standard, and consequently she was always having someone read to her things about the enslaver of Mark Antony. She carried her notion into an imitation that was as near the original as she could figure it out.*

The article stated that Miss Davis/Elias had *a fountain in her bedroom,* which he happened to know was true. That she liked to listen to the trickle of water while she made love. That her practice of making *her white servants dress in Egyptian costumes and stand there fanning her with a huge feather duster* had begun several years ago, when she found one such duster *in a Japanese place downtown.*

Inspector McClusky's feverish gaze blazed over the rest of the article. Certain words were lost to him as he read. Others broke his thinning skin and would stay lodged in him for years.

closed carriage
kinky
Pompadour
masseuse
men of wealth

But he himself was not mentioned in the text. He thanked God above for that.

He thought of the grand jury to come. He reached for a Bible resting in the drawer beneath the one which held his special nasal spray. He thought of Hannah, who was Bessie, her unshakable calm when he had first spoken to her at the mansion. The mistakes he had made on that first visit.

Then his attention fell on another line in the *New York*

American article, and he reread it, and reread it again. It was a sentence in which the writer described the subject's life as *stranger than any story told by the most lurid fiction writer*.

People said such things often, about fact and fiction, and it was, in his opinion, foolish in the extreme. Life was being invented every day. Each hour of existence was written to challenge the straight-faced pursuer of truths.

As if in a dream, a hot one, he staggered out into the corridor and paused at Acting Captain Daly's desk. A city directory, the one recovered from Cornelius Williams's most recent lodgings, sat atop it.

McClusky flicked through the thin pages, looking for the letter G.

On pages 529 and 530 were columns headed GOTTLIEB, GOULEY, GOUNDIE, and GRADY. The adverts above and below these G citizens' addresses were for carpet cleansing, kindling wood, Old Coronet rye, and a commercial detective bureau whose slogan read *We report "FACTS" only*.

Facts in capitals and quotation marks. Loud but provisional. That was about right for such agencies, McClusky reflected, while also not ruling out, in the small corner of his brain he reserved for the future, the possibility that in retirement he might earn a few easy dollars, so to speak, working for just such a private agency. It would be a relief, after years of diving into pools of blood, to work in the friendly fields of infidelity and missing aunts. He turned to a double-page spread, and then the next. Lists of citizens in tiny type named GRAHAM, then GRANH, then GRANICH, then GRAS, GRASE, GRAVURE. An interesting advert for Horton's Ice Cream, *the standard of the world,* then GRAY, and more GRAY, and then . . .

McClusky blinked. Pages 537 and 538 were missing. Ripped out. Only the slightest jaggy remains of the leaves.

He looked up. Everybody seemed to be at lunch. Almost everybody, almost always, seemed to be at lunch.

He wiped his nose on his sleeve and his forehead on his other sleeve. He stormed around the station, stupid with excitement now, until he found, at the sergeant's desk, another copy of the city directory.

He turned to pages 537 and 538.

There they were, full and present. The pages bore three columns of citizens named GREEN. And in the second column, a quarter of the way down, was one of the few Greens who had, listed next to his name, a prominent occupation, and prominent address.

Andw H lawyer 91 Park av

28

NATURALISTS' GATE (II)

O
n Tuesday evenings, between eight and nine, he ordinarily takes lessons in the German language. But lately Andrew has become frustrated with not being able to express all the ideas he wants to express, being asked to pay so much attention to ornaments, learning the difficult declensions of nouns and adjectives, the complex conjugation of verbs. In German there seems to be a separate word for nearly every idea alive, and that word is not used to express any other idea; you put it to memory in the full knowledge that you may never use it more than once in your lifetime. It is a very precise language, and its orderliness appeals to him, but that makes it all the more infuriating to fail at fluency. There are many things he cannot say or be heard saying in the rooms he has lately been confined to.

Then on one particular Tuesday, an acquaintance named Andrew Downing invites him to join a private debate on the subject of green space in the city. The prospect of speaking only his own language for the evening is too delicious to resist.

They are in a gentleman's club south of City Hall. The walls are decorated with old maps pinned inside wooden frames. Twenty chairs have been arranged in a decent arc. The small number of invitees makes Andrew feel special, and he feels doubly special when he sees he must be among the youngest here. Most of those invited look to be in their forties, and the others in their fifties, sixties, seventies. There is an unoccupied lectern around which various small glass cabinets stand on pedestals of differing heights. Some of the cabinets contain antique pots, others tilted plates, still others a little bust or jug, and the one Andrew stands by now, as he talks to a nervous Downing, contains a vase that is painted with a scene of two women peering into an infant's empty carriage. He is still not quite at home in places like this, but he has developed the tools to pretend he is, and uses them now almost without effort—the blank gaze into the middle distance, the stifled yawn, the frown of a man with an occupied mind.

He first got to know Andrew Downing through reading his editorials in *The Horticulturist*. At first, these articles had seemed overly obsessed with championing the country over the city, a simplicity of attitude that forced every other argument into a depthless black and white. It was difficult to disagree with many of Downing's statements, but it was also unclear, at times, toward what aim they were shaped. Only this year has the focus of the pieces begun to shift. The sentence structure is improving, if Andrew's ear for such things is not mistaken, and the underlying notions of free public space are becoming bolder and more eloquent. Downing seems to have learned how to hone his ideas on paper, if not quite in a room full of people. What is needed in a booming metropolis like New York, he says to Andrew now in a terribly quiet voice, like a dead man speaking from the other side, as they stand in a corner gazing into the middle distance, yawning, and frowning, isn't a complete overhaul of urban systems, nor a population rebelling and fleeing for its borders, but rather the careful reinsertion of green spaces into the city itself, an idea Andrew himself has been championing, with Samuel's reluctant help.

Some of the legislation necessary for a significant public park is already in place. It is time, Andrew has decided, to work with Downing to make it real. And yet there is also, somewhere underlying this idea of togetherness, of actual friendship, the slightest feeling of rivalry too. A shaky faith, a question of capability. Should Andrew continue in the supporting role, or might he be, in fact, the man better built to take the lead? Even Downing's insistence on calling it the Middle Park has begun to seem, on some nights, rather irritating. A small decision that may yet speak to a broader lack of judgment.

Fred Olmsted is here tonight—landscaper, journalist. Andrew has already read much of his work, because he likes to arrive at events like these with information to press into an intimacy. That is what you become accustomed to doing when you feel like an impostor, and he does still feel like an impostor, albeit one who has grown talented in the impostor's arts.

Firm and warm, Olmsted's handshake is. Andrew and he have New England to talk about. Their money is self-made, they have both come up from nothing, an unspoken bond—though not an unusual one, these days. And Downing? He shrinks away from the conversation now, for he fears Olmsted. The man's face holds, on such evenings, the delicious disinterest of the truly talented.

Yet he does ask questions, does Olmsted. He is respectful of Andrew's achievements to date, he cares about education and he knows the world of the law, he likes to gather facts and he is friends with Samuel. It is said that if there is to be a park, Olmsted might like to submit a design.

People begin to take their seats. Only the chair allocated to Downing creaks. Andrew settles next to him in the front row.

Downing's gaze tonight is eventful but lacking in traction. He hates nothing more than public speaking, Andrew knows, and therefore he seems to have arranged for a member of the Board of Aldermen—*a large man kindly disposed to my small idea,* he whispers in Andrew's ear now—to summarize his arguments first for the benefit of the room.

So it begins. The member stands before them all, hands in motion. His tongue pokes out from between his lips during pauses. And here in this prominent position (how strange, these days, to always be in the front row) it becomes obvious to Andrew that he has consented not only to be very underwhelmed, but also to get very wet. There is also the matter of air quality. People are lighting cigars now as they listen or pretend to listen, the smoke seems to lift all the dust from the floors, it takes a special effort for Andrew to breathe. His lungs, like his eyes, seem to be worsening again with each passing year, begging for a break from the city. But in the place of the kind of bodily strength he felt in Trinidad, a heightened awareness of other people's insecurities now seems to insinuate itself.

Some of us here, assembled in this room, the member of the Board of Aldermen declares damply, a fine spray of spit erupting from his lisping lips, wish to establish a new and extensive park in this city.

A few people nod. Enough to encourage the member to continue.

We believe New York requires a large public park—a *truly* public park, he says. I support thoroughly Mr. Downing's campaign. A park for sanitation, and recreation. We need a Middle Park imperatively!

The member tugs at his right ear as he pronounces this last *park*. The lobe is long, and will only lengthen with this habit.

New York's material dimensions, the member of the Board

of Aldermen continues, are beginning to challenge and vie with the most populous cities of Europe.

Europe! someone behind Andrew hisses.

Pardon? the member says.

Andrew can feel, beside him, Downing's body tensing.

No, the member says. Yes. It is clear the impulse of the age is upon her!

Who does he mean, Andrew? Downing whispers, fingers fretting at a button.

She disdains the slow pace of ordinary increase! the member says, warming to his theme. She leaps forward in the race for wealth and greatness as if impelled by steam! She opens her wondrous portals to the wandering sons of the earth, and here they find a home!

Andrew, along with half of his comrades in the front row, wipes his face dry from the member's spittle and hears again the sound of a single creaking chair.

But no, Downing sits back down again. He does not have it in him to interrupt.

Once the member has circled several issues which are, at best, *vaguely* related to the campaign for a modest middle park, a process that takes him close to thirty minutes, referring to the city by the feminine pronoun throughout, he finally comes to the specifics of Downing's proposals, arguing that the basic legislation for creating such a space is already in place, saying that what is needed now is unity and boldness of aim, but saying it in a manner that is lonely, quiet, and unconvincing, every pair of eyes in the room fixed upon the ceiling or the carpet, the pedestals or the wall, the cigar butt or the dust, or else hiding from events behind shuttered lids, swimming through a dream.

We do *have* parks, someone says.

Expensive to access, the member says.

A public park, too.

It is very small, says Downing in his chair, but Andrew senses no one else has heard the statement, nor would care for it.

The solution, someone says, is smaller fees.

Did he say someone sneezed?

Affordable, I am saying, but not to all, someone sitting behind Andrew shouts. If a park is free, we shall have every criminal worth his salt visiting! Every lowborn. Every whore. Every lisper . . .

Jones's Wood, someone else says. Jones's Wood is the proper place for the general public to . . .

At this point in the gathering, even the man taking minutes is shaking his head. Probably the notion that this pantomime will be preserved for the ages disgusts him even more than the present failures of expression? The scribe holds the pen, but he has no power over the words or how long they will last. Andrew tries and fails to meet his eye to share this thought with him. There are always at least two histories happening: the inner and the outer, the private and the public. And sometimes both, in equal measure, disappoint.

Fred Olmsted stands up next, though there is no part of the agenda set aside for him to do so. Like many an experienced public speaker, he allows a moment for the silence in the room to grow taut.

Then Olmsted removes his spectacles and says, A city with thick, unsatisfactory air. A city where disease is rife. A city whose people hold a desperate need for recreation and open space. Can New York not do better? Look to England, her far denser population, a population crowded in by the ocean at all sides. I have only lately returned from there, from England. She manages in her great capital to set apart huge public grounds, sacred to repose. Can we really not manage one half of such grounds in your great metropolis? In the future capital of the new Continent? If you say no, I will believe you, but I submit that it would be an embarrassment to everyone in this room who claims to be an American.

Someone says, a few rows back: I have always held a hatred for England.

The laughter is general.

One of the mayor's men stands.

Public parks, the mayor's man claims, were an excellent amenity when adequate space could be spared for them. This city is overcrowded indeed, and could benefit from a future park of large extent in which an expanding sea of humankind might thrive. But is a plan to turn wild land in the middle of our island into hundreds of acres of inhabitable park space, for the sole purpose of public recreation, a priority in our current circumstances? Do we prefer to spend the coming years and limited city surplus on a park rather than on housing, space to live, space to work? On a park rather than schools? On a park rather than the creation of honest businesses and the creation of jobs and the provision of basic attention in matters of health and education for the island's swelling population? Sanitation is a great problem, but sanitation will not be solved by a large park. Public transportation is a great problem, but transportation will not be solved by a few thin roads cutting through leveled parkland. Does anyone present suppose the clean air of the Battery has any beneficial influence upon the atmosphere of Wall Street, or that the foul air of Five Points is rendered one particle better by the proximity it bears to one of the city's principal green spaces at present? Does any gentleman here, entering the crowded courtrooms of City Hall itself, perhaps on the occasion of some interesting trial of a horticulturalist seeking to misappropriate public funds for a fine but altogether misguided idea, feel that the great reservoir of refreshening air situated directly outside the doors of the hall would have any influence at all in meliorating the stench of liquor on the breath of the highly paid lawyers within? Freshness does not extend very far at all. There are green spaces in this city such as Niblo's Garden that charge only the smallest of entry fees, as someone just lately said. Is it not better to have a hundred private parks of small extent than one middling pit of public money in a city that is expanding rapidly to its own dire end and has far more pressing municipal needs?

The cigars are mostly gone now, but Andrew sees he is the only person in the front row who has not begun filling a pipe. He coughs, and thinks of Trinidad, sugar, the look of the land. He coughs and thinks of the Massachusetts farm, of waking to birdsong and breeze. Without moving from his seat, he coughs, and feels himself drifting into melancholy.

And then he thinks to himself, No. Do not be a sheep for shipping.

So he stands up. Stands taller than his father ever did in the field. And once he is up, he must say something. So he says, all at once, to the assembled gentlemen staring at him: It should be called the Central Park.

There is silence. His heart is beating heavily. It realizes what he has done before he does.

Then the mayor's man says: Mr. Green, friend of Mr. Tilden, is that you? Not all of us heard what you said.

It should not be called the Middle Park, Andrew continues, and this time the words come out clear and loud. *Middle* makes one think of the gut. Of middlemen, too, and mediocrity. It should be called the Central Park, it should be truly great in size and design, and I should be the man to bring it into being.

And beside him he sees Downing's face turn scarlet with admiration, or envy, or hate.

The administration and mathematics required to make the park real. The paperwork, the balancing of budgets, the drawing out and tearing up of maps. All this would prove to be, for him, its own sprawling, thriving, artistic space. A place for play and sharpened attention, for the fullest expression of his innermost desires. It was the kind of project a boy who sat in a tree sketching out plans for better arranging the land around Green Hill never truly believed he would have access to.

Excavation and construction of drains: $20,000
Removal of interior enclosures: $5,000
Removal of stone and other material deposited in
    extending streets and avenues: $10,000
Removal of undesirable buildings: $5,000
Cutting and removal of brushwood and briars: $5,000
Clearing the entire ground of useless roots and
    vegetation: $10,000
Preparing ground for nursery: $5,000

For him, these were lines of poetry.

Acres upon acres of rocks and swamps, so uneven as to render the cost of grading alone more than twice the present value of the lands. Keeping such a project free from the influence of jobbery would be like trying to persuade clouds to stay away from the sun. He would need to remove all the water standing in stagnant deposits. He would need to facilitate the flow of water from permanent springs. He would need to direct all surface water into proper channels. It was the work he had done on Green Hill as a boy, expanded on a massive scale, but as president and comptroller of the park he would have hundreds of workers looking to him for leadership every day. Often he would fail. Often his strict adherence to the budget would cause one or another of the designers or engineers to abandon the project for a week or month or year. The experience of instilling better drainage in Trinidad was strangely specific and useful. It was funny how your whole past came into play as you worked toward a future. The concert of barely connected moments that make up any life. No one experience can be unlinked from the next. There were times when his own past lives were the only ghosts he needed to visit for advice.

Whole years opened up. Years when it seemed he could do anything. The years when Tammany Hall was a jostle of bodies and shouts, when half the democracy of the city was crammed within its walls, and half a dozen heads would turn at once to watch him enter the space. He was the not-quite-young man who was now becoming responsible for so many of New York's new institutions. If someone wanted an art museum, they came to him—could he build one within the span of his park? If wild animals wandered freely, at risk of capture by hunters, why not invite some of them into a zoo, and if the Central Park space alone was insufficient for the creatures' needs, why shouldn't he eventually build a zoo elsewhere, perhaps in the Bronx? If he wanted the educational elements of the park to focus on natural history, an appreciation of the nature he had sought comfort in throughout his boyhood, could he not make a museum in honor of that idea too? The pocket piece would be booming. He felt a feeling of great, peeling freedom. The calcium lights would shine down from the Tammany balcony. People would ask him for his advice, his secrets. They would stare at him. Admire him! The guard at the door would say, with a strange excitement in his eyes, Oh, in you go, Mr. Green, sir. And he would move easily into the heart of the hall, greatcoat still on, gloves still on, several hundred bodies seeming to part for him, allowing this person he was playing—and it did still feel like a role, some days—to make his way to the front. In his continuing surprise at the smallest side effects of fame, he would feel an urge in his forties and fifties to take people by the hand and ask them why. Why were they so quick, all of a sudden, to decide he was worth their attention?

The Man Who Gets Things Done. That was what governors and mayors called him after Central Park began to take shape. But after the speeches he delivered on the steps of City Hall in freezing weather, after the torchlight processions he planned, and the pyrotechnic accompaniments others put on to celebrate his achievements, he still went to bed with some version of the same concerns he had always had. Who he was. Who he should be. Things he could have said or done. Fireworks were simply money exploding in the sky.

Alderman Tucker, one year, lit a firework in the erroneous belief that it was a cigar. The man paid for this misunderstanding with his life. New York is a comedy to those who think, and a tragedy to those who feel. But Andrew didn't feel tragic. He did not feel a fall was coming. He was too busy to stumble or trip.

He would give directions to the Committee on Statuary, Fountains, and Architecture: what was needed for the gates was a system of nomenclature. For what if the names of the entrances were taken, not from great men of the city, as almost everyone else suggested, but from the pursuits of the ordinary people, so trapped in their own unfulfilled desires—the vocations to which New York's metropolitan character was truly owed? Scholars' Gate. Merchants' Gate. An Artists' Gate too?

Yes, an Artists' Gate! Enticing, but recklessly narrow.

Make this particular gate open up onto a whole wide field of misery. And walk through it, this wild space, picking up litter every day. He could not rely on anyone else to be thorough in the collection of items abandoned by park visitors, foods and blankets and kites and newspapers, and he had noticed that the people who most loved to use a given place or person in the exertion of their own needs were often the very same people who spoiled the beauty they touched. There would, for example, be far more receptacles for waste in the park if it were not a particular joy of young boys to throw lighted matches on top of thrown-away paper. Maturity, he supposed, was learning not to long to see flames licking toward trees.

29

ARTISTS' GATE (II)

The city finally commissioned a portrait. Henry Mosler was the artist afforded this honor. The final sitting took place at Mosler's studio at Broadway and Eighty-Sixth Street on November 10, 1903, three days before Andrew was killed on Park Avenue and Cornelius Williams, robbed of the few freedoms his country had ever afforded him, was taken into police custody and then thrown into the Tombs.

Andrew did not like sitting for paintings. Had requested that Mosler fill out the background and accessory details later. Walls. Clothes. Nose. That sort of thing. A man of eighty-three did not have much time to waste on other people's perspectives.

Which meant Mosler didn't have much time either. Today was his last chance to perpetuate, in person, the basic form and features of his reluctant subject, achieving whatever he needed for a life-sized likeness to be hung in City Hall. Andrew knew this, but he didn't feel guilty about limiting their sittings. Mosler had made clear that he would take a certain artistic license in any event. And if imagination and intuition formed certain strokes, Andrew thought, why not let them form it all? As far as he was concerned, he had given Mosler the greatest gift any artist could wish for: a subject that did not care in what light it was painted.

But there were other cares, of course. Pains. Andrew was

sitting in the armchair, pretending his knees and feet did not cause him discomfort, that his only aggravation was an inner impatience. It was hard to reduce one's body to utter stillness, especially when the purpose was to help someone else trap you on a canvas for eternity. He was clutching a document that was intended to represent a draft of his greater city charter. He couldn't look down at it, though, because he was confined to the pre-agreed pose. Also: the page was entirely blank.

Mosler was an unusual painter in at least one respect: he was uncomfortable with quiet. He had talked and talked during their early sittings, and now he seemed to decide, as he painted, that it would be good to talk some more. His accent had thinned in the years since his family moved from Silesia to New York, but he was still a man made of questions, which was very un-American of him. Questions about wealth, work, projects. His relentless commitment to curiosity could drive a subject to suicide, in fact, and perhaps in the past it had, yet how refreshing, how invigorating, in a way, to meet someone who truly seemed to care for the notion of discovering answers. Instead of perpetually addressing his own likeness (the self-portrait! Had there been a worse idea in the entire history of art?), Mosler had devoted himself to trying to envision other people. He had Andrew's respect—for an hour or two more.

There were several coffin-sized chests on the other side of the studio. Andrew knew they were there, had them fixed in the corner of his eye, longed to stand up and walk over to them. Clothes and hats hanging out of them. Props? He was like an entertainer, Mosler, except he had no jokes, only inquiries. And an excellent eye. A beautiful hand.

Mosler wanted to know how Andrew had managed to bring the Metropolitan Museum of Art into being. Waited, paintbrush in hand, for a response.

Andrew wished there was some way to satisfy this appetite for information without feeling that the process of providing a line was itself an exercise in flattening the past.

There was a small group of us, Andrew said.

Go on, go on.

A small group of us agreed on the need for a place to put art, Andrew said, careful not to let his mouth move more than was necessary. People kept giving us objects, you see, as commissioners of the park, and we needed a place to put them. And of course I saw, we all saw, that in America there could be a move toward more productive forms of arrogance.

Mosler blinked, shook his head, looked up from his canvas. The expression on his face said, Do not make me beg.

You know, Andrew said. Encouraging the rich to donate something to our new museum, a painting or two from their private collection, in return for having their name on display. *Mentioning* their name would be on display, it transpired, was much more effective than pointing out that, without a first-class art museum, a city could never be great. At first I focused on arguing for the public good, but then I met the wealthier citizens at their . . . their private level.

Mosler—he of no jokes—seemed to find this very funny.

Next, he wanted to know how Andrew had convinced the city to build the American Museum of Natural History— a question he had already tried to ask on previous sittings.

Nature, Andrew said. History. It was part of my work for the park.

Please! Mosler said, and he sounded angry.

It took a moment to realize why he was quite so annoyed: Andrew had shrugged, moved, let his shoulders relax for one second into bliss. He had forgotten the first rule of portraiture: don't be yourself.

Some restraint please, Mr. Green, Mosler said in a quieter voice.

Restraint, restraint. That sounded right.

Mosler readjusted his easel. You are known for your passion for thoroughness, Mr. Green, he said. But not, apparently, in all matters . . . Tell me how you founded the New York Public Library with Mr. Bigelow, at least?

Andrew looked at Mosler. At the expectant expression on his face, at the flecks of paint all over the floor of his studio, at the great winding sheets draped over canvases, at the half-drunk bottle of red wine on the table, its cork leaning slightly to the left.

My friend Samuel, Andrew said. He left behind three things. Books. Money . . .

Yes? Mosler said.

And people. He left behind people. The rare books and the money were two aspects I could address. Samuel had dreamed, for some time, of a public library which new arrivals to the city might be able to use . . . Or I had. We both had. So yes, that was a thing John and I could do.

There was a long silence. The strokes that were being made were surely terribly faint. Otherwise they would make a sound.

Andrew permitted himself a small change of position now and did not apologize for it. He only sighed, and Mosler sighed too. Disappointment can be contagious that way. So can grief, and hope. He had learned these lessons afresh these last few years.

Oh, what he would give to stand up! To walk! To fall! To stroll home along Park Avenue! The ache in his back was no longer a feature of his situation. It had become the whole throbbing thing.

He now did what he had told himself he would not do: he glanced up at Mosler's wall clock. He saw, with a jolt, that he had only been sitting here for an hour. One hour! And he also realized, believed with absolute conviction in this moment, however little sense it made, that if he had not looked at the clock, or if the clock had not seen him looking, much more time would have passed by now, it would all be over, finished. If you pay too much attention to time, in certain tedious moments, it slows down to punish you. This chair was his prison. It had shaped itself around his bony body, as if lack of freedom suited him.

The afternoon, the sun at the window, trying and failing to break through dark drapes. He reminded himself that this artist had given up time—time, time, time—to try to make him look alive to future generations. In desperation and regret, he decided to tell Mosler a story.

The anecdote Andrew chose was a short one. It was about Horace Hinsdale, at the store of Hinsdale & Atkins. People liked all that Dickensian nonsense.

He started by mentioning that, back then, as an apprentice boy with no friends here, he had slept on his socks at night to try to dry them. How he was hungry all the time. How he had thought he would die of aloneness if not of bites from bugs.

Then he stopped, and asked if Mosler, too, had ever done an apprenticeship of any kind.

Mosler muttered an obscenity at his canvas. Began correcting an error. Then he said that, yes, indeed, he too, by chance, had once been an apprentice—in fact, to a man named Horace. In his case, it was the wood engraver: Horace C. Grosvenor.

Andrew now asked Mosler about the wood engraver, and about the art of engraving generally, for it had become a genuine subject of interest to him in the last few years. But Mosler saw this as a trick—be a mirror, always a mirror, in order to preserve your own secret gleam—and made him return to his own past.

Well, Andrew said. He kissed me once.

Kissed you? Mosler said, baffled. Your employer? Mr. Hinsdale?

On the edge of the lips, Andrew said. Yes. Just here . . .

And he moved his hand up to his face, unthinking, only to let it fall.

It had happened on the day he decided to leave the store, to take up another situation, at Lee, Savage & Co., whole-sale cloth merchants and importers, on William Street at the corner of Liberty, and perhaps his memory had blocked it out until now.

Mr. Hinsdale had descended the stairs to Andrew's lifeless basement room and knocked upon the door. As he entered, he had seemed about to curse Andrew or strike him, as he sometimes did, across the face. He had been utterly silent that morning when Andrew told him he was leaving for another job. But now, instead of silence or an attack, Horace Hinsdale drew Andrew into his fleshy embrace and kissed him on the cheek, the edge of the lips, and said: Good boy. I am proud. Finally you are becoming you.

And it had meant everything. It had been like having, for a moment, another father.

Are you getting tired? Mosler said eventually. Perhaps we could finish next week?

But no, Andrew thought, that wouldn't do. Next week would be impossible. Too much to do. He had to fix down plans to honor Mary Lindley Murray with a plaque—and how swiftly could the words on that plaque be engraved?

Le Retour. This was Mosley's most famous picture. Andrew admired it greatly, it was what had caused him to ask the mayor to appoint Mosler as the painter of the present portrait, but what was the point in saying so?

Another one he loved was *The Lost Cause.* It was a paint-ing in which the broken South, in the person of a soldier, was left leaning on a musket, but when Andrew had first glimpsed the painting from afar, years ago, he had seen the setting as Massachusetts, and the musket as a spade or a rake. All the best paintings made you see various levels of reality at once. They sent you inward as well as outward. He had realized his mistake a moment later, a blink revising the canvas before him, the various components of its composition, but by then his own erroneous interpretation had settled into a type of truth—to his mind, it was a painting of home. Of Green Hill. Any efforts to uncouple it from his first impression proved useless. He could not shake the sense that Mosler had painted the Green family's own personal past.

———

A few days after this final sitting, with its subject freshly dead, Henry Mosler was interviewed by the *New York Times*. A journalist visited his studio to ask questions about the portrait.

A most remarkable thing in connection with this work, Mosler was quoted as saying, *in view of the tragic occurrence of yesterday, is the manner in which Mr. Green urged me on to the completion of the portrait.*

Fearing that it would put his power of endurance to too severe a test, I never favored protracted sittings, but Mr. Green not infrequently desired me to go on even after the time for the sitting had elapsed. On Tuesday afternoon when I left him he bade me goodbye very affectionately.

I said to him: "Do not bid me goodbye. Although the sittings are finished, I hope you will come to see me some time at my studio."

Mr. Green shook his head a little dubiously, but finally said he would.

30

WOMEN'S GATE (II)

I s it foolish to talk of turning points? Days in a life that set a person on a course they cannot alter, or that lock them into a position from which they might never move?

Inspector McClusky woke in his bed with the itch of an idea in his mind. Nothing more—just an itch, an inkling awaiting expression. He lay very still so as not to lose it. Sunlight poured through the curtains, illuminating him: he had slept late. The sound of traffic rising and falling outside gave him comfort. Manhattan had endured without his protection. He had been thinking at length, before bed, about the city directory, the missing *Green* pages in Williams's copy, and also Acting Captain Daly's comment about the potential importance of names to a woman like Bessie Davis, who herself had many. Had he been hasty turning Daly away, interrupting him? The manner of some people was so irritating that their occasional truths never sounded smooth. These missing pages in the directory explained the means by which Williams had tracked down Andrew Green's address. And they were probably all that Acting Captain Daly was referencing when he was blathering on and chewing the news. But none of this went to the question of motive, and without a motive no action makes sense in a court of law. No story is accepted.

Then McClusky had a second bed-based revelation: he

could breathe through his nose. Freely. Naturally. Without the use of his special spray! He rose, stretched, made coffee, ran a bath. He massaged his cheeks—no pain anymore. His nightclothes held no evidence of sweat, and his wife was apparently out with the cat. She had left a note on the table next to Bessie Davis's ledgers. Crumpling his wife's words in his hand, he felt like a new man. He put her pencil in his pocket, then opened a window.

Yes, he could smell things again. The sickly scents of sugar, molasses, tar. They rose up from the street to sweeten and thicken the apartment's aroma of coffee. Skin fresh, hair combed, McClusky decided, emboldened, that what he'd like to inhale next was a flower, a leaf, a tree. No messages had been tucked under his door overnight. A walk in the park might be possible. Even useful. A way to clear his head, and calm down, and tease out whatever his dreams had tried to tell him in the night. Fresh air was a habit he had fallen away from, lately, and that was an error. His health was a priority now. The concern was not to fall into the same flu again. Such illnesses were always waiting to ambush a patient who became glib. He did not want to die on the street on the next Friday the thirteenth. He did not want always to rely upon cocaine to kill the demons in his sinuses.

Before he left the apartment he took one more look at Bessie's ledgers. Like Williams's directory, some pages had been ripped out. He suspected Bessie had done this in anticipation of the records being seized. She always seemed to be a step ahead. Before he reached for his keys and his coat, a name on a page caught his eye—a Mr. Hart. And next to it, a note, presumably in her hand, or the hand of one of her workers: "swap days with Mr. Braine."

Mr. Hart and Mr. Braine? It was hard to know what was serious in her, and what was laughter.

———

He entered the park through the Women's Gate at West Seventy-Second Street. He carried a few of his papers under his right arm, mainly in case he bumped into a superior. His father had worked on this park as a laborer, in its final stages, decades ago. Had helped import the fertile New Jersey soil, truckloads of it. The earth here had proven to be, so to speak, insufficiently accommodating to life. And in later years he had taken him on walks here, his father had. Walks like this one that Inspector McClusky was now taking alone. Had pointed out the shrubs, giving them their proper names. A man who existed for specifics, his father. Was hungry for detail, for neatness, just as it seemed Andrew Haswell Green, a complete stranger, had also been.

Inspector McClusky huddled close into his coat and picked up his pace. He felt on the verge of something, a breakthrough of the mind or spirit, and his cough was lovely and loose now. It gave him great pleasure to clear his throat. The idea he had from waking was still at the edges of his brain, trying to find its best shape. A revelation is like a sneeze. Sounds unlikely, but it is. It can be lost, can simply vanish, if one does not look straight into the light and ask the inside to come out.

He looked up at the sky until his eyes hurt. A cold day, but clear, and bright. The walks bent quickly north and south from here. He touched his scarf, wished for gloves. He had been all over the southerly when thinking through his last big case, months ago. He decided on the northerly today.

It was a route that took in a delightful arbor, hung with trailing vines. Shifting sunshine. Dancing leaves. Periods of stillness, of a cease-fire in the wind, when an atmosphere of glass seemed to descend on the whole park. He was feeling so much better. He remembered how he loved to walk like this, safe in all the grace. And as the walk swung him around to the north, still close by the arbor, he found masses of honeysuckle waiting for him, known easily by its leaves.

Those leaves on the honeysuckle resembled arrowheads, narrowed and elongated for battle. There was a fringe of hairs along the margins, and Inspector McClusky, with a gentleness he had forgotten rested within him, brushed his hand now along some as he passed, the undersides too, the leaves' delicate bellies. In May or early June the Tartarian honeysuckle would break out again in bloom—pink, white, or crimson flowers, with upper lips quite considerably cleft. Garlands of wisteria would come to life then too. The murder victim had achieved something here, a refreshing reality, and Inspector McClusky swallowed again and wondered how much of a person's fate rested in their own head. Police work, the great deflater. You puffed out your ego those first few years, making yourself invincible, saying foolish things to the press to build an image, and then you saw enough disaster to know how small you were, and you had to keep that sense of smallness locked inside yourself, hidden from view. A few skimming clouds above now. Someone up there had a plan, and would use it, or tear it up. Piles of paperwork. Some of it half-eaten. In a quick rush of the old pettiness, he recommitted himself as he walked to finding a route by which to fire Acting Captain Daly from the force.

As the flowers pass away, changing to fruit, the honeysuckle bush is hung full of bright scarlet berries, is it not? The delicacy of those leaves, that fruit. Bright scarlet berries. When exactly had he turned his back on all this, become a man who existed in small rooms?

He paused. Took a piece of paper from his pocket. He sat on a patch of grass—it felt cold to the touch—and tightened his scarf around his neck like a noose. Looked at the timeline of Green's life he'd written and rewritten. Squinted at it in the sunlight, then put it back in his pocket. He wondered if he should move to the countryside, so to speak. That was a thing some people did, was it not?

But no, no move to the country for him. It was perhaps true that out there beyond the city's borders people had less cause to complain. But it was also true that when they needed to, no one was around to listen. Their tedious speeches about leaving New York were caught by the wind and sent to sea.

He did not quite believe that Mr. Andrew Haswell Green, in moments of loneliness, had frequented the whorehouse run by Bessie Davis, or Hannah Elias, whatever she wished to be called. A theory felt, instinctively, wrong or right. This one did not sing. You read a man's diary, you walk through his work, his park, and you begin to trust your instinct of who he might have been. A person who created a space like this was, of course, capable of paying for sin. Look at this vastness, this magic. He created Greater New York! He was clearly capable of idiocy—even the city's most talented inspectors could succumb to mistakes of the loin . . . But why would Bessie lie? She had said she didn't know him. He was dead now. There were no consequences. Few.

His *womanly hand*, the *Herald* had once noted, describing Mr. Green's writing. The way his words looped on the page.

The fact he never married. But that could be evidence of either hypothesis, could it not? Lonely man needs woman. Or simply isn't interested . . .

The friendship with Samuel Tilden. The rumors. But it would, certainly, be an unlikely thing. Less than one in ten thousand men were said to suffer that inclination. And there were always rumors about everything. They were in the air in cities like this. They *were* the air, they made it.

His thoughts twisted back upon themselves as he stood up and walked on, then arrived at this simple idea: Bessie's self-confessed priority was probably true: to keep her top clients feeling safe. To earn their trust. And in this, she must have been a proven success. The wealthy wouldn't visit just any beautiful woman. There must have been a sense of discretion, supported by fact.

And then a thought stopped him dead. The customer in Bessie's ledgers called Mr. Hart. The one called Mr. Braine. Had there not also been, somewhere, a mention of a Mr. Foot?

He already knew she used code names. But what if code names were the key to his case? What if every customer she had ever had, in these ledgers and the many previous ledgers that likely once existed, were given a code name?

Then he sneezed. He did. It came all at once, into his elbow. Last night in the last delirium of work he had puzzled over a mention of a Mr. Newgray.

Mr. Gray.

Mr. New Gray.

Colors. What if colors had made up part of her code? What if she had once serviced men she referred to as Mr. Brown, and Mr. Black, and . . .

He had worked up a sweat on this stroll, despite the cold, as he did through almost any adventure in movement of late, and that sweat was now cooling on his face, clarifying something in his body, his mind. Feeling almost superstitious, as if the park itself was helping him make his breakthrough, he turned his attention to two blooming specimens of groundsel tree. Steady, he thought to himself. Don't rush the idea . . .

If you ever wandered over the salt meadows near Coney Island in the autumn, perhaps dreaming that Topsy the elephant were still alive, you would see the groundsel trees there too, near the beach, their seedpods fairly billowing over the velvety sedge, and your heart would sink, would fairly drop down into your stomach, at the thought you were living a life that allowed so little time out here in the open air.

Those white Coney Island seagulls, turning in the sun! The sound of the ocean surge. It all mingled in his mind now with this park, its replications of nature, its thousand shades of green.

Mr. Green.

He stopped dead. Swallowed. Kneeled down on the grass now as if to pray.

Until now he had kept wanting every component of the case to lock together cleanly, to make sense, trying to rid it all of the obfuscations of absurdity, but the point was that there was no sense, no overarching master plan, only individual foibles and errors which are by their nature absurd and at the same time sad. He tied his shoelace, then untied it, then tied it again.

What if Cornelius Williams, at some point in his invisible history, which he had the dignity to refuse to describe to McClusky's colleagues as he sat locked in the Tombs, silent these last few days, as if all the talking he had done in the first interrogation now seemed entirely pointless to him, had grown jealous of one of the rich white men who had used the services of Hannah Elias, also known as Bessie Davis?

And what if that rich customer had wanted Cornelius Williams out from Bessie's properties. Out from her life? Or at least was Bessie's excuse for finally ridding herself of a lower class of customer . . .

And what if, after Bessie bought her first or last mansion, and Williams could never find her again, never achieve an opportunity to win back her affections, he had, driven half-mad by circumstance and the feeling of having his love trampled upon, come to the assumption—rightly or wrongly—that this rich white customer was the one protecting her? Harboring her? Turning her against him even now?

And what if, once upon a time, Bessie had referred to that man, an old man, a white-bearded man, as Mr. Green?

Cornelius Williams wouldn't know his first name. Would only know he was old, and white-bearded, and named Mr. Green, and of a wealthy profession.

And Cornelius Williams would look up Green in the city directory.

Would rip out the page that held a column of possible Greens.

Would focus on the few Greens who sounded like they might be rich, and lived near enough to visit Bessie's rumored home—like a lawyer with a Park Avenue address.

And he would begin to ask around . . . And some Greens would be too young, or too happily married, or too recently arrived in the city . . . And the people of Park Avenue would know of only one wealthy unmarried Mr. Green . . . The one who lived at number 91. Andrew Haswell.

How's that, Cabbagehead! It was coming together.

Inspector McClusky did not punch the air, but he tried to grasp it. He held out his hand as if to capture the cold. He smiled, and coughed, and smiled again. He did not know yet that his own death, at the hands of an armed burglar he would be called upon to arrest, would arrive only a few years from now, an ending that would forestall whatever abuses of power his future might have held. And he did not know that Catherine would, soon afterward, pick a new partner, and fall in love for the first time. He knew none of this, and therefore he was happy.

He was not certain beyond doubt that he had solved his case, but he was sure of this: he had found a version which would work. If further digging into his theory of colors proved fruitful, it would satisfy a jury and the president's men. Perhaps even a reader of the *Times*. Yes. Andrew Haswell Green had been killed in a case of mistaken identity, he was sure of that now. A great mistake based on a whore's penchant for nicknames. A stranger—what a fate!—mistook him for someone else, not a different Mr. Green, but simply a man code-named Mr. Green. He would plant this idea in the public mind, so to speak. Watch it grow, and claim credit, for credit was properly his.

His heart was up, his blood was flowing. Murder by mistake was an ironic end for a man of such set intentions. For a person who, if McClusky's research was correct, had been obsessed with never giving accidents an excuse to spread. This park was almost entirely man-made. The only natural feature on this whole site, McClusky's recent review of Green's sometimes tedious papers had revealed, was the metamorphic rock known as Manhattan schist. All seven bodies of water here were artificial. Low-lying swamps had been laboriously drained. The park's three woodland areas were contrived by planting thousands of trees, shrubs, and plants onto barren slopes. Millions of cartloads of soil were moved—some by McClusky's father and his uncle, indeed—to create the impression of undulating meadows. The work of leveling rock outcroppings had required more gunpowder than was used in the Battle of Gettysburg, and when a member of the public strolled beneath the leafy canopy of the Ramble, an area Green and his designers had once called *the wild garden*, they would have no idea they were stepping though a space that had been imagined and realized through years of careful fraudulence. The rustic stream that soothed walkers with its music could be turned on and off like a faucet. So yes, it was not as if Green believed in leaving fate in Nature's hands. He admired, presumably, the careful construction of a suitable human story.

They were all dead now, McClusky reflected, panting as he broke into a run. By only a few months, Green had outlived Olmsted, his occasional nemesis, who had suffered a breakdown and ended up in an asylum.

Greenery. It seemed to take a lot out of a man.

East of him was dogwood. West was a cluster of tall, bald cypresses. There was, within his relief, a flicker of regret: part of him would miss exploring the victim's life and death. Inspector McClusky sprinted on toward a kind of closure when what he still wanted, most of all, was a gate.

31

MINERS' GATE

ndrew's dreams often took him back, in his final years, to the sight of the Brooklyn Bridge being built. He remembered standing on the deck of the ferry with Samuel as Brooklyn approached. The 1870s had recently arrived, which meant Andrew had been alive for more than fifty years, but afloat on that ferry he did not feel new. A half century of existence had proven to be just another marker. An ordinary buoy, when what he had been expecting was a lighthouse, some kind of all-illuminating revolution.

They were halfway through the crossing when the skies began to clear. This was the best place of all for a view of the construction site; the ferry provided a moving vantage point. *The East River Bridge. The Brooklyn Bridge. The New York & Brooklyn Bridge. The Great Bridge.* So many different names raised for a structure that did not yet cross any water.

Three towering boom derricks were putting the day's work into motion, swinging huge blocks of limestone into place, and tiny figures swarmed about the masonry and climbed the stacks of lumber, circling great heaps of coal, appearing and disappearing through adjacent yards at a steady pace, no pausing, as if it were deep in their nature to know exactly where to go. Black smoke scribbled up into the blue air above and the symbols it created meant nothing.

Washington Roebling greeted them at the foot of Fulton Street. His skin looked chalky, his eyebrows dull with dust, the bones of his face elegantly formed but far too sharp under his eyes, as if the efforts of seeing, of envisaging an ending to a project that still looked only half-started, had wasted the surrounding flesh away. It was hard to believe he was still in his thirties, though he had retained the upright posture of a military man, and he had an undefeated mouth. That mouth made Andrew always want to please him.

Was it possible that Roebling already knew that the work here would try to kill him, just as it had killed his father? This morning he was spitting regularly into a handkerchief, a habit that Samuel's eyes at first seemed to refuse to fix upon, because he did not like to confront illness in others; it put him in mind of his own.

What of the plot to eliminate Mr. Tweed, gentlemen? Roebling said, slapping Andrew on the shoulder with less force than he might have intended. Quite a campaign you two are waging.

Roebling coughed, and his eyes filmed over as he swallowed. Samuel was looking away. Observing the birds, sky, workers at work.

I suppose you have abandoned the possibility of poison? Roebling added.

Andrew laughed. An impractical volume would be necessary, no?

Indeed, Andrew! A great expense, for a man that size. His murder will bankrupt the city, if his statue does not. Poison and bronze—both expensive.

Is he here yet? Samuel said.

He's *somewhere*, Roebling said. I can hear his footfall. Would you care to stroll, gentlemen? The trustee tour, it's been a while.

Andrew smiled through the headache the crossing seemed

to have left him with. Had three decades really passed since he had boarded that infernal brig to Trinidad? It was strange to acknowledge to himself that New York would be very different if he had drowned.

The fresh granite blocks, Roebling explained as they walked at his side, had been quarried and shaped in Maine, and delivered here by schooner. All the progress was here in Brooklyn, all the workers were here in Brooklyn. On the New York side, so small, so distant now, the first stone had not even been laid. There were plans, approved by Andrew and the other trustees, to rent out large vaults on the anchorage for the storage of wines, and the design included numerous passageways and compartments designed specifically for this purpose, areas inside the tower that could be kept at the appropriate temperatures and leased out, at an extraordinary price, to those seeking a wine cellar in a public place—one that could provide a topic of lofty conversation, perhaps, while a portion of its contents was being consumed. Roebling was good at this kind of thing, at envisaging ways that a great project could sustain itself in a world of self-obsessed wealth without compromising his more essential central aims. He knew that the dirty parts of a bargain had to be made and he delighted in keeping them out of sight.

As they walked, Roebling asked more questions about Tweed, and Samuel repeated a favorite lie, one which he seemed to have convinced himself was truth: that there was no corrupt ring before 1869, that it simply didn't exist. If there had been, Samuel said, touching his chin as he always did when lying, he would have begun his fight against Tweed far sooner.

Tweed's plan in supporting this bridge, in pouring so much money into it, in becoming such a huge holder of stock, seemed to be to skim yet more money from public contracts. And yet was it also possible that Tweed, egocentric as he was, nonetheless had an eye for grandeur? For architecture that would outlast him?

More than one hundred men were engaged on this site today. Most were sandhogs earning less than two dollars. They used shovels and dynamite to clear away boulders at the bottom of the river. More highly prized men, though not necessarily the most highly skilled, were employed in the caisson itself—the huge, airtight wooden cylinder sunk into the riverbed. Down in the deep, at enormous risk, they were building the foundation for the tower. In theory their health would improve with each day—they were building up; next week they would be on a higher platform!—but that didn't seem to be how the strange disease took effect. The caisson illness was cumulative. It punished you for your past, as far as Andrew could gather. Time spent down in the depths could not be unspent, mistakes made could not be unmade. It was said that those who went diving in oceans experienced a similar sickness. When the workers in the caissons had reached a sufficient depth—forty-four feet here in Brooklyn, and a planned seventy-eight for the corresponding tower on the New York side—they would begin laying granite, working their way back up to the surface, the conditions becoming less deadly week by week, until eventually a solid column of masonry would be produced to a point above the waterline from which the span of the great bridge could extend.

Voices, laughter. Coughs, sneezes. The dust that catches in your throat as history makes itself.

Members of the press were gathering now by the caisson site. In public, when Samuel was angry, Andrew could hear the stifled passion in his breathing, and see it in the tiny movements of his tensed jaw. Samuel's reputation for lawyerly calm was at this point in their lives only that: a widespread belief, accurate on the very surface of the surface, for those who did not know him well.

Andrew stood side by side with Samuel now, smelling but not seeing smoke, as Roebling was called forward to shake William Tweed's hand—gingerly, no smile, no welcome—and escorted him very slowly onto a stage made from upturned crates.

The writers fell silent as the wood creaked under Tweed. The expectation of disaster or success. That huge peach-colored face. The beleaguered frame that carried close to three hundred pounds of flesh. One diamond stickpin on his shirt shining in the sunlight as he began his speech. But somehow the platform under him held.

Who did William Tweed really fear? Not his supposed opponents, the Republicans. They admired money too much to present him with problems. They had touted themselves as the party of victory ever since the war, and what better example of the American spirit than William Tweed? He had created his own wealth. He had played both parties. He was happy crossing the line. With half a million dollars in bribes he had brought the power of state commissions back into Tammany Hall. He ran the city now, and the New York Democrats feared that if they unsettled his grip they would lose their own small share of his power. Governors enjoyed being invited to his mansion on Fifth Avenue for a quick glass of fine Champagne, and then a second slightly slower one, and in time the rest of the bottle. Once through the door, their presence recorded by a friendly journalist in attendance, their gift bag light with dollars, or perhaps heavy with a diamond necklace for their wives, their pact with the devil was sufficiently sealed.

Beyond Tweed's voice now, a hammer was hitting metal. There was the sound of water flowing. Wind.

As he spoke, Tweed eyed the press with suspicion and

a hint of humor. He was making a comment about three assembled sketchers at the front. Most of his supporters could not read, he said, but they knew an unflattering cartoon when they saw one. He told the sketchers he'd have them locked up, and the audience Andrew was part of laughed uneasily. Tweed assumed a statesmanlike stance. He said, No, in truth, I am glad to see all these faces around me today. I have a few words to say.

He was not a skilled orator, and yet his lack of skill in this respect seemed only to enhance the message he conveyed: that he was a man of the people, a humble chair-maker made good, here to turn the City of New York into the greatest metropolis in the world.

If a Democrat, Tweed said, does not support me . . .

The press held their breath. A few of them turned to look back at Andrew and Samuel.

Then it must be because they do not share my notion that any man in this Union, however humble his origins, can become rich and powerful, provide for themselves, provide for their wives and children too. Perhaps such Democrats do not have wives and children? Perhaps they have rich ancestry? Perhaps they have unscrupulous professions, or habits. Perhaps they are speculators.

Samuel's elbow dug into Andrew's side.

Tweed continued his speech, smiling. The reported division of the Democratic Party in New York, he said, is but a delusion, that is what I am here to say! A scheme devised by unscrupulous Republicans to make men believe that the Democratic Party can be defeated! We are united. Yes, we are good people, we are united. If it is doubted, look now and see that Mr. Samuel Tilden back there—he stands with me here today, a spotless Democrat such as he!

This time a greater number of heads turned to look at them. Andrew saw that Samuel's face was reddening. That

Tweed was staring, smiling, enjoying it all. A man most often depicted as a walrus in wingtips, but whose oversized appetites had him frequently drawn of late as other animals too. In the *Harper's* cartoons that he tried to remove from newsstands, and many other images like them, he had the head of a dog one week, the head of a brutish bear the next, and at Thanksgiving he had been a thickly feathered turkey big enough to feed the entire city—but determined to feed only himself.

If these artists could see the truth, why didn't the assembled newspaper writers follow suit and try to remove Tweed from his position of power? Their advertising departments were fat on Tweed's money, that was why. Their editors were scared. For every negative article they ran, a more positive portrayal would follow, all in the name of balance, fairness—the very qualities Tweed had spent his life trying to destroy.

Tweed talked now about the American Institute Fair, the Empire Skating Rink, the show of machines, the engines and drills and wonderful pumps, the emery wheels and the hatching machine. He said, The great bounty of American manufacture was on display! I shall never forget it! And this great bridge, in its becoming behind me, shows also that manufacture. Our country is making more iron than ever. A man with an eye patch showed me specimens of American steel yesterday. American steel now has no superior! The manufacture of saws began among us only ten years ago. Now the whole country is supplied from domestic sources! Screws, once brought in on ships, are now largely exported. Good people of Brooklyn want such successes to continue. But there are bad people. Yes. There are those, too. Bad people who stand in our way.

Andrew watched with a sinking feeling as Tweed paused

and nodded. His face for a moment took on a somber expression, as if he really was feeling something for his fellow man.

British laborers, Tweed said, are on railroads across Asia and Africa—they dig with spades and shovels of American manufacture, gentlemen! What if there is another war, another emergency? My supporters are good people. The people who oppose our economy are bad people. The great metropolises of the world are growing, becoming worlds. I shall make New York great, and greater still! This is the age of inventors! The age of miraculous materials shaped by human hands. An age of American greatness. Yes, life can be comfortable for all, even a humble chair-maker like myself.

It was not so very different from a speech Samuel himself had given recently. The more erudite touches had been omitted (Recall the ancients and teach them the power of steam! Put Columbus on board the *Great Eastern* and see how fast he sails! Furnish Galileo's tube with Alvan Clark's lenses! Send the armies of Caesar by rail into Gaul! Give Homer an edition of *The Iliad* set by a small American press!) but the rest of the message was there.

Andrew listened. Watched Samuel shaking his head in disbelief, as if any of this should be a surprise. It seemed not to have occurred to him until now that theft was Tweed's most obvious specialty. Stealing words was a sideshow to the main event—pickpocketing the public. If Tweed and his cronies in the comptroller's office were not removed and replaced with honest men soon, the whole city would sink into the water.

Before the war, Tweed said, we were unarmed. Before it ended, ten thousand anvils rang. Colt and Parrott and Spencer built ingenious weapons. Now we need more parks—as Mr. Andrew Haswell Green back there, who I hear votes

Democrat, is oh so skilled at building! We need more art, more of Mr. Green's museums, and science for doctors—and we need this great bridge!

A whisper from Samuel now: *Science for doctors?* We really must kill him.

It was difficult to disagree. Good to hear a joke turning serious. The word *park,* delivered by Tweed, had made Andrew's ears burn the way they did sometimes when John Bigelow called Samuel *Sam.*

Andrew saw now how Roebling, forced into this whole performance by Tammany Hall, was standing very still at the side of the stage, blank and embarrassed.

Tweed began recounting a story from his boyhood. His father, running a small store—humble, so very humble— sent his porter out for tobacco several times a week. Every time the negro porter came back—wanted to grow his hair out, this negro, but wasn't allowed—Tweed's father would say to him, How much change have you brought for my tobacco, then? And the porter would say, Four cents, sir.

Tweed laughed. Roared like a bear. The platform beneath him creaked again, and held again. Do you know what my father would reply? he asked.

Silence from the assembled press.

My father would say to his porter, every time: Four cents? *Four cents?* You'll never be rich if you bring me back my full four cents! Why on earth didn't you pocket one of 'em, and tell me three?

The expected laughter came: half-hearted, and quickly lost. The writers scribbled down the anecdote, grateful to have something for tomorrow. It had come this, and so very quickly: holding dishonesty up for amusement. But Andrew knew times would change. He would make sure of it. There would be no more Tweeds in such high power once this one was destroyed. The public's memory could be relied upon, surely, to some extent.

Of course, Tweed added, turning now to his true moral, the real change from the purchase, my father found out, was *six* cents! The negro had been pocketing two at a time! My father had to let him go. Would you have done the same, Mr. Green there, at the back—let the negro go? Would you, Mr. Green . . . ?

It took a moment to surface, to realize he'd been addressed again. Every pair of eyes found him dumb.

Come, Tweed shouted across the heads and hats. Andrew Haswell Green—a great man in our presence! You are known for nickel-and-diming, sir. You criticize my own wealth in the press, but you do not even tolerate Mr. Vaux spending a cent on flourishes for your park, do you? So I ask: Would you, too, not have let the thieving negro go? Thrown him out? Perhaps even had him punished? You are known as the Bean Counter, after all.

Andrew managed to drag some words from his throat. The situation, he said.

Speak up, Mr. Green!

Everyone was watching him now.

The situation, Andrew said, lifting his voice. It would not have arisen with me . . .

Tweed said, Oh? Why is that, Mr. Green? No one in your circle would ever wrong you. Is that it?

The press were unblinking. The wind was in Andrew's ears, then gone.

It is rather more simple, Andrew said. He waited a moment. Had found his answer. Relief coursed through him before he uttered his final words: You see, Mr. Tweed, I do not smoke.

One heartbeat—two—and then the laughter came, so

much louder than any before it. Hands slapped him on his back. Samuel was giggling like he had last spring.

A good answer, my friend, William Tweed conceded. A very good answer, my good friend, my fellow Democrat, very good.

Sometimes, when Andrew looked at Tweed, what he saw was Horace Hinsdale, a different decade, a different domain, the advertising of ideas and favors instead of jars of foreign teas in a tower. Salesmanship on a great scale. Is that what a city is?

The speech was over.

A man on the eastern side of the work site was stripping naked, careless as to who might see. Andrew watched him disappear into a wooden shack.

Roebling had arrived back at Andrew's side, following his gaze with a look of amusement. The warming house, he said. You and Mr. Tilden will be in there soon enough. But first—an entertainer's flourish of the hands, as if he had found an extra reserve of energy from somewhere—I wish to know if you'd like to go deeper than you have ever been? Deep under the river.

32

STRANGERS' GATE (11)

ased on the evidence of a respected alienist that he was *deeply troubled by delusions of persecution,* and given Inspector McClusky's conclusion that the shooting had been an instance of mistaken identity that no sane person could conceivably have committed, Cornelius Williams was assessed by further doctors, put before a jury, and remanded to the Matteawan State Hospital for the Criminally Insane in Beacon, New York. There he died the kind of death that history prefers not to preserve.

Few traces of Williams's life would survive, no solid framework for future generations to imagine themselves into, and presumably that was exactly what the judicial system had intended. He was described in court as *a man of all work.* He had been employed by various white families in New York, often to tend the furnace. He carried himself with such dignity, and dressed so smartly, within his means, that one observer said his name might as well have been Cornelius Vanderbilt.

In 1901, to supplement the small wages one wealthy family chose to pay him, Cornelius was offered some of their unwanted items of old clothing. A decent coat discarded in a passion for fashion. Gloves. A bowler hat that seemed to almost fit.

Some witnesses to his life said Williams was *quiet and capable.* Others described him as *lonely but kind.* He had complained to neighbors once or twice of hearing voices, and of needing to see a lawyer to discuss an urgent matter. To one acquaintance he spoke of wanting to track down a man he suspected of sheltering Miss Davis, a woman he loved, and whom he hoped would one day love him back—a Mr. Green, or was it Mr. Brown?

A local pastor had told him not to worry about the voices. Said everyone in this metropolis heard them from time to time. They were *the words of God's ghosts, taking their fashion and tone from the prevailing temper and condition of the day*. As for finding Mr. Green or Mr. Brown, had he tried the city directory?

That was an idea, he said. He would try that, yes he would.

Readers sighed and folded the *Times* after reading its account of the final trial. They had expected that each week would hold more clues, that they might enjoy a frothing courtroom drama, culminating in a concluding testimony that was unexpected and yet satisfying, shocking and at the same time drenched in sense. An explanation beyond the act of doubting. A solution to the mystery of why, why, why. Instead they were left to contemplate the accidents within their own lives.

Mistaken identity! It would have been better, much better, if Green had more plainly deserved to die, and if the man in the bowler hat had meant to kill him. The tale would have possessed a logic. The idea that the killing came about through a piece of random bad luck—on Friday the thirteenth! That it was an act of pure caprice, wrapped in a history of injustice, representing an ending that any one of them could have suffered! The best thing was to try to forget it, which over time almost everybody did.

And yet something, an idea of aloneness, still kept some strangers thinking. Witnesses to the crime, people on the street, or those who had known Andrew at different moments in his life, they thought about privacy in the midst of public space. About a person who, in his last twenty years, had campaigned tirelessly against the idea of isolation, while himself remaining isolated. Who had become the chief champion of consolidation, of seeing bodies of water and land as links rather than barriers, as if he were afraid that Manhattan Island, its grass, its roads, its people, might grow overly lonely one night in the distant future, as lonely perhaps as he himself was, so lonely that it would start to sink into what lies beneath New York City today, the millions of miles of telephone wire, the thousands of miles of electrical cable, the water mains, the gas lines, the cable television wiring. Sink into the steam pipes and the sewage lines and the subway tunnels. Sink into the darkness and dirt that lives underneath all the surfaces citizens traverse as they walk to and from work, wearing one mask or another, their feet touching the streets.

On Friday, November 13, 1903, he rode the Fourth Avenue streetcar uptown. Alighted at the Thirty-Eighth Street stop. Walked the final few minutes to his house. Hungry along the avenue. Almost home . . .

There was once a statue made of Andrew Haswell Green, but it was crated up and lost. A laboratory in his name was built on New York University's Bronx campus, but it became outdated and was torn down. Henry Mosler's painting of him still hangs in City Hall, but it has been placed in a restricted space, and you may only manage to view it by pretending to be someone else.

There is a dog run in Andrew's name on the East River Esplanade, where the river tries hard to capture the clouds. Recently this area, which the *Times* calls *an unlovely slice of land*, has been expanded into a public park, but the pilings that support its structures are being eaten away by water organisms, and it has proved difficult to find the money for repairs. There are signs designating a play area for large dogs, and signs designating a play area for small dogs. Medium dogs can presumably choose.

The best of the small memorials that still exist to him today is the one in Central Park. It is not situated in an obvious place. You will discover it only by a roundabout route, perhaps climbing the Great Hill one morning with a sandwich in your pocket, following a path through Glen Span Arch and along Montayne's Rivulet, one of New York's original streams. You might see the Lasker to your left, a sheet of water or ice not yet dotted with bodies, and notice to your right a set of shaded stone steps ascending through maple leaves. Perhaps you'll imagine that at the summit you will watch birds flying over the ravine below, or across the open greenery of Fort Fish. But instead, surrounded by ordinary silence, growing tired of the life behind you and the life ahead of you, you will come upon a marble bench engraved with his name and read the dedication before you finally sit.

IN HONOR OF ANDREW HASWELL GREEN
DIRECTING GENIUS OF CENTRAL PARK IN ITS FORMATIVE PERIOD
FATHER OF GREATER NEW YORK

Several characters are covered in bird shit. There is a half-eaten apple on the ground. Distant tourists are taking photographs of other, greater landmarks. You could decide, then and there, to begin.

33

MINERS' GATE (II)

So they climbed onto the deck of the caisson, he and Samuel, on that day they visited the construction site for the great bridge that would bring two worlds together. Andrew was looking down into one shaft, Samuel into the other. The caissons, the huge channels, plunged all the way into the private darkness of the riverbed.

One of Roebling's men had bought them long cloaks to protect their clothes. The insanity of air pumps, the percussive rush of the sand pipes too, the sudden lurching feeling of fear. Andrew could say he no longer wanted to go down. He could say it, but nobody would hear.

A test ahead. A risk to your ears, your eyes, your better senses. Your lungs. Your heart. This thing we call the future.

The engineer who had been chosen to guide them down into the depths was now enacting a mime over all the noise: how to hold your breath, how to pinch your nose to relieve the pressure. The only other recipient of this performance was Samuel. When the man had finished, he pointed to the western side of the site. It wasn't clear to Andrew what was meant by this last act.

Speechlessness made a person seem cold, Andrew thought. Overly committed to truth.

They descended a narrow, steep staircase, the engineer leading the way. Thin sunlight on the back of the man's protective hat. Only darkness down beyond it.

Five steps, ten. The faint smell of sewage rose to greet them now.

Fifteen steps, twenty. The slow care of each breath he and Samuel took together in the gathering gloom. His ears felt blocked. His heart seemed to swell. He held his nose and tried to swallow. A few seconds of relief, this brought. It was embarrassing, often, to be a human being, a body with needs to nurture.

The three of them stood tight now in a kind of coffin. The engineer pointed to a small oval opening to their right. Samuel looked rigid amidst the ever-increasing noise, he seemed to be becoming a ghost, and he kept pointing to the surface, jabbing with a frozen finger, but the engineer didn't care, or else it was too late. Must happen all the time: gentlemen fearing a few minutes of ordinary, subterranean suffering.

They moved through the opening. Arrived in an iron chamber that was just big enough that they no longer needed to touch one another. A little trapdoor—also iron?— came into focus under Andrew's feet.

The engineer stamped his foot. Seconds passed. Andrew reached out, held Samuel's hand. A squeeze returned: the miracle of reciprocation.

The little trapdoor now opened downward. A glimpse of a human hand down there, and Samuel nearly fell into it. They steadied themselves, giggling. Stood their feet at the very edges of available space. A dark face, a flicker of white teeth. They descended the little ladder, one by one, toward this figure. An exercise in trust.

The heat now was extraordinary, it surpassed the noise, it was as if they were climbing inside a dark artery in a massive human heart. The engineer shouted, The lock!, or words that sounded like The lock!, and as he did so the cords in his neck looked livid.

A stopcock, perhaps? Hot air rushed up from below like a reputation on the rise. It was science that seemed like art.

Andrew felt his hair come alive, thought at first it was burning, but he was distant from his own fear now, he had left it behind somehow, everything was slow and muted, it took a long time to think and blink. The trapdoor had closed above them, the pressure itself seemed to have sealed it shut. The engineer blew out his cheeks, his bulging eyes asking them to do the same. A dull pain in the eardrum as Andrew swallowed, and swallowed. How deep were they now? It seemed strange that a person could survive the sinkage they had spent the last few minutes enacting.

When they finally stepped out of the chamber they were in a corridor of dirt and stone. A beautiful coolness came. They were invisible here, underwater, the East River all around them. They had been drowned, without feeling a single drop. A vague perception of mud came as they walked along a footway of planking, the space opening out, glowworms pulsing in the gloom. Or no—only candle flames, perhaps.

By calcium light, five men were digging. Huge spades thrust into a space in the middle of the vault. Six of these! the engineer was shouting.

Vaults? Samuel shouted.

Vaults, Andrew said. In his wonder he felt he was talking only to himself.

The deep-flitting shadows cast by the calcium lights seemed to lend a supernatural depth to the thin sound of drills and chains. In a hundred years, as people crossed the great bridge above, would they imagine all these decades of effort beneath their feet? Would they learn about it? Would they remember the dead?

Andrew had heard some workers say, in open meetings he had attended while campaigning with Roebling, that they preferred life down here to life lived aboveground. And it had seemed, at the time, such a sinister thing to say—at best a fearful repetition of a politic line provided by an unscrupulous supervisor, and at worst a reflection of the misery of working life up there on the streets. But Andrew saw now, in this space where the sight of anything was such an enormous effort, that there really was a strange allure to being here, down deep, everything aglow with a soft lack of reality. He felt now a strange nostalgia, mixed with relief at having made an escape—an escape from his own daylit life. At this moment he did not care who might be standing over him, or what they might say about him. He only cared that he was not alone.

He was here with Samuel. Their hands again were almost touching. He felt light-headed, a fraction drunk. His pulse seemed to quicken and fade with the sounds of the spades and within his own veins the blood felt sluggish but sure, as if, down here, there was no such thing as a false move. And then Samuel's hand disappeared from Andrew's yet again, by choice or accident, and Samuel's voice sounded unnaturally distant as he shouted questions for the engineer.

He could not have gone far, he must still be close. And yet . . .

Samuel will die before me. This was the thought he succumbed to now, surrounded by the spades and pulsing drills, the efforts of men intent on finding further depth where perhaps there was only mystery remaining.

Parks. Bridges. Great institutions. Art. They were the only affordable forms of immortality Andrew had ever been able to imagine in his adult life. And yet it occurred to him here, briefly, pointlessly, belatedly, with the airy abstraction of a weather forecast, that all this public work might not mean as much as having a friend holding your hand as you die.

Love. This was the way not to fall into forgetting. Love, and a good publicist.

He squinted to find Samuel's face again, the surface expressions and the ripples of real feeling beneath, the comical hide-and-seek of the soul. In this darkness, words were foolish things. Their context was killed. You could only guess at how they shaped a person's face, or fate. Imagine that. Imagine anything.

Andrew felt the clamor of New York above him, a city deafening us with its continuance. He felt enclosed by the current moment, safe but suffocated, governed by emotions that had been buried for far too long. Then he prepared to ascend again toward the heavens, stopping for a while at the city's surface, where there was work to do before he slept, many years to pass before his ending.

ACKNOWLEDGMENTS

This book exists thanks to:

Andrew Haswell Green.

The New York Historical Society, the New York Public Library, and the Central Park Conservancy.

My exceptional editors: Diana Miller, Anne Meadows, and Rowan Cope.

Jin Auh, Tracy Bohan, Kate Prentice, and the teams at the Wylie Agency and 42.

Everyone at Knopf and Granta, especially Josefine Kals, Pru Rowlandson, Emily Reardon, Bella Lacey, Sigrid Rausing, John Gall, Sarah Wasley, Christine Lo, Simon Heafield, Noel Murphy, Dan Bird, Nathan Burton, Pei Loi Koay, Matthew Sciarappa, Kathleen Fridella, Lisa Montebello, and Vanessa Rae Haughton.

Andy Hunter and the Catapulters.

Clare Alexander, Jason Arthur, Gillian Stern, Dwyer Murphy, Dan Sheehan, Jonny Diamond, Stefan Merrill Block, Liese Mayer, Emily Stokes, Ben Samuel, and Katy Simpson Smith.

Martina Testa, Marco Cassini, Ursula Bergenthal, and all of the staff and translators at work on different editions of this book.

Amy and the family.

Keep in touch with
Granta Books:

Visit granta.com to discover more.

GRANTA